THE SURVIVALIST 12
THE REBELLION

Hands grabbed at Natalia's legs, dragging her down. Her right arm was twisted behind her — a little more pressure and she knew it would break. Hands held her ankles pinned.

A voice . . . she couldn't see the face clearly. "Hell — this cable'll be as good as a rope. Good enough for her."

The cable was snaked around her neck. "Tie her to the back of Rourke's truck — drag hang her!"

And then, "Fun's over!"

Natalia opened her eyes — it was John Rourke's voice.

The lights from the camp backlit him and in silhouette she could see the Detonics .45s in his hands.

"Let her go," Rourke said with an edge in his voice. "Help her up and let her walk over here. First person who does otherwise dies — end of story."

**The Survivalist series by Jerry Ahern
published by New English Library**

The Survivalist 12
The Rebellion

Jerry Ahern

NEW ENGLISH LIBRARY
Hodder and Stoughton

First published in the USA in 1985 by Kensington Publishing Corporation

Copyright © 1985 by Jerry Ahern

First NEL Paperback Edition 1986
Second impression 1987

British Library C.I.P.

Ahern, Jerry
 The rebellion.—(The survivalist: 12)
 I. Title   II. Series
 813'.54[F]   PS3551.H4/

 ISBN 0-450-39988-5

Printed for Hodder and Stoughton Paperbacks, a division of Hodder and Stoughton Ltd., Mill Road, Dunton Green, Sevenoaks, Kent TN13 2YA. (Editorial Office: 47 Bedford Square, London WC1B 3DP) by Richard Clay Ltd., Bungay, Suffolk

Especially for all those in England who have come to feel for John Rourke et al—all the best and many thanks.

Prologue

John Rourke sat in the open fuselage door of the Soviet helicopter, Natalia Tiemerovna at the controls—Eden Two was clearly visible on the horizon. A mile distant, the soaking cold of the rains gone, Rourke could see the second helicopter, the one piloted by Kurinami. Standing by the third machine, still on the ground, was the commander of Eden One and the overall Eden Project commander, Capt. Christopher Dodd. An M-16 was across Rourke's lap, slung cross body from his left shoulder. Two more M-16s were secured beside him with tie-down straps improvised from their slings.

Natalia's voice came over the radio headset. "John—I don't see any sign of Vladmir's forces, or that other helicopter unit."

"The Nazis," Rourke commented. "Hope it stays that way."

Eden Two was closing now on the road surface that had been converted to a runway—but this time no burning helicopter hovered nearby, imprisoning his best friend. No technologically advanced Soviet helicopter gunships pursued the shuttle, firing missiles and machine guns in an attempt to shoot it down.

That he and Natalia were airborne in one craft, and that Kurinami had taken a second stolen Soviet machine airborne, was precautionary only.

After Karamatsov, in what was presumably the last of the Soviet gunship force nearby, had vanished in the wake of the landing of Eden One, there had been no additional hostile action.

Rourke did not actually hold the M-16 that was across his lap—movement of his hands was painful and started the knuckles bleeding again.

He shivered in the cold of the rotor downdraft, despite the battered brown leather bomber jacket that he wore—he was drenched still and there had been no time to change clothing, so he had merely let the clothing dry on him. He smiled at himself—a doctor should know better.

He focused his attention on Eden Two. There was a thundering crack as it broke beneath the speed of sound. Below him as he looked down, he could see some of those already awakened from the criogenically sleeping company of Eden One jumping, waving their hands—he could imagine their shouts, their silent prayers of encouragement.

Eden Two was coming, low on the horizon—too low? He watched.

"Slow," he whispered.

"What, John?"

"Nothing—just talking to myself."

"I'm getting Eden Two again for a second on the sideband."

He waited, hearing the crackle of static as she switched bands, then hearing the voice of Christopher Dodd on the ground. "Lookin' good, Ralph—from here it looks like you should bring your nose up a couple of degrees."

"Roger on that, Chris—correcting. Gears down. Eden Two out and comin' in."

Rourke realized he was holding his breath—but he forced himself to look away, to scan the skies for enemy gunships.

Twenty-three people were alive aboard Eden Two, three of them awake, the other twenty still in the criogenic sleep

8

they had begun almost at the very moment The Night of The War had begun five centuries earlier.

Twenty-three people.

He was still holding his breath—he could feel the screech of rubber as the landing gear touched down, not hear it.

His eyes drifted downward, below the hovering gunship in which this time he was only a passenger, a door gunner—he thought he could pick out Sarah, waving her blue bandanna in the wind. A face that from the distance looked black. It would be Elaine Halverson.

He refocused on the Eden Two—it was slowing, slowing. Eden One had been towed a considerably greater distance up the road to provide adequate runway distance.

Slowing.

Eden Two stopped. John Rourke breathed. Twenty-three more souls had reached an earth nearly depopulated—to try to start things over again.

"They made it," Rourke heard Natalia's voice whisper through his earphone.

There was nothing Rourke could say.

Chapter One

The doctor aboard Eden One had done his work well—
assessing the situation as soon as he was able after reviving
from the criogenic sleep, he had ordered an additional
transfusion for Michael and then begun to work on Paul
Rubenstein, Sarah acting as his nurse, Rourke's hands
bandaged and unable to physically assist, but aiding the
man through consultation. Natalia had initially bandaged
his hands and Rourke smiled thinking of it, remembering
that she had almost seemed to blush when the doctor from
Eden One—Jim Hixon—had told her it was a better
bandage than he could have done himself. And Rourke had
laughed—as an M.D. himself he knew perfectly well that it
was, however sincerely meant, a hollow compliment. Doc-
tors rarely bandaged, and nurses always did it better. But
Hixon had undone the bandages and treated Rourke's
hands—rope burns, abrasions and cuts. And Rourke had
laughed again, because Hixon had asked Natalia to do the
fresh re-bandaging.

John Rourke sat now, the rain stopped long since, on a
broad flat rock beyond the perimeter of the camp, his rifle
on the rock beside him. He wore the double Alessi shoulder
rig with the twin stainless Detonics .45s. With his hands
bandaged as they were, however, he doubted he could get to
the Detonics pistols with any alacrity. But his CAR-15
would be accessible.

Eden Two had landed an hour after the rain had stopped. The four remaining shuttle craft would be landing over the next two days. Dodd, Lerner, and Styles had, at Rourke's urging, taken over setting up security details composed of the gradually reawakening passengers. But Rourke, the only living man as best he knew to have taken the sleep twice, well knew the physical state of the revived sleepers. Jim Hixon had several times during the operation on Paul Rubenstein been forced to stop, to sit down, to rest.

The human body was not made to bounce back easily from five centuries of inactivity.

Rourke lit the thin, dark tobacco cigar that he had held clenched in his teeth for more than an hour, tossing the Zippo in his hands, by the moonlight almost able to discern the initials J.T.R. engraved there. He pocketed the lighter, careful of his bandaged knuckles, inhaling the smoke deep into his lungs, then exhaling it. The cigars Annie had learned to make for him were good—and again he wondered if part of the flavor was because his own daughter had made them for him, knowing he would want them when he awoke. But he had determined to cut down his consumption—good health would be even more important in the weeks and months and years to come.

He assessed their situation.

Michael was already stronger due to the transfusions and—Rourke admitted to himself—his own surgical abilities. Paul's wounds should heal, though Paul too had lost considerable blood. He worried now not seriously about either his son or his best friend. Madison, the girl Michael had saved from the savages which had surrounded The Place, the girl whom Rourke was certain even now carried his grandchild in her womb, would care for Michael, nurse him as no other could. And Paul—he smiled at the thought. His best friend would soon be his son-in-law. Annie.

The way Rourke had used the criogenic chambers had played strange games with age and time.

Michael was thirty. Annie would soon be twenty-eight—biologically, Rourke was not old enough to have parented either of them.

But Annie would care for Paul—with her life if necessary.

He had not seen Sarah since she had assisted Hixon in the operation on Paul, except that distant glimpse of her from the air. And Natalia—battered, tortured by her husband, her husband a living ghost—had busied herself as well, working with the M-16s and 1911A1s of the two landed Eden Project shuttle craft to ensure reliable functioning after more than five centuries of being packed in something the consistency of cosmoline.

It was curious, Rourke thought, that despite the much-heralded changeover that had come before The Night of The War, the pistols packed aboard the Eden Project shuttles had been .45s and not the newer Beretta 9mms. The Beretta had been a superb pistol for the caliber, but Rourke was just as happy the designers of the Eden Project mission had done as they did. He had greater stores of .45 ACP available and personally preferred the large caliber.

He sat, contemplating loved ones, weapons for their defense, and old and new enemies.

The helicopter gunships which had arrived on the scene as he, Sarah, Kurinami, Halverson and Madison had effected Natalia's rescue had been clearly marked with the swastika. A new enemy, but one from the past. But his old enemy, his worst enemy he realized, still somehow lived.

He would never forgive himself for the carelessness. Vladmir Karamatsov had appeared dead five centuries ago after the gunfight on the streets of what had been Athens, Georgia. John Rourke would never forgive himself for not firing an extra round into the head to be sure.

That Karamatsov still lived was in itself a threat—but

13

that somehow he had gathered about him a large, heavily armed force with technologically advanced small arms and helicopter gunships of almost undreamed-of capabilities was an even greater threat.

Hence the watch that Dodd, Lerner and Styles had established at his urging. But if the helicopter gunship force of the twisted, unspeakably evil Karamatsov were to return, there would be little defense against it: the helicopter Rourke himself had flown into battle, the one Kurinami had flown and the one Natalia had flown. Three against how many, Rourke wondered.

He watched in the darkness—he watched the sky, still wondering as he had five centuries earlier, did men everywhere destroy themselves with such insanity? And he heard a voice. "You are the one from the radio communications—Rourke?"

Rourke's knuckles screamed at him with pain as he brought the CAR-15 up, throwing himself from the flat rock to the ground, swinging the CAR-15 into an assault position toward the voice from the darkness.

"I am unarmed, sir—except for my pistol. And it is holstered."

Rourke could see no face, but at a distance of perhaps a hundred yards he could faintly discern a figure stepping from behind the shelter of high rocks. "I come in peace to you, sir."

"Who the hell are you?" John Rourke hissed.

"Your entire encampment is surrounded by my men, and their machines are nearby. If you fire a shot, there will be battle, and gallant men on both sides will die. Let us talk first, and then if you must, use your antique weapon."

"I said it once, I'll say it now. I won't say it again. Who the hell are you?"

Rourke chewed down harder on the cigar, never moving the muzzle of the CAR-15 from the silhouette beside the rocks.

"I am Colonel Wolfgang Mann, field commander of the Expeditionary Forces of the National Socialist Defense Forces. And other than being John Rourke, who are you, sir?"

John Rourke swallowed hard, then answered, "I'm just John Rourke. I'm a doctor of medicine. My family and I are here to help the returning space shuttles."

"How many of them are there?"

"More than the two on the ground."

"I like a cautious man—may I approach, sir?"

"Keep your hands where I can see them," Rourke warned. He wanted to set down the rifle—he could feel the bandages becoming wet with blood at his knuckles.

The silhouette approached—tall, the skirts of some sort of overcoat reaching to a few inches above the figure's ankles, the stride confident, brisk, a type of peaked baseball cap visible now. A cloud passed from blocking the moon, the ground suddenly bathed in pale gray-blue light. And Rourke could see the figure more clearly. The face appeared chiselled from some rock harder than granite, the eyes deep set and wider apart, their color not discernible. And Rourke recognized the badge of rank on the uniform blouse when the heavy trenchcoat above it flew open. "You said colonel—I see SS *standartenfuehrer*," Rourke growled.

"Who are you that you recognize such rank?"

"A man who's seen it before," Rourke answered, his hands numbing now to the pain, the wetness of the bandage increasing.

"No man has seen this before—no living man. Unless he is one of us."

"You're wrong," Rourke answered softly, easily.

"These space shuttle craft that I have read of in books of twentieth century history—from where do they come?"

"The sky." Rourke smiled.

"You are making this difficult, Herr Doctor Rourke."

"You're a Nazi—I don't like Nazis."

"But we Nazis saved your life and the lives of your comrades when we attacked the Soviet base. Where do you come from?"

"The same place, basically—the same time is probably more apt."

"But that is impossible. You would be almost five and one-half centuries old."

"Physical fitness, vitamins and regular bowel movements—that's the trick." Rourke smiled again.

"A criogenic process, I think. You, you are in truth from—from before—"

"The Night of The War."

"These others?"

"Except for one of them—the blond-haired girl. Except for her."

"And the Communists?" the *standartenfuehrer* asked.

"One of them at least is from my time—perhaps more of them. The rest, I don't know. And you?"

"It was called Argentina before the final war of the superpowers. We lived beneath the surface—my people—for generations until the earth was once again fit to inhabit."

"A cradle of National Socialism as it were—nice." Rourke nodded. "What do you want?"

"Why do you say you do not like Nazis?"

"Six million Jews, millions of Poles and Russians and gypsies, hundreds of thousands of others who just happened to be in the wrong place at the wrong time, a war that spawned the military use of nuclear weapons."

"This business of the six million Jews—it is a Zionist lie I have been taught.

"It is not a Zionist lie. You have been taught wrong," John Rourke whispered.

"I cannot believe—"

"That you're descended from inhuman butchers?"

"The sins of the father," the *standartenfuehrer* began.

"Are to be laid upon the children," Rourke finished for him.

"This is true—you know this is true?"

"My father fought against your ancestors. When I grew up and became a man I encountered men—crazy men—who fancied themselves Nazis, carrying on some God-damned comic opera traditions which were just an excuse for racial bigotry, racial hatred. It's true."

"Your father," the *standartenfuehrer* began. "He fought against the cause of Nazism?"

"It was called World War II—and then when everything ended, that was World War III, I suppose. Yes, he fought in World War II. He was in the OSS."

"The American intelligence commando raiders."

"You could call it that."

"And you?" the *standartenfuehrer* asked, the confidence that had been in his voice when Rourke had first heard him speak seeming to have drained. "How did you come to fight National Socialism then, if your father—"

"I was in something called the CIA. Have you heard of it?"

"The secret police of the United States for extra-national affairs—yes."

"It was the Central Intelligence Agency," Rourke corrected. "I was a case officer. Most of the time, I fought the Communists—but sometimes—"

"But the Communists were the allies of the United States until the superpowers came to warring among themselves over the domination of the countries peopled by the inferior races—"

"That's not quite the way it was," John Rourke almost whispered. "After World War II there was a long period of distrust and deterioration of relationships. At the same time, the nuclear arsenals grew and grew. The Soviets perfected a system known as particle-beam technology—

they were about to use it. As a defensive system and for offensive use against Western communications-and-intelligence-gathering satellites. The United States government saw installation of the system as a step closer to thermonuclear war. We issued an ultimatum. Somebody pushed a button—them as far as I came to understand it. And everyone died. Except your ancestors in their hole in the ground in Argentina, some other groups—at least one I know of here, a very small group. Perhaps—I guess so—some of the Soviets. Maybe the Chinese survived somehow, I don't know."

"Why are we speaking like this?"

"You came to me—if you have us surrounded, outnumbered and have airpower, why haven't you attacked?"

"My ancestor, generations ago—if your words are true—he was a mass murderer."

"My words are true," Rourke whispered. "I'm sorry if you thought otherwise. But the truth is the truth."

"Where I come from, Herr Doctor . . ."

"Yes, Herr *Standartenfuehrer*," and Rourke exhaled a thin stream of gray smoke that looked white in the reflected moonlight as he watched it dissipate on the air.

"Our leader—the successor after more than twenty generations to Adolf Hitler—there are some of us, who are not SS in our hearts, who wish a democracy where men can govern themselves and the passions of a handful of political zealots do not dictate insanity for all. I have come to offer you an alliance—against our common enemies, the Soviets. And to establish a new order of freedom for my people."

"I—ahh . . ."

"On January thirtieth, it will be Unity Day."

"One, thirty, thirty-three," Rourke whispered.

"You know this date?"

"All feeling men know this date or should—when Hitler assumed the chancellorship of Germany and the evil began."

18

"The leader—he will announce our territorial victories—
he will launch our people into the maelstrom by proclaiming that there are traitors in their midst."

"There are, aren't there?" Rourke whispered. The cigar
was dead and he cast it down into the caked mud beneath
his feet, his combat-booted right heel crushing it.

"They are good men, good women—but he will have
them publicly executed. One of them—he is Deiter Bern—
he wants our science, our technology, our leadership, he
wants these elements to rebuild the world, to make it a
place where war like that between the superpowers can
never again occur."

"An idealist—and a Nazi?"

"He is a man, Herr Doctor. If I lead those of my men
who think as I do openly against the Complex—"

"The Complex?" Rourke repeated.

"Our home," the *standartenfuehrer* who spoke of liberty
whispered, his voice suddenly hoarse sounding. "If I lead
openly against the leader, against The Complex—there will
be countless women and children who will die, innocent
men as well. But if, if a small group of courageous men
could penetrate The Complex, free Dieter Bern, and if one
of these men were a doctor, then—"

"Why must one of the men be a doctor?" Rourke asked,
lowering the assault rifle.

"I am taking a cigarette. Would you care for one?"

"No, thank you." Rourke nodded.

He watched as the *standartenfuehrer* removed a cigarette
case and a lighter from the pockets of his trenchcoat, at last
seeing the man's eyes in the light of the flame—a clarity
and strength in their blueness, and a certain tiredness as
well. "Deiter Bern is kept in a drugged state, so he cannot
get messages from his confinement, so he cannot answer
the leader's charges. But were Bern to be free, to somehow
be free of the drugs, then somehow spirited to the Communications Center—then my people could choose. But

19

today's date—"

"My daughter will be twenty-eight in four days—it's the twenty-second today," and Rourke glanced at the luminous black face of the Rolex Submariner on his left wrist. "In another ten minutes or so the twenty-third."

"Then in seven days, it will be Unity Day. And Deiter Bern will be publicly executed and there will be warfare instead of freedom."

"You speak so disparagingly of warfare—yet you are a military man."

"Some men serve their country, their race, their people—some serve to guard peace."

"And in return for this help you need?" Rourke asked.

"Those men who are loyal to me would safeguard this area against further attack by the Communists—there are other shuttle craft in the night sky, are there not?"

"Four." Rourke nodded.

"My other legions have been dispatched to pursue these Soviet troops."

"And be that much further from your Complex when you attempt the coup."

The *standartenfuehrer* laughed aloud. "I am transparent, am I not?" He threw down his cigarette, crushing it under his boot.

"And you can leave a token force in this area to answer radio communications from your extended elements and from your command headquarters, while the bulk of your men return in secret to this Complex place."

"I am transparent indeed." The *standartenfuehrer* laughed again.

"What makes you think—well, in five centuries of technology, your people's medical skills must be far advanced over ours. Why do you need me?"

"You have wounded—I have a doctor who can help them, who can teach you his secrets, this new medical technology. But I would be recognized in The Complex, as

20

would any of my officers, the doctor among them. There are many thousands of our people. Were you not to attract attention, you could move about freely until you choose to strike."

"What does my being a doctor have to do with it? You could easily have your doctor teach someone the procedure of alleviating whatever condition this drug induces."

"When I learned of these space shuttle craft, I envisioned some sort of doomsday project. And for that, medical technicians would have been included. That you yourself are a medical man is sheer—and may I say fortunate—coincidence. But a medical man was a necessity."

"Why?" Rourke asked him.

"There are many who would free Deiter Bern, Herr Doctor. But none can. Because Deiter Bern is confined in a most special way. He is not behind bars. There is a shackle about his neck, electrical current running through the shackle and through the chain which connects the shackle into the wall. If the electrical current is disrupted in any way, an electronic impulse will be emitted, and the impulse will trigger a capsule which is attached to an electrode, the electrode disintegrating the capsule. Inside the capsule is a synthetic form closely approximating the ancient drug known, I believe, as curare. Once the synthetic curare is released, Deiter Bern will be dead in under four seconds. There is no antidote with which he can be previously injected. The capsule is located in the carotid artery near what my own medical specialist tells me is something called a venus fistula—you know of this?"

Rourke nodded. "You speak English well."

"The officer corps has stringent language requirements. But to further diminish any chances of Deiter Bern being freed, the entrance to and from the section in which he is confined—the only means in or out and my best commandoes have confirmed this—constantly broadcasts an identical electronic impulse. Should the current at the entryway be disrupted, an effect occurs similar to that of the claymore-type mines used prior to the warfare between the superpowers. Thousands of tiny needles the size of slivers which have been positioned at strategic locations throughout the walls and ceiling and floor of the room are released, traveling at such high velocity and of such infinitesimal size that they will penetrate up to a six-millimeter thickness of armor plate."

"Quarter inch," Rourke murmured.

"Each needle is tipped with the synthetic derivative of this ancient drug curare. Three penetrations of the needles would be adequate to kill an average-sized man in under thirty-eight seconds."

Rourke sat back on the rock, setting the rifle down—his hands, the bandages blood-soaked, pained him. "So, let me ask you. The shackle about Deiter Bern's neck—is it such that it can be slipped away from the location of the implant?"

"This is my doctor's opinion—yes," the *standartenfuehrer* nodded.

"So then the only means to free Herr Bern is to penetrate The Complex, reach the detention area and somehow perform the surgery right there on the spot while he is presumably still under guard and shackled to the wall, without disrupting the current."

"That is the only way. I understand that once men believed in a being known as God—"

"Some men still do," Rourke answered unbidden.

"That prayers were offered to this God. It is as if you came in answer to such a prayer. I observed the great daring you displayed there at the Soviet encampment, and later in rescuing the man from the burning helicopter."

"Paul Rubenstein is my friend. At the encampment, my wife, my daughter, a woman whom I have very much feeling for, a girl who carries my son's child, two friends—"

"This is a man who seeks liberty, Herr Doctor—someone with whom I should think you might have a great deal in common. My legions pursue the Communists regardless of your decision, and I personally have no desire to make war upon you. But if Deiter Bern is executed, the leader's armies will sweep over the earth. Such weapons as you might possess will be useless against us."

Rourke laughed. "I know—don't tell me. We'll be powerless to resist."

"Yes, but I suspect you might resist at any event. If the Communists have a substantial force and are well entrenched, two corps will not be sufficient to undo them. It is your choice—to aid a potential ally for peace, or to combat and eventually succumb to what I feel is an old enemy and what I fear would be a new one. And then to contemplate with your last breath that these two enemies will fight each other to the death, perhaps until this time all life on this planet is indeed destroyed forever."

John Rourke lit another cigar, weighing the battered Zippo wind lighter in his hand. "I can't speak, Herr *Standartenfuehrer*, for the Eden Project—"

"This Eden Project—"

"The Eden Project—you guessed correctly—was a doomsday mission. That was the code name given it. But I can't speak for the men and women of the Eden Project. But for myself, Herr *Standartenfuehrer*—"

"This SS rank—I am a colonel, and proud of that. I am not SS—a party member. I have read the forbidden books."

"No book should be forbidden except by individual taste or preference."

"You remind me, Herr Doctor, of some of the men whom I have read of in these forbidden books."

"Colonel, why don't you tell those two friends of yours—the one with the assault rifle about ten degrees north-

northwest and the other one with that thing that looks like a LAWS rocket—why don't you tell them to stand down? You keep your pistol—principally because I'd like to see it. And go for a walk with me."

"It, like your rifle, my pistol is an antique, a Walther P-38. There is a man in The Complex who makes the ammunition. It—the ammunition of those days—is very expensive. But this Walther was carried by my father and his father and his father before him and for generations."

"It should be quite a pistol." John Rourke smiled. And he gestured to the twin stainless Detonics pistols he wore. "These are five centuries old themselves—but I wouldn't call them antiques just yet," and Rourke slid off the broad flat rock where he had again seated himself—it was damp there anyway. His back was stiff from the weight of Paul Rubenstein when he had gotten Paul out of the burning helicopter. And he was generally sore and stiff from the exertion. It hadn't been daring, as the German-accented colonel had called it, Rourke thought. It had been necessary. John Rourke extended his right hand. "The name's John, Colonel."

The colonel took his hand—the grip was firm, like a man's grip should be, Rourke thought absently. "I am Wolfgang—I am called Wolf by some."

"Wolf," Rourke said quietly.

They released each others hands.

Rourke smiled at the man. "Don't forget your pals—they could get awfully lonely out here while we're talking. Or, if some of Dodd's security people—"

"Dodd?"

"The Commander of Eden One and the overall Eden Project commander. But if some of his people should decide to stray out past the perimeter, well, somebody could get awfully dead too, I suppose."

Wolfgang Mann's face beamed with a smile as he called out in German, "Wait for me at the edge of our perimeter—hurry!"

"P-38's a good gun, you know," Rourke began, walking beside the colonel toward the perimeter of the encampment which had clustered around the two returned Eden Project shuttles. "There's this woman with me—you'll have to meet her. But we were in this place recently—in fact it was called The Place. And of all the guns stored there, she picked only one additional handgun. A P-38. I was never much of a 9mm man myself—but somewhere back at The Retreat—that's where I live, you know—well, I've got a Walther P-38K. Hell of a good gun, despite the caliber. And in the old days, of course, before The Night of The War, sometimes when I was in the field I couldn't always get a .45. You know how that can be," Rourke said quietly. "And so a couple of times, I used a Walther P-5—ever see one of those?"

"No."

"Shame," Rourke murmured. "I bet you would've liked it." He stopped walking a moment. "Oh, I'm not trying to be presumptuous. But someone who speaks of freedom and peace—well. Don't go calling yourself a Nazi anymore. You're a German."

Wolfgang Mann didn't answer.

Chapter Two

The helicopter had barely landed. Despite his injured left arm and the field dressing which was soaked through with blood, Karamatsov jumped through the fuselage doorway to the sandy west Texas earth. He ducked his head, but too late, the wind of the rotor blades snatching away his cap. He dismissed the event, walking on. One of his subordinates would pick up the cap and bring it to him. Antonovitch was beside him in an instant, the cap in his hands—Karamatsov did not take back the cap immediately, shouting over the whir of the rotor blades and squinting against the storm of sand which they generated and blew at him, "There is no time to lose, Nicolai. You will carry out the following orders."

"Yes, Comrade Colonel Karamatsov!"

Vladmir Karamatsov altered his course slightly, toward the prefabricated shelter which had been erected as his headquarters. Aircraft landed along the runway his personnel had nearly completed carving from the sand in his absence—they would carry men, supplies, synthetic fuel. "I am abandoning plans for the destruction of the Eden Project at this time. I have never told you," Karamatsov said, slightly breathless—it was the change in humidity which affected his breathing, he knew. Part of his left lung had been cut away. He began again. "I have never told you, Nicolai—but I have an agent among the complement of the Eden Project—"

"An agent, Comrade Colonel?"

"Yes—placed there five centuries ago in the event that the Eden Project proved to be the insurance against doomsday which I had always suspected. And I was right of course."

"But, Comrade Colonel?" Maj. Nicolai Antonovitch began. "When you ordered the destruction of the six Eden Project shuttle craft, your agent was aboard—"

"My agent knew the risks. But we shall see what my agent is able to precipitate that may hasten the Eden Project's destruction. I wish activities of the Eden Project monitored by high-altitude observation craft—see that this is begun, and quickly. Meanwhile—" and he took his cap from Antonovitch, not bothering to replace it on his head, but carrying it in his left hand, slapping it against his left thigh as he walked toward the prefabricated shelter. "Meanwhile, you must see to it that Major Krakovski and his units which prosecute our efforts against the Wild Tribes of Europe are recalled immediately. Immediately. I wish for Krakovski and his forces to join me at once. We mount an attack force against these Nazis which have so brazenly interfered with our strategies."

"It is the Nazis, Comrade Colonel, who are the source—"

"The source of the high-level technology our observation aircraft have uncovered in South America. You, Antonovitch, you will take a small force and the necessary equipment."

"Yes, Comrade Colonel?"

Karamatsov stopped now, before the entrance to the prefabricated shelter. Men and equipment moved everywhere about him—more and more of the supplies he required were being flown in from The Underground City in the Ural Mountains. "You will take your small force and gather what intelligence you can without being detected concerning the Nazi headquarters base—its makeup, its defensive capabilities. You will ascertain as best as possible the size and composition of their reserve forces. As soon as Krakovski's forces arrive, if not sooner, I shall personally lead the bulk of our force against the Nazi stronghold. Once we have destroyed their headquarters and source of supply, it shall be easy enough to destroy their expeditionary force."

"But . . ."-

Karamatsov stopped—he had begun to walk inside the hut. He waited.

"But, Comrade Colonel—what of—"

"Rourke?" Karamatsov whispered. "What of Rourke and his family and my wife?" And Karamatsov allowed himself to laugh. "I have in the most likely event caused the death of his son. The Jew, Rubenstein—he is most assuredly dead. The Nazis which attacked us are at Rourke's doorstep. I have hurt Rourke—now let him suffer for a time. In a way, things have worked for the best. Rather than a quick and merciful death, he and my wife can now contemplate the inevitability of their fate. It would be impossible for the Eden Project to stand against us. But let him plan—and when we have dealt with this matter of the Nazi homeground, then destroyed what remains of the Nazi force, we shall very slowly close our grip on the Eden Project—very slowly. We shall destroy him, destroy her—destroy them all. And then Krakovski shall return to what used to be Germany and France and Italy—he shall destroy the wild tribes or subjugate them for use as our slaves." Karamatsov smiled. He clapped Antonovitch on the right shoulder with his right hand. "And I shall be master of this earth—or there will be no more earth." He left Màj. Nicolai Antonovitch—knowing the look in the man's eyes without having to see it.

Chapter Three

Ivan Krakovski watched the shadow of his machine skim across the broken ground—it was like a shadow of death, he thought. He tried to find poetry in all things because poetry had always been his first love. He knew, for example, that had he been born in a different era, he would have been one of the great Russian poets. He still indulged in verse and planned that someday after he had aided the Hero Colonel, Vladmir Karamatsov, in his conquest of the reborn earth, he would write the definitive history of the period and sing the songs of triumph in verse. And that someday in the distant future men and women would praise not only his heroic efforts on behalf of the establishment of communism as the world order, but praise also the heroic words with which he immortalized the efforts of his leader.

The shadow of death. It seemed almost to lovingly idle with the things which ran before it. The things were not men, were not women. He composed this in his mind, how he would tell it. The Wild Tribes of Europe had long ago ceased to lay claim to humanity. The French attempt at surviving the global holocaust had failed—and dismally so. They had been ill-prepared, unprepared to endure centuries beneath the ground. They had emerged too soon. Radiation had taken its toll. There were still, indeed, massive hot spots on the planet, where the background radiation was of such high level that the land would not be habitable for perhaps a hundred thousand years, perhaps twice that time. But the hapless French had ventured forth before the atmosphere had restored itself to a point where plants would grow again in any abundance. Starvation, likely cannibalism, the genetic mutations of radiation—yet thousands of them had survived. Nearly naked, their skin leathery tough, no language that could be discerned, they roamed the plains of Europe scavenging for what vegetable material could be found, huddled in caves from the cold by night, their meager, poorly designed fires barely able to warm them. The death rate among them was staggering, he knew. But yet they survived.

The shadow. It brushed at one of them and the thing—a woman only because she had dirty pendulous breasts and an infant clung to the left one—gazed skyward.

The shadow of death. Krakovski prided himself on being with his men, doing what they did, enduring their hardships, eating the same food as they. And now as he spoke into the teardrop-shaped microphone before his lips—"Fire at will"—he did the same.

He lightly touched the triggering mechanism on the throttle, activating the machine guns. And the woman and the child, neither of whom were human any more, collapsed beneath the shadow of his machine, a ragged stitch of brilliant red blood bursting across the two bodies that at her breast were one.

The shadow of death.

Krakovski wrote in his diary—of his emotions, of his appreciation of what had transpired. "As many as one hundred of the members of what is perhaps the largest of the wild tribes were liquidated this day by my own hand and the hands of my corps of loyal pilots. These one hundred were herded away from the bulk of the group which we encountered on a routine search-and-destroy mission in southern France. The remainder of the group—some forty-eight men and adult women—were less deformed and or physically ill than their fellows and were taken under our care to be employed usefully in whatever capacity will most advance the cause of global communism." The forty-eight men and women were currently penned inside the portable titanium alloy fences which reminded him of the corral structures he had seen in videotapes of the American western movies from five centuries earlier. The fence was, of course, electrified. He considered this as he closed his diary and stood, walking to the flap of his tent and opening it, looking out through the rain and watching them, the forty-eight. Sparks flew as raindrops would touch the fence rails, the forty-eight huddled together like an impossibly large litter of puppies or kittens against some invisible mother.

He thought of the Hero Colonel, Vladmir Karamatsov. Krakovski was personally disgusted that Karatmatsov used women from among the Wild Tribes for sexual purposes. Because they were not really women, only roughly in the shape of women. Morally, it was like having sex with an animal. But perhaps it repulsed Krakovski as well, because the Hero Colonel would beat the Wild Tribe women to death afterward—or during. Ivan Krakovski was not quite certain which, nor did he care to find out.

"Comrade Major!"

He looked again through the tent flap. Running across the mud flats from the communications tent he could see Brasniewicz, a yellow message blotter in his upraised, waving right hand.

"Comrade Major!"

Krakovski stood his ground beneath the protection of his tent—Brasniewcz was wet already and wasn't even an officer. Krakovski waved the man forward and then turned away from the rain and the forty-eight huddled bodies exposed to it within the confines of the electrified fence. He walked across the floor of his tent and sat down at his portable writing desk.

After a moment, he heard Brasniewicz at the tent flap. "Comrade Major?"

"Come in, comrade," Krakovski called out.

Brasniewicz appeared, his hatless head dripping water, his uniform soaked.

"You look most unmilitary, man—you should be reduced in rank for your appearance were there any rank lower than that which you already possess."

"Yes, Comrade Major. I apologize, Comrade Major."

"You have a message on that pad. What is it—read it."

"Yes, Comrade Major," and Brasniewicz straightened himself to full attention, water dribbling down his face from the wet, plastered black hair. "It is from Comrade Colonel Karamatsov."

"Read it, comrade."

" 'Ivan—' I am sorry, Comrade Major, but—"

"Just read the message, Brasniewicz."

"Yes, Comrade Major. 'New developments here. Withdraw all forces immediately—repeat, immediately—from operation in which you are currently engaged. Join me at best speed at North American Command. Advise ETA immediately.' It is signed by the comrade colonel, Comrade Major Krakovski."

"Take this message." Krakovski nodded, leaning back in his folding chair, his polished boots coming up to rest on the corner of the writing desk. "To Colonel Vladimir Karamatsov—Message received and understood. ETA North American Command—" and Krakovski looked up from admiring the shine on his own boots. "Encrypt the message and wait its transmission until I have met with my officers."

"Yes, Comrade Major."

"You are dismissed, Brasniewicz." Krakovski swung his boots down and stood, stretching, as Brasniewicz did a smart enough about-face and marched out of the tent.

Krakovski yawned, walking across the tent to where his cap and his trenchcoat hung—he took down the cap and placed it carefully on his head, then the trenchcoat, belting it firmly about his waist. He started toward the tent flap, through the opening and into the rain-soaked mud, the shine on his boots glowing dully as he watched them, the water beading on them. He kept walking, toward the fence and the forty-eight.

He approached the nearest of the two ponchoed guards on the perimeter of the fence.

The man snapped to attention, making a rifle salute. Krakovski nodded, raising his right hand to the peak of his cap, returning the salute with his customary sharpness, yet casualness. "Give me your rifle, comrade."

"Yes, Comrade Major."

Krakovski took the weapon in his hands and hefted it—it felt right. He walked away from the guard and toward the electrified corral-type fence. "Corporal, shut off the voltage and signal to me when this is accomplished. Then have a second magazine available for my immediate use."

"Yes, Comrade Major."

Krakovski approached the fence. He could see some of them looking at him, their eyes filled with fear. He looked down to his boots—the water was not beading as well as it had and already his toes were beginning to feel damp.

"The electricity is off, Comrade Major!"

"Very good, Corporal—do not forget the spare magazine!"

The dampness of his toes persisted—but he had always prided himself on enduring the same hardships his men endured. He raised the assault rifle to his hip, settling his feet firmly on the muddy ground—his boots definitely were seeping water. He worked the bolt of the assault rifle, then without looking thumbed the selector to full auto.

He opened fire, neat three-round bursts. He prided

himself that he was better than the best of his men with the issue weapon. The way in which the Wild Tribes creatures were concentrated, it was possible to penetrate many bodies with a single burst. They made the customary whining sounds, like dogs howling in pain when they were beaten. The forty-round disposable magazine empty, he buttoned it out, extending his left hand. The magazine was not instantly forthcoming and he looked behind him—the guard corporal was vomiting. "Control yourself, comrade—such weakness cannot be tolerated."

The man vomited again and pulled himself erect. "Forgive me, Comrade," and the man vomited again, Krakovski looking down, the vomit comingling with the rain water that was puddled in the mud, running toward his boots. The man extended the magazine to him.

"Put yourself on report—you are an animal," Krakovski snarled, taking the magazine. He rammed it up the well, then continued to fire. One of the more human-looking of the women was crawling through the mud away from the mound of bodies. Her left leg was covered with blood. He assumed it was a wound because the blood did not dissolve away in the rain. Her naked breasts dragged through the mud, cutting furrows there.

He did not like to waste ammunition, but he was merciful. So he shot her in the face.

Chapter Four

The light was gray still, Rourke seated on the tailgate of his camouflaged Ford pick-up, listening as Dodd, Lerner and Styles almost seemed to interrogate Wolfgang Mann. "I find it very hard to believe, Colonel, that someone who wears a uniform bearing Nazi insignia can seriously ask us to help him in restoring democracy."

"We cannot restore democracy—there has never been democracy among us. It would be the dawn of a new era, Captain Dodd."

"With all due respect, Colonel," Jeff Styles, the Eden One science officer interrupted, "you come here and ask us to perhaps limit our own chances of survival just to help you."

"We have enemies enough," Craig Lerner volunteered. "If some of our people—or even just Doctor Rourke here—if some of us go off attacking people in South America, all we'll do is provoke retaliation."

Rourke watched Mann's eyes. The *standartenfuehrer*, who preferred being called Colonel, who spoke of freeing his people, leaned heavily against the side of the earth mover which had been used to help clear the sand from the road surface at the far end of which Eden One was now parked. "I—I do not know what to say, gentlemen—except that if on Unity Day Deiter Bern is murdered and the leader goes unchallenged, no portion of this earth will be safe from the might of our armies. You have a mortal enemy already—the Russians. I view the Communists as a common enemy. It makes for the most clear of logical deductions that those who believe in freedom should unite against those who do not, to ensure that freedom will endure. If we fight among ourselves . . ." Mann's voice trailed off.

No one spoke.

But then John Rourke did. "I talked with the colonel, brought him here. I've been up all night listening to everyone argue. The colonel would have nothing to gain by lying. He doubtlessly has a superior force that could be used to attack our encampment. But he hasn't done that. His force attacked the Communist gunships when I went after my family and my friends. They made no move to interfere with our escape. When Karamatsov and his people—"

"You seem obsessed with this Karamatsov character," Dodd snapped.

"He's just that kind of a wild and crazy guy." Rourke smiled. And then he let the smile fade. "But when he attacked us, Mann and his people didn't come in for the kill. We were at our most vulnerable."

"You have a hero complex, Doctor Rourke—putting it plainly," Dodd began. "I could feel that in the first words you spoke to me over the radio, see that in the reckless manner in which you risked your life to save Eden One, and then to save your friends. Now, don't get me wrong. I'm grateful for that. Without your efforts, we would have been annihilated—"

"Get to the point," Rourke almost whispered.

"Fine." Dodd nodded, pacing the rippled, caked mud of the ground. "The point then. Nothing in my contingency plans calls for being met on this planet after the earth has been all but destroyed. And by an ex-CIA agent—"

"Case officer," Rourke corrected automatically.

"—Who is also a doctor of medicine. Who has one friend who happens to have been a very high ranking KGB agent before she saw the light. Who has fully grown children who are almost as old as he is. Who—"

"I thought you were going to make your point," Rourke whispered, taking out one of his cigars and putting it between his teeth, rolling it into the left corner of his mouth, chewing down on it.

"I am, sir. My point—nothing warned me about distinguishing between good Nazis and bad Nazis, fighting megalomaniac Russians who are five hundred years old, or taking the advice of one of the only Americans to survive World War III and the burning of the sky. No, sir—I have responsibilities not only to the people of the Eden Project, but to their unborn children. In my ship's computers, I carry the access for the accumulated knowledge of mankind. In my holds, I carry embryonic life forms of birds and animals and plants—"

"I don't think plants have embryos, Captain Dodd." Rourke smiled good-naturedly.

"The point is, I have the capability to return life to the earth. And you ask me to start a war, sir."

"The war has already been started," Rourke told him. "I'm asking you to help finish it. You can sit here—I won't say comfortably because it isn't that—but you can sit here. And you can bury your heads so you can't see, can't hear. You can ignore the situation that exists now and the worsening of the situation to come. I truly believe you are concerned about the welfare of the Eden Project—every man, woman and every child to be. I'm concerned as well. The first child to be born to the Eden Project will be the child Madison carries in her womb now, the child given to her by my son, Michael. In a very real way, that child will be a symbol." Rourke smiled. "Madison has survived through the generations, and she is a child of the world as it is today. Michael survived through the criogenic sleep

37

from the era of The Night of The War. The child will be the first child born since life which left the earth has returned, the first child to grow up on this planet in five hundred years who will be able to see birds, smell flowers. And maybe the first child to grow up in peace instead of fear. We can make a beginning here—or we can make the same old mistakes all over again. Somebody said that no man is free while other men are not—something like that. But for centuries, some men were free and most were not. And it'll be that way again unless we stamp it out—stamp out tyranny right now. I've said my piece." Rourke nodded, lighting his cigar, punctuating his words with the blue-yellow flame. He inhaled smoke into his lungs, then exhaled through his teeth.

"That was beautiful, Herr Doctor," Mann murmured.

Rourke looked at the colonel, then smiled. "If a Nazi can sound like an idealist, I suppose an ex-CIA man who, ahh, has just killed too many people—well, it's a dumb thing to say—"

"Can be an idealist as well?" Dodd supplied.

Rourke smiled, nodded. "Yeah, I guess."

"What kept you going, Doctor?" Flight officer Lerner asked, his eyes squinted tight as though thinking, or as though staring at some strong light.

"The twentieth century allowed few virtues, Mr. Lerner. If you trusted your fellow man—you could wind up dead. If you vowed that you would never take a human life, there would always be somebody somewhere who would be twice as eager because of that to take your life. But I discovered one virtue—you just don't give up if something is the right thing and you know that it is. You might die—I guess that's an excuse to give up trying. But that's the only one I know of," and he slid off the tailgate of the Ford. He felt self-conscious, as though climbing down from a soap box. "So—what is it, Captain Dodd?" But he didn't wait for an answer, but turned to Wolfgang Mann instead. "Whatever,

38

I'll help you—and you'll help these people."

"You just—you just—"

Rourke looked at Dodd.

Dodd licked his lips. "You just dismissed—dismissed any decision I could make."

"I suppose I did. I didn't intend that. Perhaps you should take a vote. Or make a command decision. I can't tell you what to do." Rourke looked at Mann. "But anyway—what I said stands."

"Doctor?"

And Rourke turned again to look at Dodd. "Yes?"

"I'll commit." Dodd looked down toward his boots. "I'll commit. And the responsibility is mine. You can take a few nonessential personnel who might volunteer. It'd be foolish of me to suggest we loan you any weapons."

Rourke laughed. He was better equipped than the entire Eden Project fleet.

"But we'll do what we can to help the colonel here in his cause. Without directly, at least, jeopardizing our people."

"Then allow me," Mann said suddenly, "to begin our alliance with a gesture of good will. I noted the Herr Doctor's hands. I understand from our conversation that Doctor Rourke's son and his friend are injured as well. Allow me to contact the chief medical officer of my legion. In five centuries, not only have our means for making war progressed, but healing too, I think." And Mann's face beamed with a smile. "I suppose healing is, after all, what we have been discussing since before dawn."

John Rourke walked away from the group—he was very tired.

Chapter Five

John Rourke had grabbed a few hours sleep—but it was not enough, he knew, his eyes burning more than slightly. His muscles still ached from the ordeal entailed in Paul Rubenstein's rescue from the helicopter. He walked now, slightly stiff, working the kinks out as he moved his arms, twisted his shoulders under the harness of the double Alessi shoulder rig that carried his twin stainless Detonics Combat Master .45s. Through the ultra dark lenses of his sunglasses, he peered toward the east—the sun was perhaps an hour from its zenith. There was a chill in the air and he was happy for the warmth of the battered brown leather bomber jacket he wore.

There had been no warmth in the night. Again, Sarah had not slept with him. She had sat up through the night alongside Madison and Annie, keeping the vigil over Michael and Paul Rubenstein. Rourke looked at his hands—and he was amazed. After the initial chill of the aerosol spray Wolfgang Mann's staff doctor had provided, there had been a sudden warmth where a moment earlier there had been discomfort and even pain. As he had slept, he had awakened often with the strange itching sensation beneath the bandages which swathed his knuckles. When Rourke had finally awakened for good, he had removed the bandages from his hands. In the space of a few hours, what his professional eye gauged as two to three days of healing had taken place.

Rourke had shaved, then showered and washed his hair in one of the portable units from Eden One's cargo bay, then taken the duplicate aerosol can Mann's doctor had provided and resprayed his knuckles. The coolness, then the pleasant warmth.

By the time he had finished a light breakfast of Tang— the astronaut corps really did use it and he smiled remembering the product's advertising campaign from five centuries ago—and freeze-dried coffee and some dehydrated fruit, the itching had begun again. But he left the new bandages in place this time.

John Rourke had walked to the edge of the camp. There had been no need to race to the impromptu hospital tent where Michael and Paul were. Had a crisis arisen in the brief period Rourke had slept, his wife would have awakened him. He stood now, staring at the mottled skin of Eden One far down the road and beyond it Eden Two. Soon, Eden Three would be landing.

He sat on a large, flat rock, thinking. Little had changed in five centuries. There were still men in the world who would deal in unbridled death and destruction to achieve their ends. Apathy still governed the souls of the good. And he—John Rourke—was still in love with two women. One would not sleep with him because he had used the criogenic chambers to age their children so as a family unit all of them would be able to survive. One he would not sleep with, though he had wanted to for five centuries. But he would not because he was married.

He had long ago determined that there was a certain innate stupidity about humankind—and he had never been so egotistical as to exclude himself from the generalization.

"Dr. Rourke?"

A woman's voice—not a voice he knew. Rourke turned toward the voice. A pretty girl, her hair more red than auburn, her eyes indeterminate, her face very pale. She

41

smiled at him. He stood and allowed himself to smile back. "I don't think I know you—but I've met so many people since Eden One and Two landed. Forgive me if we've met."

"No, no—we haven't met. I've seen you from a distance, that's all and—" she smiled thinly—"you're the only one not dressed in NASA coveralls or one of those German uniforms."

He had seen a half dozen of Mann's men about the camp that morning—engineers, medical personnel. It was clear Wolfgang Mann intended, at least at the present, to live up to his end of the bargain. "Can I help you?" Rourke finally asked her.

"My name is Mona Stankiewicz. I'm the back-up flight officer for Eden One—under Craig Lerner?"

"Right." Rourke nodded.

"I wanted to talk to you later."

"We're talking now, aren't we?"

"Well, yes." She smiled. "But, well, with Eden Three coming in—well, I just saw you out here and I didn't have to get together with Captain Dodd for a few minutes."

"Can I help you with something then?" Rourke asked her again, lighting one of the thin, dark tobacco cigars in the blue-yellow flame of his Zippo.

"I needed to tell you about something. But I can't now. But later? After Eden Three lands?"

"I'm not in charge here, Miss—ahh—Miss Stankiewicz. Captain Dodd is the overall commander for the Eden Project." Rourke exhaled a stream of gray cigar smoke through his nostrils, watching it dissipate. "If there's a problem," he continued, "Dodd is the man you should confer with."

"But you're the only man I can tell, Doctor—please! After Eden Three is down?"

"If it's that important—why not tell me now if you feel you have to?" Rourke asked her.

"It, ahh, it would take too long. There's a lot—a lot to

explain, Dr. Rourke. And then after I tell you, if you feel the best thing is to tell Captain Dodd—well, well, then I'll do that." She looked at her watch, then smiled embarrassedly. "I'm late now—I'll look for you after Eden Three lands?"

Rourke nodded, his voice almost a whisper. "If that's what you want, then."

And the girl smiled, then turned and ran off.

Rourke stared after her for a time, smoking his cigar. His schedule was "loose"—Kurinami and Natalia were already airborne in the Soviet choppers, as were two of the Germans under the command of Wolfgang Mann in their own machines. Rourke had not yet had the opportunity to weigh the relative merits of the Soviet and German machines against each other. He had told Natalia before she had taken off, "Watch for Karamatsov's men of course—but keep an eye on Mann's people. I think we can trust them—but I don't know that we can."

Rourke stood up from the rock on which he had again seated himself, then started back toward camp. More of the Germans had trickled in but they seemed, like their international counterparts from Eden One and Eden Two, only obsessed with giving themselves terminal neck injuries by staring skyward at the helicopter guards and vying for the first glimpse of Eden Three.

Rourke moved through the camp, returning the nods and smiles from Eden personnel, walking toward the tent in which Michael and Paul were recovering from their injuries. He glanced upward—Natalia's helicopter hovered virtually overhead. Rourke had memorized its fuselage number. Rourke knocked on the tent pole and waited. The flap opened. Sarah. She smiled at him, her gray-green eyes holding a warmth in them that Rourke felt happy to see again.

"Hi."

"Hi—you look tired. But you look pretty."

"The tired part I'll agree with. Come on in," and she held open the tent flap for him and Rourke stepped through and inside. The walls and ceiling of the classic shaped military tent diffused yellow light in the darkness, the darkness otherwise unbroken except for a single Coleman lamp which burned on the table set between the two beds.

"Father Rourke." Madison smiled, looking up at him from where she knelt on the tent floor beside Michael's cot. Michael appeared to be asleep. "He rests well. The wonderful medicine of the German doctor—it seems to be working."

Sarah, beside him now, whispered, "It's working on both of them."

"Don't talk about me as though I weren't here." Rourke looked toward the voice, into the shadows on the opposite side of the table. Paul Rubenstein—awake. On the tent floor, curled up in a sleeping bag, seeming impossibly small, Rourke saw his daughter, Annie. "She's asleep," Paul whispered to him.

"You're supposed to be asleep." Rourke laughed.

"Look," Sarah began, her voice low. "I'm going to find something to eat. Madison hasn't eaten since yesterday afternoon and neither have I."

"Didn't anybody bring you anything? I made certain someone would. I'll—"

"One of the Eden people did," Sarah interrupted, "but I was changing one of Paul's bandages and Madison wasn't hungry. So Annie ate it all."

"Wonderful—what a kid." Rourke grinned. "I'll keep an eye on things here. Give Madison an airing too."

"All right," and Sarah turned to speak to the blond-haired girl who was her *de facto* daughter-in-law. "Come on—buy you breakfast."

"Buy?"

"Never mind—come on," and Sarah reached down to

44

Madison and took the younger woman's hand and helped her to stand. Rourke noted that Madison looked stiff from lack of movement. The girl brushed her blond hair back from her face and smiled. "John," Sarah began. "We'll be ten minutes—that OK?"

"It's fine, Sarah."

Sarah only nodded, then still holding Madison by the hand, exited past the tent flap, letting the flap fall back closed behind them.

Rourke sat down on the canvas camp chair beside the table and let his eyes become more accustomed to the light. He looked to his son. Michael was breathing evenly, regularly. And then Rourke heard Paul's voice. "Thanks— for saving my life, John. Again. You have a real problem breaking habits—you seem to save my life all the time."

Rourke let himself smile. "Best friends are hard to find, buddy."

"Sarah was telling me about the Nazis."

"They're Germans, Paul. They just call themselves Nazis—lack of a better term."

"I'm a Jew—so maybe I can't be too objective. You really trust this guy Mann?"

"I think I do—but I'll plan ahead just in case I find that I can't."

"So what's the deal with him?"

Rourke wanted to relight his cigar—but he didn't. The smell might awaken Michael or Annie. "Basically, he's involved in a sort of palace revolution against somebody he refers to as the leader—very Hitlerian type, it seems. You wouldn't like the guy."

"Touché." Paul laughed.

"Anyway—Mann promises to help us out against Karamatsov if we help him out in his revolution. And I'm elected."

"Argentina?"

"Yeah, hear it's lovely this time of year."

"Even with this miracle what's-it they sprayed on my wounds—"

"You won't be able to come," Rourke finished for him. "Natalia?"

"Probably." Rourke nodded. "Maybe Kurinami and Halverson—back-up on the outside for us. Couldn't very well get a black woman and a Japanese man to pass for Germans that easily. Natalia's a logical choice—if she doesn't speak German, I'd be very surprised."

"And of course you speak German?"

"Not well—I'll get by." Rourke nodded, his voice low. He watched Annie as she slept—he envied the peacefulness of her face. She was very pretty and he was very proud of her. "She's a hell of a girl—you take care of her while I'm gone."

"Maybe Dodd can marry us—you know, captain of a ship and all that—I love her." And then Paul laughed. "You'll be my father-in-law."

"Hmm," Rourke murmured.

"I mean it—it's, ahh, all right?"

Rourke studied his hands for a moment. He didn't look at Paul as he spoke. "You and Annie—if you have a daughter some day, you'll know what I mean. But a man has a daughter, and you can't help thinking about what kinda guy she'll marry. You know—God help the son of a bitch if he harms a hair on her head, will he love her as much as you do—like that. Well, with you I don't have to worry. And no, you can't marry her—until I get back so I can give the bride away."

Paul Rubenstein laughed. "So—what you want us to do while you're gone—start building a new world or what?" Rubenstein laughed again. "It really does hurt when I laugh."

Rourke looked at the younger man and just shook his head. "No, I think the Eden Project people have their own plans for our brave new world. You just keep an eye on

46

what's happening and keep them out of trouble. You should be up and around on a limited capacity in the next few days—Doctor Munchen and Doctor Hixon'll both be looking after you. Get Michael rolling again as soon as he's able. The two of you—and you've got more experience— make sure Michael understands that. He's got his father's ego. Just keep an eye on things and don't interfere unless what they start to do is impossibly stupid. Ohh, and keep after Michael to teach Madison more with her driving. And you work on her marksmanship or get Annie to help. If Michael takes care of it alone, Madison'll be running around with .44 Mags just like he does." Rourke laughed.

"Four of you—I don't like it," Paul began.

"Don't change the subject—we'll be fine down there. You just make sure you're well enough to go with me after Karamatsov and his men when I get back. You and Natalia and me—it'll take the three of us. And I don't like involving her in it."

Paul Rubenstein said, lowering his voice, "You didn't know—that Karamatsov stayed alive was a miracle. He should have been dead that day on the street in Athens."

"Miracle?" John Rourke stared at his friend. "No—my stupidity maybe. But not a miracle. I'm no theologian, but I somehow don't think Karamatsov qualifies for a miracle. This time when I do find him—only a miracle could keep him alive." And John Rourke stood up. "This time I'll be sure."

Chapter Six

John Rourke had waited for the red-haired girl named
Mona Stankiewicz—but it had been no good. Bone tired,
he had asked Akiro Kurinami, "Look—there's a girl supposed to come by and see me. Ask her if it can wait. And if
it can't, wake me up, huh? Otherwise, let me catch a few
hours."

Kurinami, who had set a folding canvas chair outside
the tent earlier and had been reading technical manuals
when Rourke had approached, had agreed, moved his
chair from in front of the tent he shared with six others and
placed it outside Rourke's, then said, "Of course."

Rourke had passed inside to the tent, checked his
blankets—he would have been happy to find an insect or a
snake—and then sat down on the edge of the cot and
untied his combat boots, pulled off his socks, shrugged out
of the bomber jacket and the shoulder rig, then laid down.

Mona Stankiewicz called across the dried, caked mud
ruts toward the tent front. "Akiro—you see Doctor
Rourke? That's his tent, isn't it?"

"He is asleep. He was very tired. Are you the one who
was coming to see him?"

She had narrowed the distance to the tent front—she was
close enough now as she stopped to read upside-down a

portion of the page of technical manual that lay on Kurinami's lap. "He put in a hard day yesterday, I guess. You tell him I'll come back. I guess it can keep a while longer."

"I'll wake him up—if it's important, Mona."

"No, no, Akiro—it's fine. Just tell him I was by. Maybe he can look me up."

And she gave Akiro Kurinami a smile and started back across the compound. Kurinami was a funny sort, she'd always felt. People talked about the Japanese as being quiet, humorless, sober people. She smiled thinking about it—the time Kurinami had put one of those rubber air-filled cushions that when compressed sounded like someone passing gas—the time Kurinami had put it in Captain Dodd's chair when Dodd had stood up to deliver part of a briefing. And then Captain Dodd had sat down. Kurinami had been the only one with a straight face—at least for thirty seconds.

But she had heard Dodd say once, "Kurinami's a damned good pilot. Lucky for us he wasn't alive during World War II."

Mona Stankiewicz had nowhere to go—but there was one place she didn't want to go. Near the just-landed Eden Three. She was sort of engaged to one of the sleepers aboard Eden Three—and she wanted to see him very badly. But after she told John Rourke what she had to tell him and only him, her man on Eden Three probably wouldn't want to talk with her—let alone love her.

She kept walking, heading away from the camp, passing one of the Germans—the man smiled at her and gave her the sort of salute polite military men sometimes gave civilians. She smiled back and used her one German phrase, "*Guten tag.*"

The man smiled again and said something that ended with "*Fraulein*" as he passed her.

She kept walking. Her legs tired easily, she had noticed—but she imagined that in a few more days, her normal stamina would start to return. Captain Dodd had exercise programs already organized for them. But she had excused herself from them as had most of the women. And for the same reason; after awakening, she had begun to menstruate, more heavily than she ever had. And some kinds of movements just weren't pleasant at all.

She found the rock John Rourke had been sitting on when she had approached him earlier in the day, and she sat down on it herself, brushing her hair back from her face when an errant gust of wind blew it in front of her eyes.

"John Rourke." She said his name aloud. He was a very handsome man. Tall. Muscular but not heavy—more massive than lean. He had dark hair, neatly trimmed—she wondered who cut it for him. His forehead was high, but naturally so—not from hair loss, she thought, because his hair seemed thick, healthy. There were a few strands of silver grey in the short sideburns, perhaps more noticeable because of the deep brownness of the rest of his hair. There was talk about him throughout the camp, most of the women talking about him as being good looking and did you see the way he looked at the Russian woman and the way she looked back at him and the way his wife looked at them both? But some of the women talked about—he was good looking. He had a texture in his voice that you could almost feel touch you.

But there was a warmth in his eyes when he took off his sunglasses.

But she would have thought that a man in his position would have grown a beard—she wondered why he hadn't? It looked like he shaved every day. Even her father when she had been a little girl wouldn't shave on his days off.

She found herself smiling. Perhaps John Rourke never had a day off.

She considered what she knew about him—from what

Dodd and Craig Lerner had told her, from what Elaine Halversen had said.

John Rourke had been a Doctor of Medicine before joining the Central Intelligence Agency—the three words chilled her. After he had left the—left it—he had taught survivalism and weapons training all over the world, even written books on the subject. He had never practiced medicine on a regular basis. But she understood from what Doctor Hixon had said that at least as far as Hixon could tell from the surgery John Rourke had performed on his son Michael Rourke, Rourke was very good—very good.

And that amazed her—that he had a son nearly as old as he was, and a daughter too.

She had heard about what Rourke had done to save his friend—it was a Jewish sounding name and she couldn't remember it—climbing from one helicopter to another one when the second helicopter was already on fire and about to explode.

It was part of the reason she wanted to talk with him—to explain it to him rather than Capt. Christopher Dodd. John Rourke sounded like the sort of man that legends were built around. Christopher Dodd was a good man, a strong man—but Christopher Dodd wasn't that sort of a man.

It would have to be John Rourke.

Mona Stankiewicz heard movement behind her—maybe it was . . . "Ohh—it's you. Where—where?" It was a gun and she knew she should be hearing something because it had just been fired, but she didn't hear it. It was because her attention was focused on the burning in her chest. And then her head felt as if it were going to explode.

Chapter Seven

John Rourke opened his eyes. It sounded . . . like a woman screaming? He threw his bare feet over the side of the cot.

It wouldn't be a dream—he didn't dream anymore. A woman . . .

"Doctor Rourke! John!" The tent flap flew open. It was Kurinami. "A woman screamed. I—"

"Yeah." Rourke licked his lips—they were dry. "I'm right behind you."

Rourke pushed himself up, grabbing up the double Alessi rig, ripping first one, then the second of the twin stainless Detonics .45s from it, barefoot now, running through the tent opening, stuffing one pistol in each hip pocket of his faded Levi's, running.

He squinted against the fading light—he had left his sunglasses in the tent. But he could see Kurinami ahead of him running. Kurinami stopped, six feet or so from the body of a woman.

Rourke kept running. The wind played at the hair on the head of the prostrate body—the hair was red, more red than auburn.

It was Mona Stankiewicz.

Rourke passed Kurinami, skidding to his knees on the caked mud and gravel and sand, slowly raising the woman's head in his hands. Two bullet wounds—one in the center of the chest, another perhaps an inch from the heart.

The woman's eyelids fluttered as Rourke held her head across his thighs, his hands cradling her there. "Don't try to talk."

The eyelids opened. The eyes were very beautiful. They held neither fear nor pain. Peace, he would have almost said. And then Mona Stankiewicz's lips moved and Rourke bent his head to her mouth to hear her words. Kurinami knelt beside him now. "So-Soviet—Soviet agent—did this. . . ." The eyelids didn't close. The pulse Rourke had purchased a finger against in her neck stopped.

"The Soviet agent," Kurinami murmured. Rourke looked up—others were around them—Dodd, Lerner, Elaine Halverson, Sarah.

Dodd spoke—his voice was very soft, very low. "That flashy looking automatic pistol Major Tiemerovna carries in that shoulder holster—isn't it fitted—"

"With a silencer," Rourke finished for him. The Stankiewicz woman had been shot twice—but the only sound had been her scream. Rourke looked back to Dodd, at the man's eyes. "If Natalia had done it, she would have been neater about it."

John Rourke closed the Stankiewicz woman's eyes. They were a very light shade of brown with what seemed like green flecks in them.

Chapter Eight

Examining the dead was never pleasant—especially when the dead person was someone you had known in life, John Thomas Rourke reflected. He had observed at the autopsy performed by Doctor Hixon of Eden One and Doctor Munchen, the physician attached to the military command of Wolfgang Mann. Rourke had urged Munchen's presence on the assumption that a military doctor's knowledge of gunshot wounds might be useful.

But as Hixon had opened the body, Rourke peering past him, it was all too obvious. She had been shot at close range by an indifferent marksman. The bullets extracted from her were clearly of 9mm diameter and little deformed. Rourke judged them as being fired from a .380. Whoever had killed her had thought to pick up empty brass from the ground nearby.

Natalia carried a .380 stainless Walther PPK/S in her shoulder holster. And as Dodd had observed at the murder scene, it was fitted with a suppressor.

Dodd, observing at the autopsy, said slowly, "What more do you want, Dr. Rourke? Mona Stankiewicz named a Russian agent as her murderer. She was shot with what you call a .380—"

"9mm Browning Short," Rourke whispered.

"And the pistol was evidently fitted with a silencer since nobody heard a shot. Major Tiemerovna is a Russian agent—"

"Was!" Rourke snapped, his voice low.

"Fine—was. But she might easily be identified as a Russian agent by a dying woman who might not have been able to recall her name. Major Tiemerovna carries a pistol with a silencer in that shoulder holster of hers. What kind of pistol is it—the caliber?"

".380, 9mm Browning Short—one and the same."

"And the gun that was used to kill Mona Stankiewicz is one and the same with the gun owned by Major Tiemerovna."

Rourke looked across the body, the skin flaps laid back across the chest—he suddenly felt embarrassed for the woman, her breasts in public view, yet her secret still hidden. Dodd's face in the yellow light of the Coleman lamp and the diffused sunlight through the canvas held something in it Rourke had not seen there before. Hatred, and mingled with it the stupidity that came from the absence of logic. Rourke said to him, "Think for yourself. Natalia is the enemy of the Soviet force sent against us. She is the friend of the Eden Project—why would she kill one of its members? It is totally illogical."

"Logic be damned, Doctor Rourke. The woman is or was a Russian agent. She owns the murder weapon."

"No—logic won't be damned, Captain. You think. Mona Stankiewicz had something she wanted to tell me— only me. Not you. If it were something damning to Natalia, then why tell me, Natalia's friend? Why not tell you—you seem more than willing to assume the worst. Mona Stankiewicz wouldn't have labeled Natalia as a Russian agent. She knew better. It's obvious, at least in part, what Mona Stankiewicz intended to talk with me about. You're right—there is a Russian agent, but aboard the Eden Project. And whoever it is, assuming the person didn't smuggle his own weapon with him, must have somehow gotten access to Natalia's pistol. Who else to implicate?" And Rourke let himself smile. "What if the reason Mona Stankiewicz wanted to talk with me instead of you is because you're the Russian agent?"

"Look, Rourke." Dodd leaned over the dead girl's body.

Rourke said nothing for a moment, then his voice low, said, "Let's find out if Natalia's gun is missing. For openers. Whether it is or isn't, we can get Natalia's help. If the real Russian agent was concerned enough to implicate Natalia by using her gun or one like it—if that is a real consideration—then the Russian agent might fear that Natalia could identify him. Evidently Mona Stankiewicz could."

"A Russian agent aboard the Eden Project? You're daft, Rourke."

"Fuck you," Rourke told him evenly. "I'm going to talk with Natalia—if you wanna come along, fine and dandy." Rourke looked down at the dead girl. He drew the sheet up to cover her. To no one in particular, Rourke whispered, "She's revealed all the secrets she's going to."

"I'll see Major Tiemerovna on my own," Dodd said suddenly.

Rourke looked at him as he lowered the sheet. "I gave a sedative to her—she didn't sleep well last night. She'll need her strength—she'll be going to Argentina with me tomorrow. If she took the sedative, after Eden Three got down, she might still be asleep. We won't disturb her—you won't."

"I've got Eden Four landing in about an hour. There isn't any time to fart around, Doctor Rourke. We have a murderer to contend with."

"Then I suggest we try to find him." Rourke snapped off one, then the second of the rubber surgical gloves and threw them down.

He started toward the tent flap.

"Dr. Rourke—I can have you disarmed sir, if you interfere."

Rourke didn't look at Dodd as he answered. "Yeah—you go ahead and do that, Captain." Rourke pushed through the tent flap into the afternoon sun, finding his dark-lensed aviator-style sunglasses in the pocket of his bomber jacket and putting them on. "Damnit," he hissed under his breath.

Natalia Tiemerovna sat cross-legged on a blanket, the warmth of the fading sun pleasant on her bare legs. She had to be careful the way she sat, because she wore nothing but underpants and one of Rourke's blue chambray shirts. If she moved the wrong way anyone passing by in the camp would see that. Her mind elsewhere, her hands worked with the cleaning gear for her guns. She was replacing the screw in the forward portion of the L-Frame Smith's frame, tightening it now, the crane returned to its proper position and the cylinder closed up into its recess. She had cleaned all the guns thoroughly after the dousing they had taken in the rain, oiled her leather gear as well. She put the L-Frame down beside its twin, both pistols—gleaming stainless steel and customized with crane lock and champhered charging holes and a butter-smooth action tuning—originally a gift to the first and last president of U.S. II, Sam Chambers. And he had given them to her for her role in aiding the evacuation of penisular Florida. She had kept them with her ever since. She studied the American eagles on the right side barrel flats. She remembered her uncle, Gen. Ishmael Varakov—he had talked of the Eagle and the Bear fighting to exterminate each other. They had all but succeeded.

Natalia sniffed back a tear at the thought of her uncle. Dead—like almost everyone else.

She picked up the stainless Walther PPK/S American and thumbed the magazine release catch button, automatically then jacking back the slide and catching the chambered round in her palm.

She set the magazine and the loose round on the oilcloth which occupied a corner of the blanket. And something struck her as being odd.

The brass of the round she had popped from the chamber was very shiny, as though just taken from the box. But it shouldn't have been. She had chambered the round innumerable times, touched it with her hands. She examined the top round in the magazine. It too was shiny but, like the chambered round, should have been tarnished. Like most people who used a Walther that she had known, she carried it chamber loaded and with a full magazine. Since there was no manual slide stop, the convenient way to load the chamber after checking the pistol's condition of readiness was to work the slide and strip the top round from the magazine. Then take the round popped out of the chamber and load it into the top of the magazine. This constantly rotated the first two rounds. And they would tarnish and show scratch marks from being worked in and out of the chamber. But these rounds showed neither.

Natalia bent forward—the thought of showing flesh was secondary now. She examined the magazine. She had dropped it once during some shooting and the base plate had taken a scratch against a rock. The scratch was still there.

She grabbed up the black canvas bag that she carried most often as a huge purse but which converted to a day pack. She began fishing inside it—of the two spare magazines, one was without the finger-rest extension at the base, the other with. The finger-rest extension magazine—two of the witness holes in the magazine body showed empty, two rounds gone.

Natalia threw the magazines down on the blanket and picked up the empty Walther, sniffing at the silencer tube still threaded to the muzzle. It smelled and it should not have. The last time she had used it—she shivered at the thought. But she had cleaned the baffles afterward and replaced some of the packing as needed. There should have been no smell.

Natalia unscrewed the silencer from the muzzle, the muzzle specially threaded to accept it. She dismounted the slide, then picked up the Walther cleaning rod—she used it with all her handguns. She inserted a patch in the slotted tip and ran it down the barrel—but she already knew from the smell of the weapon. It had been fired.

The patch came out black streaked from the rifling.

"Major Tiemerovna, please stop cleaning that weapon."

She looked up from the stainless Walther—it was Captain Dodd and beside him, his dark-lensed sunglasses masking his eyes, stood John Rourke.

"John, what—"

"Major Tiemerovna," Dodd began again. "That pistol—it appears to have been fired, judging from the patch."

"Two rounds are missing from one of the spare magazines. And I believe two fresh rounds were placed in the gun."

"That pistol is a .380, is it not?" Dodd asked.

"Yes, what—"

"And that thing on the blanket near the slide—the thing that looks like a miniature automobile muffler?"

"It's a suppressor—yes—the principle is the same. What of it?"

"As commander of the Eden Project fleet in lieu of any other civil or military authority, I'm placing you under arrest for the murder of Mona Stankiewicz."

John Rourke's head turned toward Dodd. "Fuck off."

"Rourke—one more outburst—"

"And what? Go on, tell me what?"

"Murder—of whom?"

"Mona Stankiewicz—back-up flight officer for Eden One. She was shot with a .380-caliber pistol. A silencer was evidently used since no one heard the shots, but only her screams. She spoke only a few words as she died—she implicated 'the Russian agent' as her killer."

"And mine is the only 9mm short pistol in the camp, isn't it?" She didn't wait for an answer. "And mine is the only suppressor, isn't it? And I am the only Russian agent, aren't I? And so I have to be the killer—but I'm not." She started to reach into her purse—but she remembered she had no cigarettes, had not again begun the habit. She looked up into Dodd's eyes instead. "You actually believe this?"

Rourke asked the question before Dodd could respond. "How long was the PPK/S out of your sight, Natalia?"

"I didn't give myself the sedative—but I did get a little sleep. And then I got up and went for a walk. I only carried these—" and she gestured toward the twin Metalife Custom L-Frames with the American eagles engraved on the right barrel flats. "I left the Walther here. And, well, after I came back, I took another shower and washed my hair." She touched at her hair—it was still damp. "And I just slipped on these things and came outside to clean my guns."

"Where was the Walther while you were out?" Rourke asked her.

"I had it in the shoulder holster and left it in my bag." She gestured toward the massive black canvas purse. "I wore the pistol when I had the helicopter up while Eden Three was landing and I took it off afterward."

Rourke turned to face Dodd. "All right, so somebody who knew Natalia had the only silencer in the camp got into her things while she was walking or washing her hair and killed Mona Stankiewicz and replaced the pistol, but shifted the loads around so she wouldn't catch on right away."

"Did anyone see you when you were walking, Major? Or when you took your shower?"

"I have a tent here at the edge of camp as you can see—

and I share it with Elaine Halverson and I haven't seen Elaine since Eden Three came down. I left camp by the most direct route. No one saw me. And I usually shower alone." She made herself smile up at Dodd. "And no one saw me go to the showers unless someone was watching me that I didn't see."

"I find this very hard to believe, Major. Doctor Rourke has weapons. So does his wife. So do his son and daughter. And so does Mr. Rubensein. Why were yours used?"

"Perhaps because of the silencer—I don't know."

Dodd punched his right fist into his left palm. "What I said, Major—it still stands. Please consider yourself under arrest. Rest assured, however, that I'll leave no stone unturned in attempting to get to the bottom of this. And if you are innocent, you will certainly have my apology." Dodd began to draw his .45 from his holster. "I'll have to ask you to stand up and come with me."

Both of John Rourke's Detonics .45s seemed to spring of their own will from beneath his coat, his fists closed around the butts, both pistols inches from Dodd's torso. "Breathe wrong and you're dead," Rourke whispered.

"No, John!" Natalia was to her feet, putting her left hand between the muzzles of Rourke's pistols and Dodd's body. "No, not this way, John. I've done nothing wrong. And Captain Dodd will be able to prove that. I know he will."

"I'm—I'm supposed to leave for Argentina tomorrow. I wanted you with me."

She searched for some image of his eyes behind the lenses of his sunglasses, but saw only her own eyes reflected in them. She reached up to his face, slowly, gently removing the glasses, holding them in her fingertips. "Nothing will happen to me. It will all be settled by the time you get back, John. And Paul will still be here, won't he? And Michael and Annie and Madison? Take Sarah with you—she's very good. She'll help you as well as I could have."

"No, no."

"I can show you how to use my lock picks—if Captain Dodd doesn't need them as evidence. You or Sarah can take the Walther so you have a gun with a silencer. Any other things I have—they're yours, of course."

"That's—that's not what I want," Rourke spoke, barely above a whisper.

She reached her right hand up to his cheek—it was warm to her touch with his anger. His dark eyes were squinted against the light. She realized how much she loved him—and that she would never fully be his. "I'll be all right, John. I can look after myself. I really can. And I'm innocent. You taught me to believe in your system—that it was the best system. Now here is a chance to prove it." She didn't believe that Captain Dodd would uncover evidence that would implicate someone else. Whoever had killed this woman with the Polish last name had evidently decided that the crime should be connected to her—her gun. No alibi. And then the damning words of the dying girl.

John Rourke spoke—she listened. The soft, quiet assurance not so much in his words, but in the way he said them. "I can't leave you."

"You have to leave me. We both know that."

Rourke closed his eyes—he simultaneously lowered the hammers of both pistols, letting them hang at his sides. "Did Karamatsov—could he have had an agent aboard the Eden Project?"

"I don't know, John."

"Don't be ridiculous, Dr. Rourke—every man jack of us has a security clearance that's lily white," Dodd snapped.

Rourke looked at him. "Those are the worst kind—a perfect security clearance is always the one that's flawed, because nobody's perfect."

"And what about you, Doctor?"

Rourke looked at Dodd. "If you'd moved for that .45 on your hip, you'd be dead."

Rourke shoved the pistol from his left hand into his belt, making the right hand pistol disappear under his brown leather jacket. Then he repeated the process. It took two hands always to conveniently reholster his guns because of the trigger guard break design of the holsters.

"I'll change, if I may," Natalia began. "And, then, I'll accompany you, Captain." She didn't wait for an answer—she handed back John Rourke's sunglasses, leaned up on her bare toes and kissed his left cheek lightly, then started for her tent.

She didn't delude herself. Dodd thought she was guilty, believed it. And nothing would convince him otherwise.

But if she let John Rourke commit some act of violence against Dodd, John—all of them, all the people she loved—they would be outcasts from human society forever.

She let the tent flap fall closed behind her, then sat on the edge of the cot.

Her mind was functioning on two levels. While she awaited the inevitable, she might as well be comfortable. She wouldn't be going into battle. On impulse when she had left The Retreat she had taken a skirt and a pair of sandals. She also wondered how they would punish her for this murder—and how she could prevent John Rourke from ruining his life and the lives of his family by interfering.

Chapter Nine

Michael was awake, but not sitting up—his eyes seemed alert and clear though, as clear as they could with the medication. Paul Rubenstein had sat up, Rourke cautioning him before the younger man attempted it. Sarah sat at the small table beside the lit Coleman lamp, Annie and Madison respectively sitting beside Paul and Michael, at the edges of the cots. John Rourke stood near the tent flap, too angry to sit.

"I'm supposed to leave for Argentina tomorrow—I don't want to. Dodd's going to railroad Natalia—I can feel it in my guts. But if I don't, and Mann's faction loses and this Deiter Bern is executed, we'll be facing Karamatsov's forces alone and we may wind up facing the Nazis too—a no-win proposition, at least on the surface."

"On the surface?" Sarah echoed. "Now I went through a lot since the Night of The War—and I learned you were right about a lot of things John. Don't ever give up like that. And I know that if the Russians and these Nazis attack us, you never will give up. None of us will. But they have weapons that are a whole lot more sophisticated than ours, and there are at least hundreds of them—more likely thousands of them. And we'll lose. I mean, maybe all of us here and Natalia—we can stay together and keep fighting from the mountains and harassing them—but we won't win, John. You've got to go."

"Momma is right," Annie said softly.

"She—she is, Dad," Michael agreed.

"It isn't my place to speak, Father Rourke. . . ."

"No, of course you have a voice in what we do. Go ahead, Madison."

"We will care for Natalia. But I think we will all die—Natalia, too—if you do not help the colonel-man in his fight for freedom."

"She's gonna make a hell of a sister-in-law," Paul began. "Michael and Annie and Madison and I—we can take care of things here, John. Because if you don't go—you and Sarah and Kurinami and those volunteers he's been rounding up and Elaine Halverson—if you don't go, well, I've been doing a lot of thinking. And the whole idea of Nazis—it gives me the creeps. But if this guy Mann is what he says he is—and I don't think he'd have anything to gain by lying to us—but if he's what he says he is, then he wants to kick the real Nazis out of power. I gotta be for that, ya know?"

Rourke only nodded, staring past the Coleman lamp at his wife's shadow.

"And as far as Natalia is concerned," Paul continued, "like Madison said—she'll be safe."

"There's a Russian agent at work in the camp," Rourke answered. "That's probably how Rozhdestvensky and Karamatsov before him knew so much about the Eden Project in the first place. One of the men or women aboard fed the information to the KGB. And whoever this person is, it's important to him or her to get Natalia out of the way. Perhaps Natalia might be able to recognize him, or recognize something about him that would betray his identity. I doubt Mona Stankiewicz was murdered just to be a victim—if I'd forced her to speak her piece when she first talked with me. Shit," he groaned. "Anyway, Karamatsov will assume this person is still alive, and find a way of using him against us. The key to proving Natalia's innocence is one of the keys to our survival here. Get the KGB agent—and with Eden Four just down and two more to go, this place is starting to look like a used space shuttle lot—and the whole thing . . ."

John Rourke stopped.

Sarah Rourke looked up at him, smiling thinly as she pulled the blue and white bandanna from her hair, then ran her fingers through it. She was a pretty woman, Rourke thought in the instant. "What's the matter, John? Too many people?"

Rourke sat down on the chair opposite her, reached out and took her hand—she didn't withdraw it. "Yeah," he laughed. "I was used to it for so long—and it looks like everything is starting all over again. Maybe the people who propounded cyclical views of history were right—I don't know."

"What did you fight for, you mean?"

He leaned across the table, touching his lips to her hand that he held in his. "I always knew what I was fighting for. I always knew that. To stay a step ahead of the insanity. But the crazies are still out there, Sarah. It hasn't changed. People are still running around trying to kill one another. Violence is still everybody's answer. Human life is still cheap. I don't know," he whispered to her, his throat tight.

"You've always tried, John, to do the right thing. For us more than for yourself. You lost the youth of our children. You're in love with Natalia, but you remain faithful to me."

He started to speak, but she touched her fingers to his lips.

"You're a decent man. A fine man. Maybe—maybe you're too fine, there's too much nobility in you. It would be easier to live with you—you've always been so good at everything you did, John. Your honor's like a suit of armor to you. Your knowledge. You could never accept the fact that the rest of humanity wasn't perfect just like you—and so you fought against the idea and you isolated yourself, John. If this is all over, someday—what do you want to do?"

Rourke looked down at her hand in his. "A clinic, maybe—get a real hospital going. Pretty soon there'll be babies born, life starting up again." And he looked up at her, across the table, into her eyes that were only half visible in the lamplight. "But I don't think it's ever going to end, Sarah—I just don't."

"You've never been an optimist—just a pessimist who refused to give up. You are that. And I love the idea of you—so very much." It was as if they were sitting all alone in their house that was no longer there. And it was late at night and the children were in bed. "A woman couldn't ask for a better man to love. I'll never agree with you—I can't see life the way you do. I'm just not that logical—but it's a conscious choice with me, John. I refuse. I'm very sorry— sorry that you were right. And you're sorry too. You carry a burden I couldn't carry, John. I never could. It's been hard trying to share it—and I know I really haven't. It'll be good to go with you to Argentina. A lot of places, well, a man can't get in, I think. But a woman can. I don't speak German—but one of the people Kurinami got to volunteer, Forrest Blackburn, I think his name is, he does. So at least there'll be two of you. It sounds silly after all these years— these years of being married. But I don't think we ever really knew each other. But we can now. And whatever happens between us—we'll be better for it, I think."

"I love you," John Rourke told her.

"I know you do. And I know you love Natalia, too—and I can't help with that. Because this is real and you don't get story-book solutions to things, do you, John?" And she smiled.

John Rourke laughed. "No, no, you don't—you don't at all, do you? I don't think I gave you a very good life, did I?"

"No, John—for once you're wrong. You've always been bigger than the reality around you. I never wanted to be. But I don't think a better man has ever lived than you." And she stood up and drew his head against her breast and Rourke felt her breath against his face and her lips touched at his forehead.

It was then that he heard the first shout of anger from beyond the confines of the world they had drawn around them for a few moments.

Chapter Ten

"Stay here, miss," the Eden Project guard holding the M-16 said, sticking his head inside the tent flap briefly, then disappearing again.

From outside she heard the shouts. "She caused it— she's the one. Kill her now and be done with it!"

"Kill the Goddamned Commie bitch!"

She perched on the edge of her cot, drawing her feet closer to the side of the bed, pulling her skirt down lower over her tightly squeezed knees. She realized she was frightened.

She could hear Captain Dodd's voice shouting above the din outside. "All right—Major Tiemerovna is Russian, but her guilt hasn't been clearly established. And if it is, she'll be punished, but in a lawful manner and only for the death of Mona Stankiewicz—not for causing World War III."

"Mona and I were engaged, Goddamnit, Captain!"

"Haselton—I know how you feel, man—but this isn't— no!" Gunfire. The M-16 fired into the air, she surmised.

Her right hand moved up from her knees along the tops of her thighs, pulling up the beige linen, moving to the inside of her left thigh—with a scarf she had tied the Bali-Song to her leg. She undid the scarf now, the knife coming alive in her right hand as she stood, the full skirt dropping to below her knees as she moved toward the rear of the tent, the scarf in her left hand, her left hand thrusting into the pocket on the side of the skirt, freeing her of the scarf.

Her left hand moved along the interior rear wall of the tent, the Bali-Song's Wee Hawk pattern blade biting into the canvas and then ripping downward from the height of her chest to the level of the canvas floor panel. She looked back toward the front of the tent and the flap. Another burst of assault riflefire. Screaming. Shouted threats.

Natalia Anastasia Tiemerovna reached back to the cot—the dark blue cardigan sweater there. She caught it up and pulled it over her shoulders, tossing her hair free of it, buttoning the top button at her neck to keep the sweater from falling. She pushed her sandalled left foot through the opening she had cut in the rear of the tent, the Bali-Song open still in her right hand, thrusting into the darkness ahead of her as she stepped the rest of the way through.

She was out of the tent—more gunfire, then a shout. "Get out of our way, Captain!"

Natalia started to run, cursing herself for dressing like a woman—the sandals were impractical for running. The sweater would give her scant protection against the evening's chill with the sleeveless blue knit top she wore beneath it. The skirt would catch and rip on briars and thorns if she made it far enough away to start for the mountains. And the Bali-Song was her only weapon.

She ran, hearing behind her, "The bitch got away. The Commie's loose—hunt her down!"

Another voice—a woman's voice—the words made Natalia's breath catch in her throat. "Hang her!"

Natalia ran—as she reached the edge of the camp, she slowed, stopped. "There she is! Over here!"

"Look out. Shit—she's got a knife!"

Two men—neither of them was armed except with handguns. At the distance, she doubted their ability to hit with them except by accident.

She wheeled to her left, starting into a dead run—but something hammered at her legs and she fell, hacking into the darkness with her knife. "Jees—she cut me! Cut me!"

Natalia's left hand hammered up and out, the heel of it contacting bone. There was a groan, and the weight rolled off of her.

She pushed herself to her feet, but arms reached out for her. The knife in her right hand hacked through the darkness. There was a scream of pain—something was coming toward her face and she dodged, feeling something slamming against the left side of her head. She started losing her balance, falling. Hands—her right arm was twisted back and around and she felt her grip go and the Bali-Song fall away.

"Bastards!" she screamed, her left knee catching one of the men in the crotch, her left hand straight-arming another man in the face—but her left wrist was caught in a grip that felt solid as a vise and her arm was wrenched back. Hands grabbed at her legs, dragging her down, the weight of a man crushing her down. Her left arm was pinned to her side. Her right arm was twisted behind her—a little more pressure and she knew it would break. Hands held her ankles pinned.

A voice—she couldn't see the face clearly. "Hell, this cable'll be as good as a rope—good enough for her."

And then a voice she recognized—the one Dodd had called Haselton. "I'm doin' it. Mona and I were going to be married—I'm doin' it!"

"Then do it!" Natalia screamed at the attackers surrounding her.

Dodd's voice—from the edge of the knot of humanity crushing and twisting her. "For God's sake, you're supposed to be the cream of humanity—and you're a mob. For God's sake, don't do this thing!"

Natalia was dragged to her feet. Her right knee found a target. "Fuck you!" The voice was washed with pain. A hand slapped at her and her head sagged back and she felt her knees buckling.

She was being pulled—she didn't know to where, but when she tried using her feet even to walk, the pressure on her right arm was increased and she screamed, "Stop it!"

But the pressure didn't decrease.

The cable—it was snaked around her neck now. "Tie her to the back of Rourke's truck. Drag hang her!"

And then: "Fun's over!"

She closed her eyes. It was John Rourke's voice.

Natalia opened her eyes. The light from the camp backlit him and in silhouette now, she could see the Detonics .45s in his hands.

"Dr. Rourke, I can handle—"

"Shut up, Captain." Natalia felt the cable loosen slightly at her throat. "Let her go. Help her up and let her walk over here. First person who does otherwise dies—end of story."

"John," she whispered. The pressure on her arm was eased—then gone. The noose of cable fell from her neck to her chest. She sat up, took the noose from her body and threw it down.

She tried to stand up—she looked at her skirt and mechanically began dusting it off as she stood there, her knees weak.

"I've got Natalia's Bali-Song, John!"

It was Paul Rubenstein's voice.

She heard John Rourke shout to him. "You should be in bed, Paul."

"Coverin' this end with my Schmeisser instead, John." She heard the familiar and now very reassuring sound of the German MP-40's bolt being drawn back, open.

"Give my friend some room." It was Sarah's voice from the far side to Natalia's right. "Go over to John. Natalia—can you walk?"

"Yes, yes, I can walk." Natalia nodded. Her throat ached and her right arm felt as though somehow it weren't an arm at all but a tooth gone bad very suddenly and very painfully.

She started—slowly—toward John Rourke, seeing faces now as the glare of headlights washed at a tangent across the crowd surrounding her. She could see John Rourke's face now, half in shadow, half in light. She could see the gun in his left hand dully gleaming, the gun in his right hand still in shadow. "I've got the truck, Dad." It was Annie's voice.

It had been the blue pick-up, the one she had nearly been tied to to be drag hanged. It would be the camouflage-painted truck Annie drove now.

"Get my bike and Natalia's," Rourke rasped. "Annie—do it quick. Sarah—"

"Right."

Natalia saw a figure stepping beside Rourke—she saw Rourke's body tense in silhouette and then the tension faded. It was the wiry frame of Kurinami backlit in the glare of the headlights, a pistol in his right hand. "I am here, Doctor Rourke. Elaine Halverson is with me."

"You and Dr. Halverson—get on the truck, back it up and keep the lights on the mob."

"Dr. Rourke—what the hell are you doing?" Dodd's voice called out. "I can take charge here now!"

"I'm going to Argentina, Captain—remember? Hmm? And I'm taking Natalia with me. And Sarah and Akiro and Elaine Halverson. And I won't even insult your intelligence by mentioning what'll happen if anybody tries stopping us."

"This woman is a murderess."

"Yeah, Captain—and I'm your great-aunt Fanny and the Easter bunny's gonna be here in ten minutes or so—hitched a ride with the tooth fairy on the back of a unicorn. Yeah, Paul and Michael will represent my interests here. And if you or anybody else takes any reprisals against them, then you'd better hope the people under Karamatsov get you—or I will. And just to keep you busy while I'm gone, why not look for the real murderer and find Karamatsov's agent before Karamatsov comes back and you find out you've got an enemy outside and an enemy inside."

"You'll be a wanted man, Doctor."

John Rourke simply laughed—Natalia was nearly beside him now, her legs still felt weak. And then—as she sagged toward him, his right arm reaching out to her, enfolding her, supporting her—John Rourke said to her, "I got Madison to round up your clothes. Sarah found your guns and put 'em in the truck Annie was driving."

"John—I—you—you'll be an outcast now."

"I was never anything else," John Rourke whispered as she rested her head against his shoulder.

She could hear Paul's voice from the far side of the crowd—and she wanted to go to him, to kiss him. He was her dearest friend, someone she had shared secrets with. Paul said, "John, you guys do what you've gotta do in Argentina. I'll find the murderer—and I'll kill him."

Natalia looked up at John Rourke's face, feeling his breath against her skin as Rourke whispered, "I know."

Chapter Eleven

Antonovitch was sorely tempted to reach to his hip and draw the Stechkin Mk 7 from its holster—but he did not. If he drew his pistol, it might make the men around him think that he was nervous or afraid.

He kept walking, instead, slowly, looking from right to left and then behind him, his men forming a ragged wedge on both sides of him as they moved through the jungle.

Scouts had confirmed what electronic surveillance had earlier indicated—that the surrounding area of habitation which ringed the mountain was unfortified except for guard towers at the four compass points. The mountain which was apparently the stronghold of the Nazi force seemed so well fortified that it would take firepower beyond that available from the helicopter force alone to penetrate it or destroy it.

But Maj. Nicolai Antonovitch had to see for himself.

He kept walking, slowly to avoid noise, the jungle heat surprisingly bearable and springlike seeming. He could remember jungles once teeming with wildlife, with birds and insects.

But this one did not.

Wild fruit grew in abundance. The foliage was ridiculously bright in its greenness.

But there was no life—except for the sound he heard just ahead. He signaled his men to a halt with hand and arm movements.

Now he drew his pistol—it had been the sound of a human voice speaking something that was not Russian and was likely German, though he had no way in which to tell. The Hero Colonel, Vladmir Karamatsov, spoke the German language. So did a few of those who had taken the sleep with him.

The Stechkin Mk 7 clenched tight in his gloved right fist, he moved ahead, signaling his lieutenant to accompany him.

The voice was clearer now as he parted the foliage ahead of him—a child's voice. And then a woman's laughter. He dropped to his knees and moved forward beneath the cover of the foliage, the debris of the ground—rotted leaves—clinging to his field trousers.

He crept forward, glancing once behind him to ascertain that his lieutenant was still there.

He parted another of the low-to-the-ground broad-leafed plants—and he could see. A woman wearing a filmy-looking summer weight dress, blond hair restrained at the nape of her neck with a large bow. A child in khaki shorts and a short-sleeved shirt running and playing, throwing a red ball to the woman who on closer inspection seemed little more than a girl. The woman caught the ball, and threw it back to the child, almost bowling it across the manicured green of the grass. As the little boy caught the ball, the boy and the woman laughed, the woman rearranging her dress, then clapping her hands and calling something in a musical sounding voice to the little boy. The little boy threw the ball toward her again and she caught it.

Antonovitch looked to his right: the guard tower, glass enclosed—air conditioned, he imagined.

He would not risk a stray reflection from his field glasses, so he studied the tower with his naked eyes. Perhaps two men. One stood by the nearest window. The second appeared to be sitting—Antonovitch could barely make out the top of the head when there was movement.

They were more watchers than guards, he realized.

The other tower, to his left, was merely a speck against the horizon.

But less far to his left, well back from the woman and the little boy with the red ball, rose the mountain. An exposed pinnacle of granite. Massive doors were at its base, the doors—brass, perhaps. He could not be sure. And two massive stone pillars rising, flanking the doors on either side, the pillars becoming huge torches, flames that were apparently natural gas burning from the top of each.

He heard the laughter of the child again—and Antonovitch turned his attention back to the boy and the woman with him. As he did he saw a bronze bust the height of a pillar set in the middle of the garden. He recognized the face. It was unmistakably the face of Adolf Hitler.

He forced himself to look away and to the mountain itself. It rose so high that its summit was all but obscured in wisps of white cloud. Perhaps a hundred feet above the doors were long parapets, and on these parapets he could see armed men moving in some sort of regular pattern. There would be fortifications at the top of the mountain— aerial reconnaissance. He thanked his own foresight that he had kept his reconnaissance far back and relied on electronic observation rather than visual. Anti-aircraft emplacements ringed the summit, the nature of the guns he did not know. It was suspected by heat source identification that the entire mountain and the green space which seemed carved from out of the jungle were ringed with surface-to-air missiles.

His helicopters would stand no chance against the Nazi fortifications, regardless of the disposition of the Nazi troops who were now thousands of miles away from protecting their stronghold.

Fighter bombers were the only thing—fighter bombers

and a ground assault to penetrate the main entrance. If it were timed perfectly, it could work, he thought.

He watched the pretty young woman and the child for a moment longer—they reminded him of things he could not afford to consider until the conquest of earth under the leadership of the Hero Colonel was completed.

But he wanted to reach out to her very much—and touch her gently.

Chapter Twelve

There was a French term for it that she had forgotten. She massaged gently at the sides of her distended abdomen, watching Frau Mann as much as she listened to her. "Helene? You are all right? I cannot help but notice—"

"I am fine, Frau Mann. I have had many babies and this one is just telling me that he will be coming soon—but not too soon." Helene Sturm smiled, moving her hands from her abdomen to the table that separated them. It was a favorite place for the women of the officer corps, located on the top floor of the field officer's quarters and overlooking almost the entire complex. The streets below bustled with pedestrian traffic, the few private vehicles and the mass transport machines. The Educational Center could be seen in the far distance beyond the government buildings.

She thought of Manfred and his loyalty to the youth.

"You are not listening to me, Helene." Frau Mann smiled.

"I am sorry, Frau Mann—I was thinking of my oldest son."

"Do you think that he spies on you?"

Helene Sturm realized that the teacup she had been lifting from its saucer was making a rattling noise in her right hand.

She looked about the huge room. Other women like

herself populated the tables dotted about it—she recognized most of them. As her eyes scanned the room, Maria, the fiancé of her brother Sigfried, noticed her and waved. Helene smiled and waved back. Sigfried was with her man, her husband Helmut. They were in North America, fighting—under the leadership of Frau Mann's husband. And she was afraid for them both, and for Col. Wolfgang Mann as well. Because if he failed, the conspiracy against the leader would doubtlessly be found out in its entirety and there would be many arrests. She touched again at her abdomen, shifting her position on the smallish, wooden-framed armless chair—the seat of the chair was not padded enough.

"Helene?"

Frau Mann's voice brought her back to the present. "No, I do not know—I think that Manfred watches and listens very carefully. He is very political, I think. But he does not spy on me for anyone—not yet."

"If he were to learn," Frau Mann began, then stopped. The waitress came with their sandwiches, asked if they wanted more tea, then left. Frau Mann began again. "If Manfred were to learn—we would all be executed."

"He would not inform on his own mother—I cannot believe that," Helene Sturm insisted. She had no appetite for the sandwich, thinly sliced sausage with lightly scrambled egg. The smell of it was making her nauseated. But she needed to eat regularly for the baby. She picked up one of the quartered pieces and nibbled at it.

Frau Mann was talking again, stubbing out her cigarette as she spoke. "My husband did not attempt a radio contact last night—I was informed. This means that either something has gone wrong or that he feels the time is too close and he cannot risk a radio message being discovered."

"I think it is that—that he doesn't want to risk discovery. I just know he is all right."

"I spoke with a member of Field Marshal Richter's staff this morning—official communications are still coming in. They have encountered a strong Soviet force in the southeastern segment of what was the United States. Their first skirmish was successful for our forces."

"That will only make the leader more powerful—he can use the Soviets as a threat to increase his demands for a total war footing."

"But there was a message for me from Wolfgang—that he had found a rose. I think this is a code that he has found a means for aiding Deiter Bern."

Helene Sturm looked anxiously around the room—to mention Deiter Bern was to risk arrest for treason. "I pray that you are right, Frau Mann."

"And if," Frau Mann said slowly, "my husband and his legion should be unable to reach The Complex in time—then we shall do it ourselves. We are agreed in that still?"

"Yes—still," Helene Sturm answered. And she touched at the life in her abdomen. "Still."

"If—if he—if he is executed, all is lost," Frau Mann whispered. Helene Sturm watched Frau Mann. She looked at her sandwich, the same as Helene had ordered, then neatly folded her napkin beside the blue willow pattern plate. "I will be right back." Frau Mann pushed her chair out and stood, smoothing her skirt along her thighs with her hands, the fingers splayed. She slung her bag over her right shoulder and started toward the rear of the restaurant—the powder room, Helene Sturm knew.

She watched Wolfgang Mann's wife. The clothing, the hair, the walk—the casual smiles and more casual nods to the women she passed. Her husband was the ranking field officer under the general staff and would, after the first phase of the campaign, be promoted to general officer's rank. But if he attempted to save the life of Deiter Bern and smash the power of the leader and were to fail—he would be publicly executed.

Helene Sturm took her own napkin from her lap and set it down beside her own plate. She could eat nothing now.

Chapter Thirteen

Aerial observation had confirmed considerable activity at the site in the west Texas desert where Helmut Sturm had tracked the Soviet force, as per the orders of his commander, *Standartenfuehrer* Wolfgang Mann.

"Herr *Hauptsturmfuehrer!*"

Sturm turned to the voice of the young soldier. "Yes, Corporal—what is it?"

"A message from *Untersturmfuehrer* Bloch, Herr *Hauptsturmfuehrer!*"

Sturm took the folded message form, returned the man's salute, "Heil," and unfolded the message. "Helmut—my men are in position. We await the signal. Sigfried." He folded the message and dropped it in the left outside pocket of his battle dress uniform tunic. "Very good, Corporal— return to your unit."

Again the corporal saluted and Helmut Sturm returned it, the younger man doing a very sharp about face and breaking into a dog trot, his assault rifle at high port, his steps carrying him leadenly across the drifting sand.

Sturm turned away, licking his dry lips against the sun and the wind.

He scanned the area distant from him where the helicopters awaited, looking for his *obersturmfuehrer.* He saw the man, shouting, "Fritz—give the signal—we attack!"

"Yes Herr *Haupsturmfuehrer!*" And his *obersturm-*

fuehrer saluted, Sturm this time returning the salute with added sharpness.

He began to walk, ignoring the background sounds of the helicopters' rotor blades picking up speed, tugging his gloves into position, breaking into a run now for his machine's open fuselage door. And as he ran, he patted at the full flap holster on the belt at his waist—his pistol.

He had estimated the Soviet force on the ground—planes were coming in with alarming regularity as though a full-scale invasion were in process—at being in rough parity with his own. And he would have the element of surprise.

He ducked his head, slowing his pace, then vaulted aboard. He clapped his sergeant at the shoulder, shouting, "Herman—to victory, eh?" He didn't wait for a response, moving forward and sliding into his seat beside the main control panel and his pilot. He settled his radio headset into position, jerking his left thumb upward.

His pilot nodded.

The machine started to rise.

In the distance he could see the mirror signals from the highest of the dunes, signaling those elements on the ground under the leadership of Sigfried and Sturm's two other line platoon leaders to begin their attack. He had ordered radio silence lest a message be intercepted by his quarry, the Russians.

And radio silence would be his excuse with *Standartenfuehrer* Mann—that he had not obtained proper authorization for the attack.

As he stared groundward through the machine's chin bubble, he considered *Standartenfuehrer* Wolfgang Mann. Born to one of the best families, among the original elite who had founded The Complex more than five centuries ago. His party membership assured—he had never sought party advancement. His wife one of the most beautiful women Sturm had ever had the good fortune to see in his entire life. And she from a family equally as good as that of the *Standartenfuehrer*. But it was rumored always that theirs had been a love match, not one of the doomed arranged marriages within the elite, marriages that were publicly strong and privately weak. The *Standartenfuehrer* had been a superb athlete in his youth. He had revamped the air cavalry force to his own ideas and methods while still a junior officer, sometimes in direct opposition to the general staff. And soon, he would be appointed to the general staff as the youngest field marshal in the history of the military organization of The Complex—the first true field commander in five centuries. He was called in some quarters "the modern Rommel"—and it was this which worried Helmut Sturm. The business with Deiter Bern, whose name even whispered was punishable by death. Wolfgang Mann had been one of Bern's supporters against the leader's drive to re-Nazify The Complex, but Mann had been too highly placed to touch because of family and influence, his career too meteoric to crush.

Not a pilot by training, he could fly as well or better than his best pilots. He was at once a strategist and a tactician, beloved by his men.

Helmet Sturm at once saw his *Standartenfuehrer* as an idol and a danger.

"Herr *Hauptsturmfuehrer*!"

He turned from his reverie to the face of his pilot. "Yes?"

"We are in position, Herr *Hauptsturmfuehrer*!"

"I know that," Sturm answered evenly.

It was time to break radio silence. He flicked the switch on the console to which his headset was wired. "Eagle Strike!"

On the ground to the north, he could see the puff of smoke from the first of the mortars.

Vladmir Karamatsov sat bolt upright in his cot. The

sound of the explosion rang in his ears.

He swung his feet over the side and stuffed his feet into his boots. Another explosion, this one closer. Mortar fire.

He was up, grabbing his black flight jacket in his left hand, his shoulder holster with the five-centuries-old Smith & Wesson Model 59 automatic in his right.

He was at the door of his quarters, shrugging the shoulder holster onto his frame, twisting his feet to push them all the way into his boots.

He was through the door—one of his officers was running toward him. The sunlight bright, Karamatsov squinted against it for a moment—and he thought of John Rourke, the sunglasses.

"We are under attack, Comrade Colonel Karamatsov!"

"Get our gunships airborne!" He ran past the man, dismissing any further conversation, dodging right, throwing himself to the sand as another mortar struck, a wave of sand crashing down across his back. He beat the sand from his body as he forced himself to his feet, running, shaking his jacket free of the sand and shouldering into it.

His personal gunship was waiting for him, its rotor blades already turning.

But he heard different sounds—vehicles. He looked to his right—gunfire, flames. And things which looked like miniaturized tanks were crossing over the high dune at the far edge of the encampment's perimeter. They were roughly the size of the efficient Volkswagen Beetles of five centuries earlier, but rode high off the ground, heavily armored, from the look of them, balloon tires instead of treads. The first wave of the machines bounced over the dune and was coming toward him.

Karamatsov ran—emblazoned in his mind was the image of the swastika which had adorned each of the mini-tanks.

He was cut off from his machine now, a second wave of the mini-tanks coming from the opposite end of the camp.

Gunfire—machine guns, but not his own.

He looked skyward as he dove for cover behind a rank of packing crates, chunks of wood splintering off as machine gunfire raked across them. Helicopters—some were his own—but others, the majority of the others—they were not.

He cursed in English, "The devil with you!" He pushed himself to his feet, running again. He had to reach his machine so he could take charge of the response—otherwise defeat would be certain. He reached under his jacket, breaking the Model 59 from the leather, working off the thumb safety. He shifted the pistol to his left hand, patting at the outside pocket of his flight jacket—the little Smith & Wesson Model 36 Chiefs. He opened the pocket flap and drew the snubby barreled revolver. A pistol in each hand now, he ran.

He looked behind him. The mini-tanks were consolidating on the central section of the encampment—his men were resisting but had no armored vehicles and even the new assault rifles would not penetrate armor.

A small squad of the Nazi troopers were racing on foot and cutting him off from his machine. Karamatsov threw himself to the ground near the dead body of one of his men, stuffing the revolver into his hip pocket, picking up the assault rifle.

Gunfire hammered toward him; Karamatsov rolling, fired the assault rifle toward the small squad of Nazis. He could hear—see now—gunfire from the open fuselage door of his helicopter. Two of the Nazis were down. He fired again—the third went down, the fourth dropping to a crouch beside a fallen comrade, firing. The sand near Karamatsov's head seemed to explode over him and he rolled left, firing wildly.

The roar of heavy machine gunfire—he looked up. One of his own helicopters. The Nazi who had been firing at him was down, draped clumsily across the body of one of his comrades, the back of his khakis laced with the red of his blood.

Karamatsov threw down the assault rifle, running now, across the ground and into the storm of sand made by his beating rotor blades. He threw himself through the opening, shouting to his pilot, "Take it up—now!"

He crawled forward, out of the opening in the fuselage, the machine rocking and swaying under him, around him. It was then that he glanced at the digital chronometer on his left wrist. As he hauled himself to his feet, fighting the sway of the machine as he moved forward, Vladmir Karamatsov laughed.

If the jet fighters of Krakovski's lead elements were on schedule . . .

As if to echo his thoughts, he heard the sonic boom, then another and another and another and another.

He was fully forward now, sinking into the seat opposite his pilot.

"Pull back—so I can see this!"

"Yes, Comrade Colonel!" The machine banked hard to port, Karamatsov watching the horizon line for a moment through the chin bubble, then as the machine leveled off, watching through the windshield. Black streaks through the sky, tan Nazi mini-tanks erupting as contrails dissipated in the black and orange fire-balls of air-to-ground missiles. The sand rippled under the impact of submachine gun bullets, the Nazi infantry forces falling back toward the perimeter of the camp.

His own helicopters were closing in battle with the Nazi machines, but some of the fighter bombers were breaking off, engaging more of the Nazi helicopters. He had seen an anti-aircraft bombardment once—shells exploding in mid-air. And it was the same effect now—but rather than shells exploding, the Nazi gunships were exploding, vaporizing before his eyes.

* * *

The windshield through which he stared was smudged black with oil that had gushed toward his machine when another from his force had caught fire from a peripheral missile strike and a secondary explosion had then vaporized the craft.

He kept his hands locked in his lap—to prevent anyone seeing them shaking.

War—it was no longer something talked about at night, or studied from books, or an exercise—it was reality.

And Helmut Sturm, his forces triply decimated at the least, knew inside himself that had *Standartenfuehrer* Wolfgang Mann been in command, somehow the roles of victor and vanquished would have been exchanged.

And the worst of it—he had witnessed as machine gunfire from one of the shadow black fighter aircraft which had appeared seemingly out of nowhere had stitched across the position held by his wife's brother. And her brother's men.

Helmut Sturm wondered how he would tell his wife Helene that her brother Sigfried was dead and that he could not even retake the boy's mangled body from the field.

He closed his eyes—it was unmanly to cry, he had been taught.

Chapter Fourteen

Annie Rourke squeezed the towel tighter, the water dribbling from it into the basin, then refolded it and laid it across Paul Rubenstein's high forehead, smoothing back his thinning hair, murmuring to him, "You were so brave—I love you."

He opened his eyes then, and she leaned over him more closely, kissing his lips lightly.

"What, ahh, aww, shit—I'm—I'm sorry—I—"

"After Daddy and Momma and Natalia got away with Lieutenant Kurinami and Doctor Halverson—"

"I remember." Paul Rubenstein smiled up at her thinly. "Dodd—he—"

"No, it wasn't Dodd. He was at the other side of the crowd. It was that man Blackburn, the one who spoke German and was supposed to go with Daddy to Argentina. He hit you with that wrench and he tried to take your submachine gun."

"What—where, ahh—wow, my head hurts."

"I shot him in the left thigh—just a little," Annie admitted.

"What—are we under siege here—what?"

Annie put her hands into her lap, smoothing her skirt, studying the pattern in the material rather than looking into Paul's dark eyes. "Ahh, well, no, ahh—no. After I shot Blackburn in the leg, Captain Dodd and Craig Lerner and Jeff Styles and Jane Harwood—she's the commander of Eden Three—they all got guns and forced the crowd to disperse, after they forced all of them to put down any weapons they had. He, Captain Dodd, he had an assault rifle pointed at you. I laid down my gun," she sighed. "So Captain Dodd, Lerner, Styles and Jane Harwood are the only ones in the camp who are armed. Right now. There wasn't anything else I could do."

She watched Paul's eyes—the lids fluttered and his jaw was hard-set, as though he were in pain. "What happens if the Russians come back and pay us a visit?" Paul asked her.

"That's the same thing I asked Captain Dodd. He said then he would rearm us."

"Gee whiz, that's smart. Ahh—"

"Dr. Munchen came by. He said your head will be all right—and he told me Momma and Daddy and Natalia got away with Colonel Mann. They're on their way to Argentina. They're safe—for now."

Paul reached up his right hand and she took it in hers. She waited for him to speak. "Annie, how's—"

"Michael's asleep. Madison's asleep too," and she gestured behind her to the opposite side of the tent. She had her father's bad habit of second guessing what people were going to say and answering questions before they were fully asked.

"You've gotta get something going—so we can find out who the murderer really is. With a Soviet agent in the camp and Dodd disarming everybody—hell, if—"

"I know," she whispered, touching her lips to his hand a moment. "What can I do, Paul?" She knew what to do, but wanted to let him tell her.

"You're gonna have to go to Dodd and demand that he let you help. The killer has to be from Eden One or Eden Two—Eden Three wasn't on the ground long enough for any of the criogenic sleepers to be awake. Unless somebody from the flight crew—the commander or the flight officer or the science officer. Eden One has a master computer with all the personnel files. Dodd told me his instructions indicated that that was in case they landed and reviving all of the sleepers proved impossible or impractical. The files were to allow him to pick and choose who he needed for specific tasks from among the sleepers. There's gotta be something to link somebody from Eden One or Two or the flight crew of Eden Three to Mona Stankiewicz. I'd say it was her boyfriend maybe—"

"Haselton?"

"Yeah, but he was on Eden Three, I think. So he wouldn't have been awake yet. If Dodd'll let you use the computer and you can find some kind of link—it'll be subtle."

"I can use Daddy's Apple IIE—and I taught myself Basic. I should be able to use the onboard computer."

"Good girl." Paul smiled. She touched her lips to his hand again. His plan had been exactly the same as hers—but she was glad she'd let him say it. "See if you can find Dodd—and be careful. Even if that Soviet agent doesn't have a gun anymore—"

"I know," Annie interrupted. "Don't forget—Daddy taught me martial arts."

"When Natalia gets back, you'll have to get her to teach you a few things. She knows a lot and the techniques she uses are probably better for a woman."

"All right, Paul. Will you be all right here?"

"Fine—if I need anything, I'll shout for Madison."

"Dr. Munchen told me you should stay in bed for at least twenty-four hours in case you got a slight concussion."

She watched Paul as he started to laugh and the laugh turned into a wince against pain. "All I've got's a big bump. And as soon as I'm up and around, I'm gonna find that Blackburn guy and give the Eden Project dentists something to do."

She leaned over him and kissed his mouth lightly—she was very much afraid of moving about the encampment, and of leaving Paul alone. But if she didn't find the murderer of Mona Stankiewicz, the murderer would find them. She felt that inside herself.

She stood up, pushing her hair back from her shoulders. She smiled at Paul. "Don't get into trouble," she whispered, laughing.

"Be careful," she heard as she started through the tent flap.

Chapter Fifteen

Captain Dodd had been reluctant, but it was Jane Harwood, the commander of Eden Three, who had finally convinced him that Annie be allowed access to the onboard master computer of Eden One.

She had spent the first ten minutes in the cockpit just staring at the instruments. Very vaguely, from when she had been very little, she remembered seeing one of the space shuttles taking off—she had watched it on television. And her father had videotapes of several of the space shuttle launches that she had watched at times over the years on his machines at The Retreat. She had seen every tape he had several times over.

And of course she had seen the landing of the Eden fleet.

But the fascination at actually sitting behind the controls of one of the shuttle craft awed her.

After what she judged as ten minutes or more, she began to attack the computer.

It was not as difficult a task as someone might suppose, she reflected, settling herself more comfortably in Craig Lerner's chair. She was only recalling information, not programming, and the master computer was programmed to accept English.

She booted up the disc and started typing. "Recall Personnel File s Eden One." She punched Return.

The display terminal printed, "Syntax error."

She stared at it a moment, then activated the cursor. She eliminated the space between the "e" and the "s" in "Files," then retyped "Eden One." The display printed, "What system?"

She considered that. They would be listed alphabetically certainly, but also by job specialties.

She decided on alphabetical order but for the heck of it typed, "Catalogue Systems."

A lengthy list appeared on the terminal—alphabetical, job specialty, sex, blood type, military experience, age—Annie let the catalogue run itself out, then selected the alphabetical listing. The first name was Abromowitz, Arthur A. Annie closed her eyes for a moment—it would be a long job. . . .

She walked through the camp, the sun setting toward the west, a breeze blowing which toyed with her hair and caught up under her skirt at times as she walked. She felt stupid that she had not seen it earlier. Because if the secret of Mona Stankiewicz's death were to be found, it had certainly been with Mona.

And Annie had found it there. She had not found the killer yet.

But she had found the reason.

She stopped before the tent, looking behind her—no one lurked beside another of the tents, and no one watched furtively from the edge of the camp.

She pulled back the tent flap and went through, sitting down beside Paul on the small chair next to his bed.

Annie stared at him—and Paul opened his eyes.

She had learned she could make him do that, and it frightened her a little. "Annie?"

"Paul, are you awake?"

"Yeah. What—ahh—"

"It's almost sunset. I found something in Mona Stankiewicz's personnel file. I haven't found a clue to who the killer is, but I know why anyway."

Paul started to sit up and she gently nudged him back. "You rest. You can lie down and hear this just as well."

"Not even married yet." He smiled—"and you're telling me what to do."

"You can tell me what to do all you want and I'll do it—or I'll make you think I am." She perched on the edge of the chair, the hem of her skirt brushing at her ankles as she moved her feet. "All right. Mona Stankiewicz was first generation American. Her parents were born in Poland—that do anything for you?"

"Before The Night of The War—"

"The Russians invaded Poland—it was a good number of years before, wasn't it?"

"Uh-huh." Paul nodded. "Yeah. Polish trade unionism was the apparent rationale—but Poland was becoming too uncontrollable and the Russians cracked the whip."

"What if Mona Stankiewicz had relatives living in Poland and the KGB threatened to harm them? And the only way she could prevent that was to sell out? I talked to Jane Harwood for a while after Captain Dodd gave me permission to use the onboard computer. And I found out something very interesting. The primary and back-up flight crews had been given special briefings and special training sessions that were with classified material. All of the primary and back-up flight crew personnel were Americans except for the flight officer on Eden Six—an Englishman. Jane Harwood insisted they had no inkling that the Eden Project was a doomsday contingency, but some of the special training included use of radiation monitoring equipment, landings with various types of aircraft on various types of runway surfaces, stuff like that. So Mona would have had all the special training and the secret information. This is the juicy part—"

"Women." Paul Rubenstein laughed.

"All right, smarty. But anyway—the flight crews and the backup flight crews were the only ones that got any detailed information at all about the criogenic process, hmm? And the serum. The way you and Daddy and Natalia talked about it—well, Karamatsov had a lot of information he shouldn't have."

"So, someone in the flight crews was a KGB agent and threatened Mona Stankiewicz's relatives and forced her to give information."

"That's what I just said." Annie heard Madison stirring behind her and turned and smiled at the girl as she sat up. She had been sleeping curled up in a ball near the foot of Michael's cot. Michael's breathing seemed even and Annie dismissed checking him. "Hi—you slept for a long time, Madison."

"I—I didn't know I was so very tired, Annie."

"Pull up a chair. We're solving a murder mystery."

"The poor Mona Stankiewicz?"

"That's the one." Annie nodded, smiling still.

Madison stood up, stretching like a house cat—Annie had seen house cats in videotapes and read about them in her father's Britannica. Madison straightened her clothes, walking across to their side of the tent, then turning around and taking the second chair. Annie watched her—Madison still looked half asleep as she sat down in the chair placed near the foot of Paul's cot, then began adjusting her clothing. The skirt was impossibly wrinkled.

"Annie found out," Paul began, "that Mona Stankiewicz had relatives in Poland—"

"What is Poland?"

"It was a country before The Night of The War which the Russians occupied," Paul supplied.

"The Russians are the bad people—yes. Except for Natalia who is very good."

"Not all the Russians were bad people—just some of

them. And the worst ones were in the KGB," Paul told her.

"But this cagey-bee—was not Natalia a member of it?"

"But she was the exception," Paul told her.

Annie interrupted. "Anyway, we found out that the Russians were blackmailing Mona Stankiewicz into giving them special information about the Eden Project."

"Black-male? Some of the men aboard the Eden Project are black, like Doctor Halverson is black."

"No, not black male—blackmail," Annie tried to explain. "They threatened her relatives to get her to give them information. But when she woke up—" and Annie looked at Paul and smiled— "and The Night of The War had come and gone, she realized the KGB had no hold over her. And whoever murdered her realized that too and that's why he killed her."

"The black male did this?"

"No, the man who worked for the KGB—or it could have been a woman—and the person could have been black or white or yellow."

"Ohh, yellow male?"

"Aagh," Annie groaned. She needed to spend time with Madison—lots of time. Michael taught her driving, shooting and lovemaking, spending his greatest efforts on the latter pursuit.

"Whoever," Paul began again, "did kill her is gonna figure you'll get onto him with that computer. You'd better wait until I'm up and around. Dr. Munchen stopped in— he says tomorrow afternoon I can spend a little time on my feet if I take it slow."

"We don't have 'til tomorrow afternoon," Annie announced. "I'm going back to that computer right now and check for whoever seems too perfect."

"Before you do that," Paul cautioned, "check with this Jane Harwood. She's in the clear or close to it. Get her to put you in touch with a few people she feels certain can be trusted. What if the killer turns out to be someone Dodd just won't buy?"

"You're right," Annie agreed. "Then Daddy and Momma and Natalia might not be the only ones with a revolution on their hands."

Chapter Sixteen

John Rourke pulled at the canteen—the water had a sweet taste to it, different from the water in northeastern Georgia somehow, but good to drink. Several hours of daylight still remained. Wolfgang Mann walked from where he had been talking with a *haupsturmfuehrer* beside one of the helicopters, lighting a cigarette as he came, saying through a cloud of smoke, "You should have brought an American cowboy hat, Herr Doctor."

Rourke looked past Mann toward where two of Mann's men were saddling the horses. "I never thought I'd see one of them again. The Eden Project has horse embryos in criogenic freeze, along with other animals. But still."

"With customary German efficiency, we had the foresight to assume that some domestic animals might indeed be worth saving. What if a synthetic fuel had not been discovered? But a small portion of The Complex was set aside for the nurturing of livestock. Breeding pairs. And when it finally came time to return to the land, one of the first tasks was the breeding of the animals to increase their numbers. Unfortunately, no dogs, no cats—I understand from materials I have read that such animals were very amusing and actually kept as pets."

"Yes," Rourke said. He thought of the dog he'd had as a boy. He hadn't thought of the animal who had somehow been his best friend for longer than he could remember.

"But we did of course keep beef cattle growing throughout our enforced entombment as a source of protein. Chickens as well. Horses were the only other ones. Certain types of fish, of course."

"If secrecy is so important," Rourke asked Mann, "how were you able to arrange that the animals be here?"

"Since horses had a potential military value, they were naturally assigned to the armed forces. The commander of the unit which is in charge of their breeding and their training is one of us—one of those who oppose the leader and work for the freedom of Deiter Bern. Hence, the horses which await us."

Rourke found himself watching Natalia—she was slowly approaching one of the animals, a massive bay with white stockings all around and a white blaze on the head, the animal pawing at the ground with apparent nervous energy.

"I'll make you a deal," Rourke told Mann. "If this all works out successfully, after we've dealt with the Russians, if I can find a way of getting them from here to Georgia, we'll—"

"Horses? Of course. They are the best, I have read—a crossbreed of Arabian and American quarter horses. Stamina, intelligence, speed. They have been bred for nothing else."

Rourke had already seen the animal he wanted for himself—it reminded him of his own horse, Sam, which he had not seen since before The Night of The War, Sam who had so well served Sarah and his children in the earlier stages of their flight. It was darker—more gray than white, the forehead broad, the Arabian in it showing strongly, with black stockings, flowing black mane and tail.

"Are any of these animals owned privately—or a man's special mount?"

"You see a special one—which?"

"The gray—is he—"

"He is yours, Doctor Rourke, You have made a fine choice, I think. And as to the other mounts, all that you request which we can supply—for your entire family, if you like."

There was a saddle at The Retreat. A very special saddle that had been given to him years before The Night of The War when an assignment he had had caused him to work with DEA and the Mexican authorities in breaking up a ring of terrorists. The Mexican he had worked most closely with had shipped the saddle to him. With the big Mexican horn and the high cantle, the leather intricately tooled.

It was black—completely. With the big gray, it would go well.

"All right—thank you." Rourke nodded, leaving Mann, walking toward the animal. He would not call the horse Sam after his own mount from so long ago. A name was an individual thing. And he struck on the perfect name for the horse—he would call it Wolf, after the man who had given it to him. But he would not say the name aloud—not just now.

They had landed some considerable distance from The Complex, Mann proclaiming that the electronically enhanced scan of the radar system above the complex was too sensitive to be risked.

Natalia rode ahead, beside Elaine Halverson—both women rode well. Kurirnami, in the lead just ahead of them and beside Mann's *haupsturmfuehrer*, looked somehow strange, his baseball cap, his white coveralls.

And just ahead of Rourke, Rourke and Mann bringing up the rear, rode Sarah, beside one of Mann's men who was practicing his English. Rourke watched his wife—the loving way she touched at the bay mare. It was almost identical to her horse, Tildie, lost at the same time

102

Rourke's horse Sam was lost after a narrow escape from the swollen lake and the bursting of a dam.

Rourke thought of Michael—Sarah had told him of Michael's bravery, as had Annie years later.

Wolfgang Mann began speaking again and Rourke tuned the man in. "I early became fascinated with the history of the place we call The Complex. Its earliest beginnings, its construction. Like most officers, I have a degree in engineering. It was forbidden to travel in the tunnels beneath The Complex and surrounding it, forbidden because there were many possible dangers from cave in and rock slides. But like most young men, I cared little for danger and more for adventure. So I explored the tunnels without the knowledge of my parents or my friends. I became expert in maneuvering there. And, since it seemed logical that there should be, I persevered, Herr Doctor, until I had discovered a way out of The Complex via the tunnel system. When I originally planned the rescue of Deiter Bern, I entertained the thought of utilizing the tunnels as a means of escape from The Complex. I never dreamed that the leader would be launching the campaign so soon. I believe that part of his reasoning was that I would be away when the execution took place on Unity Day."

"Sounds like a sweetheart," Rourke observed.

"He is a clever man. I shall warn you now—if somehow he were to have discovered my intended use of the tunnel system, it will likely not be closed, but booby-trapped instead. I believe that is the Americanism—booby-trapped, yes?"

"Yes." Rourke nodded, uncomfortable in the English-style saddle—he had never cared for English tack. It seemed to him as sensible as riding a motorcycle mounted atop a postage stamp. "These tunnels, where do they end—how do we enter The Complex?"

"It takes some great amount of explanation, Herr Doctor. I will tonight make a diagram which will better enable you to understand."

Rourke looked ahead. The sun was lowering in the west.

Chapter Seventeen

The modern German equivalent of a Coleman stove had
been used to heat the water with which their food had been
prepared by the young sergeant who had accompanied
them and practiced English with Sarah throughout the
hours they had ridden side by side. Rourke had learned
from his wife that the young sergeant—Conrad Heinz—
had aspirations to the officers corps. From Rourke's earlier
conversations with Mann, Rourke remembered that a
command of English was one of the basic requirements.

Rourke supposed that it was somehow flattering that the
German high command had assumed that somehow the
language would still be viable and necessary.

Conrad Heinz had taken the first shift at guard duty,
along with two of the other noncoms, four in all besides
Heinz having accompanied them.

John Rourke, Sarah Rourke, Natalia, Wolfgang Mann,
Mann's *haupsturmfuehrer* and Elaine Halverson and
Akiro Kurinami sat about the stove in a ragged circle,
sharing the meager light in the darkness, as heavy as
velvet, which surrounded them. The *haupsturmfuehrer's*
name was Hartman.

And Hartman spoke, his voice rather high-pitched for a
man's, his English heavily accented but syntactically correct. "I would like to ask, Herr Doctor—and perhaps I am
speaking out of turn."

"You are free to speak, of course," Mann noted.

"Thank you, Herr *Standartenfuehrer*." Hartman turned to face Rourke. "Herr Doctor—as someone viewing this apart, so to speak. How do you then view our chances of success?"

Rourke inhaled on his cigar, exhaling a thin stream of gray smoke as he spoke. "Our success or failure in the specified mission depends on too many variables, but I'd say the basic probability of reaching Deiter Bern is comfortably high. The exact nature of the operation I'll have to perform and what in practice rather than theory must be done with that device which I remove—that is difficult to say. But the overall success of your goals, Mr. Hartman, seems to rest with how accurately Colonel Mann and the rest of you have gauged the public support for this Deiter Bern. If freeing him causes the people of The Complex to rise up against the leader, and those military forces loyal to the leader can be neutralized or held at bay, then chances for success seem very good. But some of the 'ifs' are very important ones. And can't be ignored."

"But you—but you, Herr Doctor, you and Major Tiemerovna—you are both veterans of such enterprises, is that not so?"

Natalia answered. "Perhaps that's why John is reluctant to be more specific, Herr Hartman. I think the best example I can recall is something Sarah told me."

Hartman turned from looking at Natalia, who sat at Rourke's left, to Sarah, who sat at Rourke's right. "And what is this, Frau Rourke?"

"I think Natalia is talking about an operation I was involved with through the Resistance—the people who were still fighting the Russians once our country was invaded. Many of the men of the Resistance were imprisoned—it was along the eastern coast of the United States. There was a storm, I remember. Their women were in self-imposed exile on one of the offshore islands. A group of us—all of us women—went to the prison, forced our way in and out and rescued the men just before they were to be shot. I think what Natalia means is that just looking at the odds from a clinical standpoint isn't necessarily a way to judge things. You do what has to be done for no other reason than necessity. And maybe you can get through on nerve."

Rourke folded his right arm around his wife's shoulders. Wolfgang Mann began to laugh.

Akiro Kurinami said, "In Japan, we have the legends of the samurai. One man would take on vastly superior odds—and he would win."

"You have to consider both sides of the coin," Elaine Halverson began. "This is basically a struggle for freedom. This is nothing new to people of my color. Freedom is hard won. I hope you win yours, Colonel, Captain Hartman. So that we can win ours. Wouldn't it be wonderful to know that we lived in a world where every man and woman and child was free? Where there were no dictators? No slaves? The old world that died five centuries ago—we can't afford to let history repeat itself, can we?"

Sarah murmured, "Amen."

John Rourke realized the one problem with stoves rather than real campfires—there was no flame into which he could toss his cigar.

It was odd; he felt as though somehow he were cheating on Natalia—because Mann's troopers had set up a separate tent for Rourke to sleep with his wife.

They had not slept together since before The Night of The War.

They lay beside one another now, on rigid inflatable air mattresses which rose some eight inches above the ground. Rourke stared at the ceiling of the tent. He could hear Sarah breathing.

"John," she whispered.

"Yes?"

"However this turns out, I'm glad I'm with you."

"I'm happy for it too," Rourke answered her.

"I think I've come to understand what you did with the children. I'll never like it—but as children, they might never have survived. And if the Eden Project hadn't returned—"

"I tried to do what I thought was best, Sarah."

"Why haven't you—you and Natalia, ahh—"

"Made love?"

"Um-hmm."

"You're my wife. Before I found you, I figured that if there were any chance you'd still be alive, well—I couldn't. It would have been wrong. And now—well, it'd still be wrong. At least to me it would be."

"Do you—do you—do you still, ahh, do you want me?"

Rourke stared upward. "The trouble from the beginning—it's that I love both of you. You said that yourself. I want you—but I'd be less than honest if I said I didn't want Natalia too. And I reject the idea of . . ." He didn't finish it.

Sarah did. "Having two wives."

"Yes."

"We haven't made love—for five centuries," and she started to laugh.

Rourke eased closer to her, folding his left arm around her. Her head moved to his chest. "That's crazy to think of. That we were born in the twentieth century and it's the twenty-fifth century. And—and the other thing, it's crazy too, I guess."

In the darkness he could barely see his wife's face.

"Pretend," she whispered, Rourke feeling Sarah's breath against his chest, her fingers knotted in the hair there. "Pretend—well, that none of it, none of it happened, John—please."

Rourke drew his wife's face up to his, then bent over her,

as she rolled back.

Pretending—it was something he had never been able to do, even as a child. He had lost himself sometimes—with characters in books. But he had never pretended.

But he did now—that The Night of The War hadn't happened, and Rourke crushed his wife's lips beneath his, his right hand moving beneath the blanket which covered her. She had worn only panties and a T-shirt—Rourke had seen her remove her bra, slipping the straps down along her arms and taking it off without removing her shirt.

But he raised the shirt now, first his hand, then his lips finding the corona of her left breast, touching at it. She had nurtured both their children and he too had tasted her milk. His hands touched at her, exploring her and he felt the hardness rising in him as he pushed down her panties, felt her hands opening his jeans.

John Thomas Rourke slipped between his wife's thighs—it was no longer pretending then, no longer pretending at all.

Chapter Eighteen

Had it not been for the arrival of the fighter planes from
The Underground City which he had summoned just after
sending word to Krakovski to break off any engagement
with the Wild Tribes of Europe, Vladmir Karamatsov
realized that all would have been lost against the Nazis.

But with the arrival of the planes, what had been
doomed to defeat had become a glorious, if costly, victory.
Eight of his helicopters were destroyed totally. Three more
were in need of serious repair and work crews even at this
late hour—he checked his watch, it was nearly two a.m.
here—labored over them. Sixty-three men and women had
been killed or seriously wounded.

One of the jet fighters had slight damage which was
being repaired.

The Nazi force had not only been beaten back, but
taken what Karamatsov estimated as over twenty percent
casualties and lost nine machines totally. Their casualty
figures could have been higher. Twelve of the peculiar yet
efficient-seeming mini-tanks were destroyed as well.

But at the height of his despair of the losses suffered, he
had received an encrypted radio message from Nicolai
Antonovitch—that the Nazi headquarters had been located
in a rain forested area of Argentina.

Vladmir Karamatsov walked the length and breadth of
his camp.

His plans were firm now.

Soon, Krakovski's elements would be arriving. But he would not wait for Krakovski and his helicopter squadrons and troops.

He had recalled the jet fighters from pursuit of the retreating Nazis.

He had ordered Major Antonovitch to secure a landing site where troops could be debarked, where helicopters and jets could be refueled.

Karamatsov stopped near one of the prefabricated hangars, watching as a work crew restored one of the damaged helicopters.

They worked with great efficiency.

He took pride in their work.

And after conquering the Nazi headquarters in Argentina, he would return to Georgia and the Eden Project.

And he would utterly destroy it.

Vladmir Karamatsov studied his watch again for a moment. The work crews would not have completed the repairs until dawn. And shortly after dawn there would be the perfunctory burial services for his fallen troops.

And then . . .

He had once thought that victory could be tasted. Vladmir Karamatsov longed for that taste again.

Chapter Nineteen

"He has gone!"

"Yes, Helmut."

"Where?" Helmut Sturm watched the eyes of *Sturm-bannfuehrer* Axel Kleist, ignoring the fact that he was speaking to a superior officer. He was tired, dirty, discouraged—and hours of letters that had to be written to the families of his dead lay before him.

"*Standartenfuehrer* Mann—" and *Sturmbannjuenrer* Kleist seemed to slightly regain his composure. "He has been forced to return to the New Fatherland."

Helmut Sturm lit a cigarette, staring down at his muddy boots—they had set down in a swamp in what had once been Louisiana in order to tend to some of the wounded. "Why, Herr *Sturmbannfuehrer?*"

"That is not the concern of a junior officer—or need I remind you, *Hauptsturmfuehrer* Sturm?"

Helmut Sturm stared beyond his boots—at the encampment from which a dozen of the machines and a full company of men were missing. Two dozen more of the machines were preparing for departure. "But an entire legion, Axel."

"Helmut—the *standartenfuehrer* knows what he is about."

"The Soviets cannot be attacking The Complex—not yet, at least. Nor can these Americans." He waved dismis-

112

sively in the direction of their camp several miles to the south. "Not in their antiquated spaceships. There is only one reason why the *standartenfuehrer* would authorize such a large number of men to return to the New Fatherland."

"Do not say this, Helmut," Kleist whispered, his blue eyes narrowed, his narrow shoulders hard-set in his short frame. The man was almost a miniature and barely the height requirement for an officer. Helmut Sturm towered over his superior.

"Do not say treason, Axel? Do not say that he goes to somehow attempt to effect the rescue of Deiter Bern before the execution which is scheduled for Unity Day? Do not say this. If you tell me it is not true, I will not."

"The *standartenfuehrer* has the best interests of the German people at heart."

"Wolfgang Mann has never been a Nazi—and neither have you. You have never shared the dream and neither has he, is that not so, Axel?"

"You—you overstep your bounds. You could be shot. I could have you shot."

"And I, Axel—I could have you both shot. And I will," and Helmut Sturm drew his pistol from his belt, the Walther P-38 which his ancestor had carried into battle for the Old Fatherland generations ago. He pushed off the safety catch, worked the slide back to chamber a round.

"Helmut!"

Helmut Sturm pulled the trigger once, then again, point-blank, placing both rounds into the center of his superior's chest.

He shouted to his *obersturmfuehrer* who stood some hundred yards away, gaping open-mouthed. "I have relieved the *sturmbannfuehrer* of command—take what men you can who are loyal and assault the departing gunships. Be quick, man!"

His pistol still cocked, Helmut Sturm ran toward the

airfield which had been cleared at the far end of the camp.

The gunships were already beginning to take to the air and he fired toward the nearest of them, the range hopeless, and the effectiveness of his bullets doubtful at best against the armored bodies of the great machines.

He fired—the pistol empty now, the slide locked open.

And he stood, staring skyward, hearing the rattle of small arms fire around him, his right arm hanging limply at his side. He had been betrayed. The New Fatherland had been betrayed. The leader . . .

He would gather what remained of his forces, what loyal men and officers could be gathered up from this encampment.

And before following the traitorous *Standartenfuehrer* Mann to The Complex, he would destroy these American spaceships and the men and women with them.

Destroy—it was all he could consider now.

He screamed to his *obersturmfuehrer* over the beating of the rotor blades above him, "We shall prevail!"

Chapter Twenty

She sat at the breakfast table, leaving the chair at its head vacant as she did always when her husband was away with his troops. At the opposite end, since he was the oldest man in the house, despite the fact that he was a boy, sat her son Manfred.

Helene Sturm looked at his very pretty face. "Why do you stare at me, Manfred?"

"I have become distressed, Mother."

"You worry concerning your father, then—but I am sure—"

"My father and the troops of the New Fatherland shall be invincible, Mother. I am distressed at what I have come to learn."

Helene Sturm dropped the spoon with which she had been stirring her coffee.

"I do not—"

"But you do, Mother. You understand quite well, I am afraid."

"A boy should not talk thus to his mother, Manfred—I will tell your father."

"I doubt you would tell my father any of this. For I have followed you, Mother. And I have curiosity concerning the topic of which you speak so secretly with the wife of the

Standartenfuehrer Mann."

"Frau Mann," Helene Sturm whispered. "But, but she and I are friends, Manfred."

"You are not of her station, Mother—there is something besides friendship of which you speak."

Helene Sturm set down the spoon which she had picked up, it made the shaking of her hand that much more visible. "I don't—I don't understand, Manfred."

"I want more cereal, Mother," Willy asked.

"Yes, I'll, I'll get it." She started to stand up.

"Willy, you will wait for your cereal."

Helene Sturm looked across the table at Manfred. "Don't talk to your brother like that—and don't talk to me like that either."

"Then I shall talk to the supervisor of the youth, Mother. I shall tell him what I suspect."

Helene Sturm stood up—that her hands trembled mattered no more to her. She felt the child—or perhaps there were two as her doctor suspected, but she looked at her son. "You will obey me—as you would obey your father. What I do is none of your concern, Manfred. When your father returns, if you feel that my conduct must be reported on, then tell him. You are my son—you are in my charge. And you are responsible to me, and to your brothers. And to your father. We are your family—not the youth. I am your parent—not the supervisor of the youth. Is that clear to you, Manfred?"

"My primary obligation, Mother, is to the party."

Hugo, her second oldest son, stood up. "Manfred—you should not speak this way to Mother."

Bertol, next oldest to Hugo, stood as well. "Yes, you are being bad, Manfred."

Now Willy stood, apparently his quest for cereal abandoned or forgotten—she could not help but smile as he spoke. "If you talk bad to Momma, I'll punch you in the nose, Manfred."

"Hush, Willy—he is your older brother and you should respect him."

Willy looked confused. She didn't blame him.

Manfred stood. "I leave now—to meet with the supervisor of the youth. Your reluctance that I speak with him only confirms my worst suspicions, Mother."

"You will not leave this house."

"It is an apartment, Mother—the concept of the private house is an anachronism. You live in the past—you refuse to prepare for the glory that is our future."

"Manfred!"

He threw down his napkin, stood very erect and straightened his youth scarf about his neck. "I am leaving now, Mother—and in your present physical condition, I should not advise that you attempt to interfere. I, like all members of the youth, revere women who fulfill their biological destiny by providing those who will serve the New Fatherland in the years to come. But my duty is my first concern, Mother."

He turned as though doing an about-face, then walked from the room.

"Mother?"

She looked at Hugo.

"Yes, darling."

"Bertol and I—we could try to stop Manfred, Mother."

"No, he is your brother."

"Momma, can I have more cereal now?"

She leaned forward and kissed Willy's forehead. She realized that she was holding Hugo's shoulders very tightly. "Bertol—fix your little brother some cereal. I must use the telephone," and she walked around the table and toward the small hallway by the door just as she saw the door close. Manfred was gone.

Helene Sturm's hands still trembled. She picked up the

telephone. She punched the buttons and made a mistake, broke the connection and replaced the call. "Frau Mann, I am sorry to trouble you. This is Helene Sturm. Manfred— I fear."

Chapter Twenty-one

John Rourke swung down from the virtually pommel-less, virtually canteless English-style saddle, to the rocky ground beside the already dismounted Wolfgang Mann.

"We are here, Herr Doctor," Mann announced, smiling.

John Rourke looked over the terrain before them. A massive valley, lush with rich green vegetation, sprawled before them, gray rocky abutments rising from amid the green, a river coursing through its center. It could well have been paradise.

Or the gateway to hell.

He had the uncomfortable feeling he was about to find out which.

Natalia swung down from her mount, and in the same instant so did Sarah. Natalia asked, "Where is the entrance—from your diagram, I was looking for a peculiar triangular-shaped rock."

"Ahh, but it cannot be seen from here—we must walk along a very narrow trail. The horses cannot come. I should have drawn the map more carefully. I apologize, Fraulein Major Tiemerovna."

"Are we coming in through the tunnels with you?" Elaine Halverson asked, still mounted and beside Kurinami who stood holding her animal's reins.

"John has something else in mind, I think," Sarah volunteered.

"We discussed this a little last night—because of your obvious non-Germanic appearances, neither of you can enter The Complex. And Akiro already knows his part. Sergeant Heinz will accompany Colonel Mann, Sarah, Natalia and myself. Elaine—you and Akiro will travel with the four remaining enlisted personnel. Captain Hartman has other duties." Rourke looked up at the four enlisted men—they were still mounted. None of them spoke English. "You'll position yourselves strategically outside the main entrance of The Complex, either to be a back-up for us or coordinate efforts with the remainder of Colonel Mann's forces when they arrive. From what the colonel tells us, the tunnels are too narrow in spots and far too treacherous to bring a large body of men with field equipment through. And since you speak some German, Elaine—well, you shouldn't have any communications problem with Colonel Mann's men."

Rourke began untying gear from his saddle as he continued to talk. His pack was already on his back because with the English saddle it had been impossible to tie it on. He removed the pack now. He had left the CAR-15 in his truck, taking instead two M-16 rifles for the heavier volume of fire they could lay down. Natalia and Sarah were each similarly armed and there were several eight-hundred-round containers of 5.56mm ball that would accompany them. He slung the M-16s crossbody now, one on each side, adjusting the position of his musette bag at his left side where it became entangled with the rifle. "If something goes wrong—you and Akiro are gonna have to kinda wing it." He secured the canteen—one of the round Western-style canteens, blanket covered—on his right side on its strap, opposite the musette bag. He picked up the pack and began securing it into the actual seat of the saddle, the only way it could be secured. Halverson and Kurinami would take the horses with them.

Rourke glanced to Natalia, then to Sarah—both of them

120

were doing roughly the same with their gear. He looked to Sergeant Heinz. Heinz alone bore a pack, and also two of the Nazi assault rifles.

Their rifles were apparently based on the successful G-3, but utilized a caseless cartridge, similar to those used in the new forty-round capacity Soviet assault rifles. But the magazines were not plastic disposables and the caliber seemed closer to thirty than twenty—all told, from what little he knew of both rifles, he favored the German. Their pistols—Mann alone carried one, a pistol apparently not an issue item for a noncom. And not the P-38 Mann had worn before. Their pistols seemed derivative of the Walther P-5, but with double column magazine enhanced capacity. The bore diameter was smaller than 9mm, closer to that of a .30 Mauser to which the caseless pistol round bore an astonishing resemblance as to shape.

Heinz, beside his feet, had one of the eight-hundred-round boxes of 5.56mm ball. Rourke walked to one of the still-mounted noncoms, taking down from the man the second box. Rourke found himself smiling, wondering if the exalted *standartenfuehrer* would take turns on the eight-hundred-round box his noncom carried. He made a private bet with himself that Mann would.

"I'm ready," Natalia said, settling her purse which she had converted into the backpack mode across her shoulders. She picked up first one, then a second M-16, cross-slinging them as Rourke had done.

Sarah stood beside Sergeant Heinz.

Rourke extended his hand to Elaine Halverson, and then to Kurinami, to each of them in turn wishing, "Good luck."

He didn't wait for an answer, passing Mann as the colonel issued orders in German to his still-mounted men. Rourke waited now beside the lip of the rocky outcropping which overlooked the valley, Sarah and Natalia flanking him.

"We are ready, Herr Doctor," Mann announced, taking the ammo box from his sergeant and starting ahead in a long-strided march.

Rourke followed after Mann, smiling—he had won the bet.

Chapter Twenty-two

Annie thought of her father's words—be prepared. She had done exactly that. Before leaving The Retreat she had packed with her three useful objects. One was a dark gray skirt that reached to her ankles, which on the surface she realized did not seem all that terribly useful. She had packed it with her few other clothes. The other two objects she had packed in a ziploc bag and secreted under the seat of her father's comouflage pick-up truck. Both trucks had been stripped of weapons, ammo and gear in the aftermath of her father and mother freeing Natalia.

But the hollow under the pick-up's seat was never checked. She had waited until dark and gone to it, feeling in darkness under the seat amid the springs and finding the bag.

She sat now on the edge of one of the two cots in the smaller tent beside the tent shared by Michael and Paul during their recuperation.

Madison sat opposite her.

"You have a look in your eyes, Annie." Madison smiled, buttoning her blouse, then sitting on the edge of the opposite cot and putting on her shoes.

Annie hitched up her slip and began pulling on her over-the-knee woolen stockings—they were black and they were warm and the previous night had been cold. When she had wrapped herself in a blanket to go to the showers that morning, she had nearly frozen. The weather had again changed and drastically.

She half expected snow from the gray of the clouds.

Annie stood up, her slip falling below her knees. "What look in my eyes?" She laughed.

"A look that says, 'I have a secret' is what I mean." Madison laughed.

Annie picked up the long gray skirt, then started stepping into it, buttoning it at her waist. She found a black turtleneck sweater and pulled it on, straightening the turtleneck and freeing her hair.

She bent over beside her cot, pulling out the combat boots. Her father had planned ahead with that—he had bought several pairs of combat boots in her mother's shoe size and several additional pairs in sizes smaller and larger. It had worked out, and although she liked to credit her father with exceptional foresight, she realized it had been a lucky gamble. Madison's feet fit the smaller boots; her feet fit the larger ones.

"What do you have in your boot?"

Annie placed the two objects she had retrieved from the truck on the cot, then raised her left leg, hitching her skirt up above her left knee. "This is a Bianchi leg holster—Daddy used it when he was in the CIA a few times. I took a tuck in each of the elastic bands and it fits just perfectly now." She secured the two elastic straps, one above and one below her calf over the heavy stocking on the inside of her leg.

"And this," Annie went on, raising the wooden and gleaming steel second object, "is an American Derringer Corporation .45 ACP derringer—same caliber as my Detonics Scoremaster. The derringer goes in here." She settled the derringer in the leg holster, then lowered her foot from the cot and let her skirt drop. "See—don't see it, do you?"

"A gun—on your leg?"

"American ingenuity, kid." Annie laughed.

She sat down on the edge of the cot and started getting into her combat boots.

All the time Annie had spent working with the master computer aboard Eden One had turned up dossiers that had all seemed perfect—and hence none of them had been outstanding enough to seem spurious. Hugging her coat about her, and the shawl about her coat, she entered Michael's and Paul's tent, Madison behind her.

"You could at least knock, Annie—for God's sake," Michael groused. He was sitting up.

"I can tell you're feelin' better," she said, laughing. She went to her brother and kissed his cheek and smiled.

And then she turned to Paul, walking to the opposite side of the tent. He smiled at her and she kissed the origin of the smile. "And how are you today?"

"Dr. Munchen came by—says I can walk if I take it easy. Gave me another zap of that spray, and God does it itch."

Annie laughed, finding a purchase at the edge of the cot, sitting there.

"You look like you're ready for winter," he told her.

"You stick your head outside this tent, Paul, and then you'll see why I look like I'm ready for winter. And that's exactly what you're going to do. You can walk, but you have to take it easy. Fine—you can walk over to Eden One with me. Plenty of nice soft rocks along the way you can sit on to rest. And then you can help me fool with that damned computer. I was working on it until midnight last night. Everybody's perfect—we've gotta figure out some different questions to ask the machine."

"The secret of life," Paul quipped.

She kissed his cheek. "We already know that." She stood up. "Now, do I help you get dressed Paul or do Madison and I wait outside?"

"I can dress myself—but I don't think I bend right yet—"

"Yes, I'll get your boots—men seem so obsessed with having women help them on and off with shoes and boots. You just like seeing us on our knees."

She grabbed Madison by the hand and propelled the younger woman through the tent flap ahead of her.

At Annie's request, Captain Dodd had started putting a guard on the hatchway of Eden One. She had told him, "If there is something in the computer that can help us to find our murderer, then the murderer might try murdering the computer."

Paul Rubenstein's body tensed against her as they started for the entrance of Eden One—the man standing guard (but actually sitting) was Forrest Blackburn, the one who had hit Paul over the head with the wrench, whom Annie had subsequently shot in the thigh. Dodd still had his no-guns policy in effect and she personally thought that was rather stupid—a man on guard at a sensitive site with no weapon to back up his words.

But Captain Dodd hadn't asked her advice.

"That son of a bitch," Paul Rubenstein murmured beside her.

"Hey, when you're all well—I'll call him a—what you called him—and then when he goes to punch me out, you can punch him out instead and look all gallant and everything. But right now, you're in no shape for a fight," she cautioned.

"He's still a son of a bitch," Paul hissed through his teeth.

They were nearly within casual earshot of Forrest Blackburn, the wind whipping up cold from the northwest, her skirt billowing with it, her hair blown in front of her face and partially obscuring her vision like a veil. She brushed

126

it back, smiling at Forrest Blackburn. "How are you, Mr. Blackburn?"

"Miss Rourke. Mr. Rubenstein. Leg's stiff when I walk, but no big deal."

Paul stopped walking—she couldn't tell if it were because he was tired or because he was planning something. "Blackburn, once I'm back in shape—you and I have something to settle."

"I'm sorry you feel that way Mr. Rubenstein—it wasn't anything personal the other night."

"Bullshit."

Annie said nothing.

Paul started ahead, Annie still clinging to his arm, the wind fiercer now somehow in its intensity.

Blackburn stepped in front of them at the base of the stairway leading up into Eden One. "I understand Captain Dodd is allowing you to use the onboard computer, Miss Rourke. But there's nothing in my orders about allowing Mr. Rubenstein aboard. I'm afraid he'll have to stay here."

Paul started to speak, but Annie cut him off. "Look, smartass. You can waste everybody's time by making me hunt up Captain Dodd or you can let both of us in right now. There's a killer loose around here, regardless of what you and some of the others might think. And if we don't find him or her, then when Karamatsov and his people come back, every one of us is going to have to spend more time looking behind us than ahead of us. Now, do I get Dodd to pull your plug, or do you let us both inside?"

She was gambling that Blackburn was trying to provoke Paul and at the same time just trying to be obstinate.

She waited.

She could have straight-armed him in the Adam's apple—her father had taught her how. But that would only have provoked things still more and caused relationships between the Rourke family (she lumped Paul, Natalia and Madison, even Kurinami and Halverson, under this classification mentally) and the Eden Project people to further deteriorate.

She waited still.

After a long moment, Blackburn stepped aside. He smiled. "I used to be pretty good with computers myself, Miss Rourke. And I have some training on this one in particular. I could help. I can guard this thing just as well from the inside as the outside. I'm sorry—I was only trying to do my job. The other night and now."

And Forrest Blackburn stuck out his right hand.

Her eyes flickered to Paul's eyes—she watched something that looked like a momentary flash of disgust pass across his eyes, and then he took Blackburn's hand.

Annie let out her breath in a long sigh. "I'm freezing out here, guys."

Blackburn laughed. "Both of you—go ahead, please," and he even reached out to help Paul start up the steps. Paul had only rested twice and Annie herself was worried that he might be overdoing things.

She walked ahead of Paul, waiting just inside the bulkhead, taking his arm and leading him to the cockpit seat, helping him into the chair where Captain Dodd would have sat.

He closed his eyes—weariness, she surmised. But he opened them and smiled. "I'm really not an old man—I just feel like one." He grinned.

She kissed his forehead, her hands lingering against his face and neck.

She turned around to look at Forrest Blackburn. "Now, just what are you trying to find out—and maybe I can help. Like I said, I'm pretty good with computers."

Annie looked at Paul—Paul nodded.

Annie began, "We're trying to find whoever has the most perfect dossier of any of the personnel aboard Eden One or Eden Two—so far everybody looks perfect, just from scanning their files."

"Do I look perfect, too?" Blackburn asked her, smiling.

"Yes. But no more perfect than anyone else."

"So your theory is that if you find the one with the most spotless background, it's obviously the Russian agent you believe is among us."

"That's right," Paul answered for her wearily. "So, if you believe we're wrong and Natalia is the killer, the best way to prove your point is to help us."

Annie looked at Paul—he was smiling.

Forrest Blackburn told them, "Well, I think I can ask the computer to sort through the personnel data files itself, and then determine from those, maybe in ways more subtle and logical than we could, who the killer is—who's the most perfect."

He started across the cabin to the seat Annie would normally have taken, then sat down. "I mean—if you guys don't think I'm interfering," Blackburn added, looking first up at her and then across to Paul.

"It can't hurt," Paul nodded.

"Fine—try it," she said.

Three hours had passed—she wondered just how long Blackburn's tour of guard duty was supposed to be. Blackburn was reprogramming the cataloguing of the personnel files—and it seemed to be taking too long a time, she thought.

She sat perched on the armrest of Paul's chair, just about to make some mention of the time factor, but as she was about to open her mouth, she heard gunfire.

"What the hell?"

She glanced at Blackburn, who had spoken, then to Paul. Blackburn was up, racing to the fuselage door, Annie behind him.

More gunfire now, and the sounds of small explosions. Machine guns, she guessed, and the lighter sounds of

129

assault rifles.

Annie looked skyward, over Forrest Blackburn's massive shoulders—he was a tall man, darkly good looking and well muscled it seemed. "Nazis," she whispered.

Blackburn turned to face her. "Get back."

Annie drew back inside the meager protection of Eden One. The shuttle crafts themselves from her brief view did not seem to be the object of the attack—but a half dozen helicopters, some men on foot, they were attacking, it seemed, the main portion of the camp.

"What the hell's goin' on?" Paul began, starting to rise.

"It must be the rest of the Nazis—with Colonel Mann gone, they must have found out why he's gone and they're attacking."

"Gotta get out there," Paul told her.

She started toward him, to try to keep him from getting up. But she heard Forrest Blackburn's voice behind her and turned.

In his right hand he held a pistol—it was Paul's battered Browning High Power. "I oughta thank those guys." Blackburn smiled.

"What the—"

"Shut up, Rubenstein. The two of you—stay nice and still. No sense wasting energy with this computer. I can give you the information you need."

"You," Annie whispered.

"See, I don't know if the computer would show me up as the most perfect background or not. But it might show that I knew Mona Stankiewicz. And it'd show that I went to college in West Germany. So the two of you might put two and two together and figure that while I was in West Germany, I got involved with the East Germans. Which I did. And that got me involved with the KGB. Which I did. But this—this is just perfect. With what I did to the computer's personnel files these last couple of hours, no-body'll be able to really figure out anything. And if they do, it'll be too late. See, confusion is always the best ally. Your gun for example, Rubenstein. It's a 9mm Parabellum. Some of the Germans, I noticed—some of the officers—they carry 9mms, maybe sentimental about the good old days five hundred years ago, huh, when they were killing Jews."

"You mother—"

"Shut up, Rubenstein. Initially Dodd and the others'll figure you and Miss Rourke were killed by the Germans. By the time anyone finds your bodies out there dead from fighting beside them, I'll be long gone to the other end of the camp."

"To report to that bastard Karamatsov," Paul snapped.

"No, not really. I didn't kill Mona for that—just to keep my identiy from being discovered. She was gonna fink on me. She didn't care that she'd get herself in hot water. I guess you could count this as wartime—so that means I coulda been shot. Naw, I'm not running to Colonel Karamatsov."

"Why did you frame Natalia?" Annie asked him. "It can't hurt to tell us."

"No special thing against her. She never met me—but I hadda kill Mona and Major Tiemerovna was the logical person since she was a KGB major and everybody knew it. The hatred was already there—it was easy for me to whip people up into a mob without them even knowing I was the one who'd done it. But I don't owe any allegiance to the colonel. Karamatsov was willing to shoot me down with the rest of the Eden Project. I got other plans."

"What?" Rubenstein snapped.

"Well, Captain Dodd—he dies during the attack here, see, and I become the leader. The leader of the Eden Project, for openers. My plans are flexible. Who knows after that? Now—both of you, outside."

"Fuck you," Annie snarled.

Blackburn reached out and grabbed at her, dragging her

against him, Annie hammering at him with her fists, but the muzzle of Paul's gun raised toward her face. "It's easier for me if you die outside," Blackburn rasped. "And look at it this way—we all go outside, maybe I'll stop a stray bullet, or you can jump me, Rubenstein."

She watched, Paul starting slowly up from his chair—and then he threw himself forward as Blackburn shifted the muzzle of the pistol away from her face. Annie stumbled, falling backward toward the door. Paul and Forrest Blackburn were grappling over the pistol. Annie reached under her clothes for the derringer, drawing it, forcing her thumb down against the spring pressure of the hammer to get the pistol cocked.

Blackburn's right arm was upraised—he slammed the Browning down against Paul's head, Paul falling back. Annie stabbed the derringer forward—but Blackburn's right foot snapped up as he wheeled toward her. The pistol flew from her hand.

Blackburn jumped for her, Annie throwing herself across the cockpit floor for the pistol, Blackburn on top of her now, twisting at her left arm. But she was reaching for the derringer pistol.

Chapter Twenty-three

For the last twenty minutes by the luminous black-faced Rolex Submariner on Rourke's left wrist, they had progressed in single file through a tunnel roughly the height and width of a sewer pipe, but uneven, bending, and at some times partially blocked by mounds of dirt and rocks. There was no light—Rourke thought of films he had seen over the years or watched by means of his VCR: in the darkest tunnels and labyrinths, somehow there was always a light source, and it was never totally dark.

But here it would have been, except for the synth-fuel-powered lanterns which Rourke, Sarah and Natalia carried. Two spares, as yet remaining unlit, were carried by Colonel Mann and Sergeant Heinz.

Rourke led the way, Mann behind him directing their course each time they came to a portion of the tunnel which segmented.

Rourke attempted, all the while, to memorize the rights and lefts they took—just in case the tunnel would be needed for their escape and Mann were not available to guide them. With his Gerber, he scratched arrows into the tunnel walls to mark the path, but placing the arrows to be intentionally misleading—marking the wrong passage rather than the correct one. Where there were more than two choices, he would mark the correct passage instead.

He hoped the result would be thoroughly confusing if

anyone attempted to follow.

At times, the air was close and foul-smelling, and at times it seemed as though there would be no air at all and the lanterns themselves would flicker.

But then the lights of the lanterns would steady, and their breathing too would ease and they would heighten the pace and continue on.

As Rourke checked his watch, he noted that the overall time so far spent in the warren of tunnels and caverns and cut shafts had been three hours.

As Rourke stepped out of the tunnel and into less confining space, a massive cavern opening, before them, he called a halt. He was on a tongue of rock which extended over a yawning precipice, the cavern ceiling perhaps some hundred feet overhead. At the base of the drop—perhaps a hundred feet below—a silver ribbon of stream gleamed dully as Sergeant Heinz flicked the single battery-powered search lamp from the cavern ceiling downward.

"We'll rest here," Rourke proclaimed.

Sarah walked past him toward the edge of the spit of rock, shining her lantern into the void. Because the mantle surrounding the synth-fuel flame was a lens rather than plain glass, the light was intensified and illuminated enough of the void to see that indeed nothing was there. "It's beautiful—but it's creepy," Sarah announced, her soft alto echoing among the rocks. "And that's creepy," she added, the echo once again following her words.

Natalia sat down beside Rourke on a rise in the rocks. She leaned her head against his shoulder for an instant and Rourke smiled at her. It was written all over her face that she knew he and Sarah had made love the previous night—and he was glad she knew it. That morning, she had kissed his cheek and proclaimed, "I'm happy for you both," and then walked past to saddle her horse. Now, Natalia said, "How much longer, Colonel?"

They spoke in English out of deference to Sarah who

spoke no German—and it had the ancillary benefit of aiding Sergeant Heinz.

"I think, Fraulein Major, that another two hours remain before us. From here, we must travel downward, along a steep path that would be better traveled by goats—I have read of goats. They sounded marvelously interesting."

Rourke laughed. "I used to eat goat every once in a while."

Sarah took up the story. "We had this older gentleman who used to stop by the house and sell us hindquarters of goat. I finally got to where I'd barbecue it and we'd eat the goat ribs like regular ribs and the—"

"You ate goat?" Mann interrupted.

Rourke nodded. "Tastes pretty good too—a little gamy."

"Gamy? I do not know the word."

Natalia, her English virtually faultless, explained, "That means that there is a certain wild taste to it, not like something that is bred to be eaten. Deer is a good example."

"Ahh, the hind—yes."

Rourke thought of a line from Shakespeare that had always particularly amused him. "If a hart doth lack a hind, let him seek out Rosalind." He looked at Mann's uncomprehending expression. "I always thought it was an interesting double entendre—don't mind me." He grinned.

"Shall we get started again, my friends?"

"Why not." Rourke nodded, standing, taking up his lantern and his eight-hundred round box of .223.

"It is better I think that I take the lantern and lead the way," Mann announced.

Rourke handed him the lantern.

"Herr Doctor—perhaps you should be last."

"My thinking exactly," Rourke agreed.

And Mann started ahead, back along the outcropping of rock that formed a peninsula in the air space and down, his lantern a beacon which Rourke could follow along the corridor of darkness through which they descended, Rourke following after Natalia, Sarah behind Sergeant Heinz.

The lantern Natalia carried illuminated the rocky downward path sufficiently that Rourke could see to walk. But, beyond the shaft of diffused yellowed light, Rourke could hear the sounds of tiny rock falls—they would begin but it seemed as though they would never end. On a rational basis, he knew that they had to.

And he could hear quite gradually building the rushing sounds of water, cascading over the rocks in the underground river bed below.

He imagined that in the time prior to the fires which had consumed the sky, the caverns had likely teemed with bats.

But like all other wildlife—whether beautiful or, like the bats, touching a buried nerve in the racial subconscious which inspired revulsion—they would be gone.

They kept walking, the pathway angling more steeply now, once Rourke reaching out grabbing for Natalia as she started to lose her footing, the yellow of the lantern she carried arcing maddeningly through the darkness.

They walked on. It was necessary now at times because of the narrowness of the ledge to move sideways, scraping the back against the rock surface, arms and hands and fingers splayed along it for the added fractional inch of purchase, inching ahead rather than really walking at all.

They travelled for what seemed to Rourke like an hour—but when he checked the face of his Rolex, it was only half that time. And suddenly the ledge widened and gave way to an apron of rock that bit deeper into the rock face. By stooping over it was possible to keep back from the very edge.

After several more minutes, the rock surface widening still, Rourke could see Wolfgang Mann's lantern swinging back and forth, and Rourke almost knocked Natalia down, bumping into her as Mann brought their file to a halt.

136

Rourke followed the light then as Mann drew back further still from the edge into what seemed like a shallow cave mouth, the shape, as Rourke took Natalia's light for a moment and moved it in a gradual arc around them, roughly like a shell.

He watched the light, how it seemed to linger for an instant in the darkness, and then disintegrate.

John Rourke could hear Mann's voice. "We rest here, hmm?"

"Right," Rourke agreed, all three of the lanterns set down now, the five people forming a ragged circle around them.

"We shall be soon turning, not so much downward as we have been moving, but along a pathway which is at times horizontal, and at times, from our perspective, diagonally ranging upward. It is very narrow. But there is a further complication once we enter onto this path. I discovered it as a boy but fortunately in such a manner that I myself was not discovered. The rocks—they form a natural whispering gallery here. The effect is at its greatest at the height of the path, and then decreases after several hundred yards to where it will no longer be a concern. But while we travel through the whispering gallery, we must maintain total silence—even our breathing will be slightly audible. If a loud noise were to be made, all could be lost. The gallery at its height forms what appear to be tiny fissures in the mountains into which we are crossing. And near the opening of these fissures, there is a guard post. I placed one there years ago. I realized the tunnels were a potential route for an enemy. But I did not elect to have the tunnels sealed, perhaps envisioning in the future some use such as we indeed make now of the tunnels. So posting a sentry station there was the logical answer. They would hear us clearly if anything were said above the sound of the softest whisper. I gave no contingency plans in that event, but I would assume that they would begin firing through the vents and downward. It would be possible with the hard rock surface that bullets would ricochet and strike us. The noise of gunfire would most certainly deafen us, and perhaps cause rock slides which would indeed kill us by hurtling us off the path into the abyss."

"I can see why these caverns never became a tourist attraction." Rourke smiled.

"Quite so, yes." Mann laughed. "I suggest that we rest here for a few more minutes before pressing on with our journey. Once we are through the whispering gallery, the path is wide and level and it is less than a mile by your reckoning to the entrance into The Complex."

Rourke shifted off the slings for the two M-16s, sitting in the darkness. A woman's hand moved along his thigh and felt for his left hand. He closed his hand over it—but he could not be certain if the hand were that of Natalia or that of his wife.

Chapter Twenty-four

"Tell me, Herr Rubenstein—this penchant for being hit on the head—how have you dealt with it over the years?"

Paul Rubenstein tried to sit up. Dr. Munchen was smiling. "What the—"

"Lie still, my young friend. Although your surgery seems unaffected and if anything heals marvelously well, you need to rest after this latest hit on the head."

"He didn't—didn't hit me—yeah, he did. That—Blackburn—where—" Paul pushed Munchen's hand away and sat up. "Where the hell—aww, shit." He touched at his head where his own pistol had crashed down against it. He remembered it all now. "Annie—where's Annie?"

"The battle—it goes on. *Standartenfuehrer* Mann's troops who were left here with the Eden Project fight to repel the forces under *Haupsturmfuehrer* Sturm. The idea of fighting their own comrades—it is very difficult. But, I realized that you and Fraulein Rourke were nowhere about." He smiled—but the smile was somehow a grim smile that conveyed no happiness. "Unfortunately—"

"Unfortunately what?" Rubenstein began, trying to stand, but Munchen placed his hands firmly on Paul's shoulders, Paul Rubenstein sagging back against the bulkhead.

"One of the Soviet helicopters—it is missing. After I found you unconscious I theorized that Fraulein Rourke's efforts had perhaps flushed to light—" Rubenstein's editorial training from before The Night of The War once again surfaced and he thought of badly formed metaphors.

"What?"

"The fraulein—I believe that she has been kidnapped by the Russian agent who murdered the unfortunate Fraulein Stankiewicz."

"I—" Paul again started to his feet, Munchen helping him this time, Paul swaying with a sudden dizziness and sagging toward the bulkhead, Munchen supporting him. He thought of the irony of it—that a man in a Nazi uniform should be helping him, a Jew. And he realized in its totality for the first time that John Rourke had been right. These Germans, men who wore the wrong uniform and were trying to change that. Rubenstein looked Munchen squarely in his bright blue eyes. "Doctor—it was Forrest Blackburn. And if he stole a chopper it means he abandoned his idea of killing Dodd and taking over as the leader of the Eden Project." Rubenstein shook his head and it hurt. He realized he wasn't talking straight, realized it from the puzzled look in Munchen's eyes. Paul Rubenstein began again. "Did—did any of you—" He sagged back against the bulkhead, slipping to his knees, Munchen guiding him down.

"Herr Rubenstein, you must rest."

"No," Paul whispered. "Don't you see? Blackburn. He's the Russian agent. He's got Annie—gonna kill her—but—" He shook his head to clear it, the pain enlivening him and at once weakening him again. He tried to think. "Okay, follow me if I make sense. He was gonna kill us both—blame some of your people. It was just when the attack began. My pistol—he had my pistol. A 9mm, like some of your officers still carry. Was gonna kill us and blame your people, then kill Dodd and take over—to lead the Eden Project. But, ahh, if he stole a chopper, ahh, then something went wrong. If—maybe—maybe Annie's still alive and with him."

"I am sure that Fraulein Rourke is still alive, Herr Rubenstein. Dr. Hixon and I, we tended to the wounded, dragging some of them nearer to the road surface and away from the heaviest concentrations of fighting. I witnessed as the Soviet helicopter screwed itself into the air. There was no one shooting at it. It circled and traveled toward the north. I came looking for you—and outside the shuttle craft, Jane Harwood, she was shot in the chest. I tended to her wounds and progressed inside—and I found you."

"Then Jane Harwood must've come looking for us when the shooting started—and he gunned her down."

"But she will live, Herr Rubenstein. A medical technician who accompanied me attends her even now."

"Is—is she—"

"Yes, conscious—yes. Come—can you stand again if I help you?"

Paul Rubenstein licked his lips, his mouth too dry. He stood though, with Munchen's help.

He was becoming conscious of gunfire from beyond the confines of the shuttle. He wondered how the battle went. If the attackers won . . .

He was walking—beside Munchen, leaning heavily on the German doctor for support. "How's it—"

"The battle goes—but it does not cease, I think, Herr Rubenstein. *Haupsturmfuehrer* Sturm is a loyal Nazi. What he lacks in manpower and weapons he makes up in anger, I think. A battle rages at the *standartenfuehrer*'s camp—and the battle rages here. I think that *Haupsturmfuehrer* Sturm must lose. But there are casualties among the Eden personnel and among those loyal to *Standartenfuehrer* Mann."

They started down, to the ground level—in the sunlight, the cold shocking Rubenstein into heightened consciousness, Paul Rubenstein saw something gleaming in the dirt.

"That—get it—I'm all right," and Rubenstein leaned

against the bulkhead opening. Munchen looked once at him, then nodded, dashing down to the ground level. Paul Rubenstein watched as the German doctor picked up the object.

"A pistol of some sort, Herr Rubenstein."

"Annie's—Annie's derringer." He started down the steps—almost falling, Munchen catching at him.

He was down the steps, staring at Jane Harwood on the ground, a female medical technician applying a bandage of some sort to her left shoulder just above the Eden Three captain's breast. Rubenstein dropped to his knees, calling to Jane Harwood as he balanced his upper body against his thighs with his hands for support—he was growing faint. But he would not allow himself to pass out. "Captain Harwood, did you see Annie Rourke—please."

Rubenstein took the American derringer from Doctor Munchen. He worked the lever over the spur trigger to break the action, rotating the barrels upward. Both rounds in place, neither of the primer's struck. "Shit." He closed the pistol, lowering the hammer to the safety notch, pocketing it. "Captain Harwood—answer me, please dear God answer me."

"Annie—Forrest Bla-Blackburn—she—"

"Was she alive?"

"Yes," and Jane Harwood's head sank back onto an inflatable pillow.

The medical technician turned around. She had a pretty face with pale skin and dark brown hair and green eyes. "She has passed out, Herr Doctor."

But Munchen was already on his knees beside the injured Eden Three captain. "Herr Rubenstein," Munchen began, not looking at Paul. "She will not be able to continue your conversation for some time I think. She shall need quite a bit of attention and—"

"What the hell's going on?" Rubenstein looked up from the ground. Dodd.

142

"Captain—Forrest Blackburn—stole a chopper—took Annie. He's the Communist agent. We gotta go after him," Paul murmured, barely able to hold up his head.

"We gotta do a lot of things, Mr. Rubenstein. Like win this battle for openers. What the—"

Dodd dropped to his knees beside Jane Harwood, setting down his M-16.

The gunfire seemed more sporadic now. "I heard that Jane Harwood had been shot. Is she—"

"She shall recover, I think, Herr Captain," Munchen proclaimed. "You had best listen to Herr Rubenstein. What he has to say could affect us all."

Dodd looked over his shoulder. "If you're so concerned about Miss Rourke—well, remember. If she—"

"Shut the fuck up," Paul Rubenstein snapped, his adrenalin rising, something he could feel.

"You—"

"No! Annie—she flushed him out. And now Blackburn's got her. And if Captain Harwood hadn't seen them, Blackburn was gonna kill her—Annie. Gonna kill me. Gonna kill you. It's time you grew up, Dodd!" Rubenstein raised his head, his neck aching with the pain from his head. "I want help in getting after Blackburn."

"This Blackburn," Munchen interrupted. "He evidently stole one of the Soviet gunships."

"Couldn't get more than a hundred miles in it if he did. Then what's he gonna use for gas, huh?" And Dodd turned to Paul Rubenstein. "And much north of where St. Louis used to be is mostly ice and not much else. I'm sorry about Miss Rourke. And I guess I owe all of your family an apology, Mr. Rubenstein—and Major Tiemerovna most of all—maybe. But we got a battle to win, got dead to bury, got defenses to prepare. I can't spare a pilot or one of the few helicopters we've got. Or any fuel for it. The survival of the rest of the Eden Project could mean the survival of civilization, of democracy. Especially if Dr. Rourke should

143

fail with Colonel Mann. Once we're done here," and Rubenstein was suddenly more conscious of the gunfire, the shells exploding near the main portion of the camp, "we're getting to one of the underground supply caches— and getting fortifications built. We could have the rest of the Germans, the Russians—everybody down on us. No, I'm sorry about Miss Rourke, Mr. Rubenstein—but I can't spare anyone to go after her."

Paul Rubenstein pushed himself up to a standing position, swaying as he spoke. "You son of a bitch." And he fell over and closed his eyes.

Chapter Twenty-five

They were entering the whispering gallery.

He could tell by the sound of his wife's breathing. She walked ahead of him, perhaps six feet, but her breathing sounded as loud and labored as a patient on a respirator. Rourke's own breathing—it seemed almost deafeningly loud.

Footfalls on the rock ledge now, the sound of small rocks cascading from the surface of the narrow ledge into the blackness below. And like a dull growl in the blackness, the stream which crashed along below them out of sight, concealed in the darkness.

In a cone of yellow light, he could see Natalia's feet as she edged along just ahead of Sarah.

Rourke heard a loud scraping sound as the zipper of his bomber jacket—it was open—scratched against the rock.

He stopped moving, slowly and as soundlessly as possible linking the two base pieces of the brass zipper, then starting to zip the jacket closed a few inches at the waist— the zipper sounded impossibly loud, like an animal somehow. He moved on, both rifles slung at his right side and lashed together so they would not bang against one another and issue a betraying sound. His musette bag and his canteen hung at his right side as well, lashed together as well, the musette bag a buffer between the rifles and the canteen. He had used a spare pair of combat boot laces to do the tying.

He could hear Wolfgang Mann's footfalls loudest of all, because Mann as the trailblazer encountered the largest number of loose rocks and silt and sediment.

They kept moving.

Natalia's lantern swung up and for an instant he could see Natalia's eyes—fear in them. And then Sarah's face and hair—a resoluteness in her face that he had seen since reuniting with her just before the fires had consumed the air, a resoluteness he had never seen there in the time they had spent together before The Night of The War.

The lantern swung away, and he could only see their feet and his own and the progressively narrowing ledge.

John Rourke could feel more than see that they were edging steadily upward at what at least for now seemed a gentle angle.

And now the angle seemed more visually apparent— because Mann's lantern which was shone ahead of their file was higher than Rourke's chest and should not have been.

John Rourke's right foot slipped and he splayed his arms against the wall which backed the ledge, his left knee buckling slightly before he caught his weight—rocks fell, small ones he knew, but the noise they generated sounding like boulders rolling down a cliff.

He caught his breath, regained the proper footing and moved on.

The angle of the ledge became steadily steeper; the ledge itself suddenly narrowed.

Shafts of yellow light, but paler than the yellow light of the lanterns, filtered down through clouds of airborne dust as he looked ahead, the light still too distant to illuminate the path.

As they moved forward and upward, Rourke could gradually discern the origins of the light—the fissures of which Wolfgang Mann had spoken, through which the sentries posted above would be able to hear them.

John Rourke no longer walked the ledge, but rather edged forward a few inches at a time, his guns and gear hanging pendulumlike from the front of his body. It threw his balance slightly off, but there was no other way to traverse the ledge.

Rourke watched as Wolfgang Mann's body penetrated the nearest of the downward ranging shafts of light. And it was then that Sergeant Heinz slipped from the ledge and fell away to be lost in the darkness.

Rourke caught his breath—the sound of the rockfall was like the roar of thunder. In the arc of Mann's lamp, Rourke could see Natalia stooping over the abyss, swinging her lantern downward.

And then the gunfire from above began, from the fissures in the rock.

The noise of it vibrated through his entire being, Rourke opening his mouth wide to equalize pressure with his eardrums. As he edged forward along the ledge, Sarah ahead of him, Rourke could see Sarah's hands clasped to her ears, her mouth open in a soundless scream as Mann swung his lantern upward.

Natalia was to her knees along the ledge, her mouth open wide as well, but her left hand purchased precariously against the wall of rock behind her, her right arm swinging the lantern down into the darkness.

Bullets whizzed past Rourke's head, ricochetting about the cavern and along the ledge, rock chips and rock dust spraying against his face and his bare hands as he inched ahead.

Mann too was to his knees, his lantern swinging down into the darkness. Rourke touched a hand to his wife's shoulder, drawing her back against the rock wall, gesturing with his other hand in the shaft of yellow light which now cast a pale glow around them.

Sarah understood, flattening herself against the rock

147

wall, Rourke swinging out his right leg over the abyss, his combat-booted right foot scratching against the rock wall beyond where Sarah stood, groping for the ledge. He found it, his right arm flailing out around her, his right hand brushing against her left breast in the darkness. He felt her left hand grab at his wrist, holding him.

Rourke edged around her from the portion of ledge where he had been standing to a narrow spot just beyond her, his hands clawing for a purchase against the rock surface, her left hand on his right wrist still, his left foot swinging into the abyss.

But he had the ledge.

He edged slightly forward, his rifles scratching against the rock wall, any noise they would have made, he realized, drowned out in the reverberating roar of the gunfire from above. And this he could barely hear over the hollow wailing sound which filled his ears. Another few minutes, and he and the others would suffer permanent hearing damage, and a few minutes more and it would be permanent hearing loss, he knew.

A spray of rock chips pelted at his face, Rourke's eyes already squinted, shutting tight against it.

He opened his eyes into narrow slits and edged ahead.

He was beside Natalia now, staring down into the abyss where Mann's and Natalia's lanterns shown, scanning the fringe of light and darkness for some sign of Sergeant Heinz.

And then Rourke saw it—his eyes squinted shut against it for an instant, against the comparative brightness.

As he peered downward again, the light shone again and Rourke averted his eyes. It was Heinz—still alive and signaling with his powerful battery-operated hand-held searchlight.

Rourke looked to Wolfgang Mann—the climbing rope about Mann's torso, draped diagonally, left shoulder to right hip.

Rourke thought bitterly that they should have lashed themselves together—and perhaps saved Heinz. But it might also have meant that if Heinz had still fallen, he would have pulled the rest of them after him and off the ledge.

Rourke gestured to Mann; Mann nodded. The German colonel slipped the coiled climbing rope from his frame and handed it to Rourke.

Rourke found the plastic sealed end and shook out several feet of the rope, passing it back to Mann. Mann wound the rope into a harness behind his shoulders and bound over his chest, knotting a double square knot into it. The knot would be satisfactory, Rourke considered, but it was evident that the Youth of which Mann had spoken once aboard the aircraft while en route to Argentina would never replace the Boy Scouts.

Rourke began uncoiling the remaining portion of the rope. But first passing the coil behind Natalia. She understood his intent as well, standing to her full height, securing a loop into a knot with the rope, anchoring herself to it as well.

Rourke shook the remainder of the rope down into the darkness.

The light flashed—evidently in some sort of signal code which Rourke could not comprehend. Three long flashes. Two short. Then a long and a short.

Rourke looked to Wolfgang Mann.

Mann stabbed his left forefinger downward toward the flashing light of Sergeant Heinz. And then Mann shook his head.

Rourke tugged at the rope—it was either held by Heinz or caught on a rock. It would not budge.

He looked again to Wolfgang Mann. Had they been able to speak . . . but they were not. A spray of rock chips and dust pelted Rourke's face and he squinted against it.

Mann gestured downward with his left index finger.

Natalia started unknotting her rope—Rourke grabbed at her hands, then tugged at the hitch in the rope bound around her shoulders and chest.

Sarah—John Rourke unslung his assault rifles and passed them beyond Natalia and into Sarah's hands. She took the rifles, slinging them cross-body beside her own weapons.

The musette bag and the canteen. Rourke passed these to Wolfgang Mann.

Rourke's fists closed over the rope and he gestured to Natalia and then to Mann—he was going down. He found his bloodstained gloves, pulling them on.

His ears pained him now. Swallowing, keeping his mouth open—nothing seemed to ease it.

He started downward, holding to the rope, rappelling, his feet against the rock surface beneath the ledge, his hands locked to the rope.

He realized suddenly that perhaps the gunfire had briefly stopped—because he could dully discern the sounds of more discharges from above but had not heard them in the last few moments. His hearing was not as far gone as he had thought.

Rourke looked below him. The searchlight flashed again in what was to him a meaningless signal. If there had been time—he could have noted the system of long and short flashes and perhaps deciphered it. There was no time.

He kept moving downward, the rocks beneath his feet dislodging, his body swinging outward and then slamming against the rock face. He swung there, the pendulum motion momentarily bringing on a wave of nausea.

He swung his feet right and left, at last finding a purchase, kicking against it to be certain that it was steady.

The flashing of the light again.

Rourke started downward once more, all auditory sense nearly gone, the noise penetrating his consciousness and blocking thought.

But it was no longer conscious will, but instinct which drew him toward the light.

The light—he keep shifting his weight downward, ever nearer to the light.

Downward, the roaring in his ears unceasing now, no discernible sound at all, just a steadily growing cacophony which somehow seemed inside his head.

They were shooting downward through the fissures, Rourke knew—because as he moved along the rock surface, he could feel sprays of rock and dust pelting at his face and neck and the exposed skin at his wrists where his gloves ended and below where his sleeves began.

The light seemed impossibly bright now, Rourke averting his eyes as he swung himself left on the rope, zigzagging downward over the sometimes slick, sometimes rough, sometimes knife edge sharp rock surface. He could feel through his gloves—and he could feel that his gloves were cutting.

The light—Rourke pressed his feet against a wide ledge, straightening his legs, locking his knees, his body hanging outward.

The light—he edged along the ledge now, flattening his body against the rock surface, reaching out with his left hand toward it.

The light—Rourke's right hand tightened on the rope, his left hand closing over the face of the searchlight, the light illuminating pinholes in his gloves, backlighting the hairs on his wrists.

The light—John Rourke tugged at it. Something behind the light tugged back. Heinz.

Rourke edged further out along the ledge, in the glow of the light now seeing that he was on a narrow peninsula of rock surrounded on three sides by the abyss. He sagged to his knees, crawling forward, his right hand locked to the rope, his left hand groping into the darkness that he would not suddenly fall because he could not see the far edge.

151

He sagged forward—against something which gave slightly at his touch.

It was Sergeant Heinz.

John Rourke grabbed again at the searchlight, twisting it free, turning it toward the shape he had found in the darkness.

Heinz's left temple dripped blood and his right arm was twisted at the elbow, almost back against itself.

Heinz's eyes seemed oddly clear. The German sergeant attempted a smile.

And the German sergeant gestured with his left hand downward along the length of his body.

Rourke watched the man's eyes, then followed the direction of Sergeant Heinz's gaze with the searchlight. The left leg—it seemed like a simple fracture at first glance.

Rourke reached to his belt, drawing the long bladed Gerber MkII from its sheath, inserting the blade at the pulled up trouser cuff which he had simultaneously drawn up from inside the jackboot.

The jackboots were made of a synthetic that looked and felt like leather. He preferred the real thing. He began working the blade along the trouser seam of Heinz's BDU pants. There was no redness visible as he laid back the material to study the skin. The fracture had not penetrated the skin.

He shone the light back toward Heinz's face. Heinz had passed out.

But still slung from his left shoulder cross-body were two of the German assault rifles.

Rourke checked for pulse and breathing—Heinz had simply passed out and seemed in no immediate danger.

There was no possibility of doing anything substantial with the leg. Not until they reached safety. Rourke had not assumed and did not now assume that their presence had been detected beneath the fissures—the sentries were shooting because they had heard the noise of rock slides

152

and were looking for the excuse to break the boredom of sentry duty. The shots seemed haphazard and not in sufficient volume to indicate that something was actually suspected.

Rourke—as gently as he could—unslung the two assault rifles, removing the magazines and quickly inspecting the weapons themselves to ascertain the method of disassembly. The completely assembled rifles would be too heavy and awkward to utilize as splints, but the plastic stocks would be ideal.

He found what looked like a dismount latch, working the actions first to check that no round was chambered in either weapon. Then he turned the dismount latch. For a rifle, it was surprisingly like a pistol, using the basic system pioneered in the Walther P-38. But the dismount latch served to release the bolt carrier. He lifted this away. Beneath the trigger guard housing at the very front of the guard. A knurled piece—he tugged at this, the trigger housing group falling out with only slight pressure. John Rourke shook his head. Simple, yes, but not so sturdy an arrangement as to be found with Colt, Ruger or earlier civilian or military police/assault/sporter rifles. Another latch—beneath the front handguard and inset to be recessed. It latched downward under finger pressure. The barrel and receiver freed themselves from the one-piece stock. He threw the metal parts aside, no longer concerned about noise.

He reached up to the sergeant's waist, undoing the brown web belt threaded through the man's trouser loops. Positioning one of the plastic stocks on either side of the shin, the belt beside the nearer one, Rourke grasped the leg.

As he pulled, he pressed firmly, setting the bone.

He felt Heinz's body twitch. Rourke had no time to look. Methodically, he positioned the impromptu splint and bound it to the leg with the belt.

He moved the light, shifting along on his knees to the upper body. Gingerly, he touched at the twisted and misshapen arm. It was not a break, but rather a dislocation of the shoulder, no apparent damage to the elbow.

Rourke checked Heinz's breathing. Even. The German sergeant's unconsciousness would make it easier. After a time following dislocation, the muscle which had been parted by the outward force of the bone being dislodged from the socket would form to close the gap. Without the body being relaxed, either through anesthesia or some other means, reduction of the dislocation was made that much more difficult. He felt at the shoulder, grasping the arm firmly, drawing it out straight. He began to work the arm in a circular motion, twisting it through the gap between the muscles. He could feel the pop. Gently, he rested the forearm across Heinz's chest, bending the arm slowly at the elbow.

If he were forced by circumstance, Rourke knew, he could remove his own belt to secure the arm to Heinz's chest—but there was gear on his belt that then would have to be pocketed. He shrugged his shoulders, picking up his knife. Rourke bent across the body, cutting away the left BDU sleeve at the seam where it mated with the shoulder. He wrenched the sleeve down along the left arm, then using the Gerber again sliced it open along the seam. He halved the sleeve and used the Gerber again. Resheathing the knife, closing the scabbard retainer to secure it, Rourke tied the two sections of fabric together. He gauged the length—more than adequate. Sliding the tail of the material under Heinz at the small of the back, Rourke worked it up along the torso until it was in position, secured the arm just below the elbow, then bound both sections of the sleeve together with a simple square knot, securing the arm tightly enough to the chest that it wouldn't slip down.

The rope had been a possibility—but he had nearly been to the end of it and did not want to risk excising length he might need in order to safely secure Heinz for the journey up along the rock face.

And he began to do this now, working a cradle of rope around the unconscious German's body, avoiding the dislocated shoulder, securing the right leg to the injured left leg for added firmness.

Trussed securely, Rourke dragged Heinz back along the spit of rock, after cursorily examining for neck or back injury—he found no evidence of either. The head wound seemed superficial, bleeding already stopped.

The light—he secured it to his own belt, shutting it off as he tugged solidly on the rope.

There was an answering tug.

And he guided Heinz's body toward the rock face, shining the light on it as soon as his hands were free. Heinz was being lifted upward.

He still could not hear and as he turned away from the light, all he could see was the blackness of the abyss.

According to the luminous black face of the Rolex Submariner, it had consumed twelve minutes for Heinz to make the journey upward, the rope to be undone and dropped back toward the spit of rock and then Rourke to rappel back to the ledge.

Securing Heinz's arm more sturdily, they continued movement along the ledge, first Wolfgang Mann and then after fifteen minutes, John Rourke taking the still-unconscious young soldier over their shoulder in a modified fireman's carry. The ledge was too narrow for him to be carried any other way.

After what Rourke judged as perhaps an hour, on his second tour with Heinz over his shoulder, Rourke could perceive the effect of the gunfire's amplified sound in the whispering gallery to have at least slightly diminished. The shooting had stopped—he could not tell precisely when.

155

But he could hear the breathing of Heinz over his shoulder, hear the breathing of Sarah ahead of him along the ledge, hear his own breathing.

He had mentally gauged it as ten minutes since they had left the pale yellow light of the last vent and now had returned to the total darkness of the abyss, the darkness broken only in the cones of light from the lanterns carried by Natalia and Sarah and Mann. But beyond the effective range of the lanterns, the darkness was total or seemed so.

They kept moving.

Chapter Twenty-six

The ledge had widened and, almost suddenly, what had been shadow became 'substance, the ledge gone and a cavern wall less than a dozen feet beyond the wall along which they had travelled.

Beneath their feet was solid rock. Rourke once again took the burden of Sergeant Heinz, Natalia carrying one of his assault rifles and his musette bag, Sarah with the second M-16 and the canteen. They walked in ragged formation four abreast, the going easier as well because the passageway slanted slightly downward.

Mann—his voice audible but a hollow roar like the sounds of the sea heard in a shell taken from the beach almost obscuring it to Rourke's ears—spoke. "We are at last out of the whispering gallery. Can any of you hear me?"

"Yes." Rourke nodded, shifting Heinz's weight on his shoulder. His neck ached and his back ached from the strain as well.

"I hear you—but it sounds funny," Rourke heard Sarah telling Mann.

"My ears—they are ringing. I can't stop it, but it doesn't seem as bad," Natalia announced.

"I think Heinz may wind up the luckiest one, at least in

that department. With his unconscious state, his auditory functions might have been better able to compensate for the noise level. How much further to the entrance of The Complex?"

He was debating whether to stop and give Heinz a more thorough examination now that space allowed, or continue until they reached the entrance.

"Another ten minutes—if that—and again it would be wise to be silent since we are so close."

Mann had resolved the question.

They walked on, Rourke refusing that Mann spell him with carrying Heinz—the distance remaining was so little.

The passageway narrowed as it turned sharply right and the angle increased—downward. Rourke broadened his stride—the end of the journey through the underground was near. He raised his left hand to his ear—too faintly, he could make out the ticking of his Rolex. But at least hearing was returning.

The passage took a sharp bend left and leveled off and Mann ran ahead, raising his right arm in a signal to halt.

Rourke stopped, Natalia on his right boosting Heinz's body slightly to ease the weight burden. Sarah started forward, behind Mann, one of the three assault rifles she carried—two of her own and one of his—pointed along the rock corridor.

Mann was feeling his hands along the surface of the rock at the end of the corridor. It seemed like a dead end from the distance as Rourke observed him. But then suddenly the rock beneath Mann's splayed hands shifted, outward. Mann drew his pistol and moved to the right side of the rock panel, then disappeared, stepping through.

Rourke watched Natalia's eyes for an instant—their incredible blueness. She smiled at him.

He heard a sound and looked up. Two German soldiers

158

had appeared at the far end of the corridor—Sarah was raising the assault rifle. Natalia wheeled toward the opening.

But then Mann was there—he waved a hand to signal that all was as it should be.

The two German soldiers, their assault rifles slung at their sides, ran the length of the corridor, past Sarah, stopping beside Rourke, immediately starting to take Heinz from him. In German, Rourke's voice a rasped whisper, he cautioned, "There has been a break in the left leg at the shin and the right arm is dislocated from the shoulder. Be careful how you carry him."

"Yes, Herr Doctor." The taller of the two men nodded.

Rourke flexed his tortured shoulders, walking ahead, taking one of his assault rifles from Natalia. Mann beckoned for them to come through the passageway as Rourke took the second rifle from Sarah. He took the eight-hundred-round box of .223 Sarah carried and picked up the box Mann had set beside the exit from the rock corridor, and then, ahead of his wife, ahead of Natalia, ahead of the two German soldiers carrying the injured sergeant, he passed through the cut out in the rock.

He was inside a vast power plant, pipes of enormous diameter all but obscuring the low ceiling and the roar of turbines drowning out at least temporarily the roaring inside his head which lingered on after the whispering gallery.

He looked to right and left and could see no end to the corridor formed on one side and overhead by piping, beneath his feet and on the wall behind him concrete slabs.

Mann stood a few feet away, his arms enfolding a tall, slender, patrician-looking woman who was by any standard exquisitely beautiful.

Rourke noticed that Sarah and then Natalia flanked

him.

He remarked to both of them, "I can see why Mann kept going."

Chapter Twenty-seven

In the five centuries of survival beneath the earth, the Germans had perfected a system of fusion-based hydroelectric power. In four unused drums of the type usually utilized for the transport of liquified byproducts, John Rourke, Sarah Rourke, Natalia Anastasia Tiemerovna and Col. Wolfgang Mann were transported from the power plant and through The Complex. There were five of the containers, but the fifth container was empty. Because of his injuries, it had been impossible to cram Sergeant Heinz inside one of the barrel-shaped units. So he remained at the power plant, but only after conferring with a military doctor had satisfied Rourke. The power plant, like anything conceivably defense-related, was under the direct control of the army and the officer corps was entirely SS. But, like Wolfgang Mann, a substantial portion of the officer corps was SS in uniform and rank designation only. The power plant was controlled by Mann's people.

Cramped in the drum with his weapons and gear, Rourke had felt the jostling as the trucklike vehicle which he had seen before being placed inside the drum had ferried them. At a loading dock for what Mann had hastily identified as the New Fatherland Printing Office, Rourke, his wife, Natalia and the *standartenfuehrer* had exited the drums and switched to a van-like vehicle, their assault rifles hidden beneath floorboards, enlisted rank uniforms provided for all of them. Rourke had always admired German precision—and the uniforms were near perfect fits, Natalia's and Sarah's women's uniforms however well fitting, terribly unflattering. The windowless van had stopped at the rear of a tall building Rourke had been able to observe by looking forward through the windshield. Once stopped, they had quickly exited the van. Waiting for them in the below-level parking area, Rourke again saw Frau Mann.

As they ran from the van—at her urging—to join her near what appeared to be a service elevator, Wolfgang Mann answered Rourke's unasked question. "High ranking members of the officer corps and other ranking officials are permitted private vehicles. The air-scrubbing system can only take so much here in terms of emissions and electrically powered vehicles such as the van and the private cars are in limited supply—intentionally so to prevent traffic problems."

They reached the service elevator, Frau Mann stepping inside, Natalia and Sarah following her, Natalia pulling off the khaki uniform cap and stuffing it in the pocket of her skirt. Both Natalia and Sarah carried their individual weapons in large shoulder bags.

Rourke was the last of the five into the elevator, the doors hissing shut.

Frau Mann stood before the locking panel, turning her key into one of the locked floor markers. And the elevator began to move.

The elevator stopped almost too abruptly, the doors opening, Frau Mann stepping through first. In Rourke's right fist was one of the twin stainless Detonics .45s concealed beneath his uniform tunic. In his left hand was a canvas tool bag, the rest of his weapons concealed inside.

"Bitte!"

Rourke nodded, stepping through into the corridor after

her, Natalia, Sarah and Mann following as he glanced back. Frau Mann gestured to him along the corridor. *"Geradeaus."*

Rourke nodded, starting along the corridor, his hand still on his gun. He passed a door marked *"Ausgang,"* then took the bend in the corridor.

He looked back—Frau Mann was running after him, her high heels held in her left hand, her purse in her right. "This way, Herr Doctor."

"You speak English," Rourke murmured, glancing back along the corridor, Natalia and Sarah running just ahead of Mann.

They stopped at a door, Frau Mann glancing over her shoulder as she turned a key in a lock—some things never changed, Rourke observed silently. She swung open the door. *"Schnell!"*

Rourke stepped back, letting Sarah and Natalia through first, then following after them, the Detonics .45 out in his fist now as his eyes scanned the dwelling—a large apartment, a vaulted ceiling above a sunken living room, drapes drawn at the far end of the living room over what he assumed were windows looking out over The Complex.

Rourke heard the door close and turned to face Wolfgang Mann. Mann swept his wife into his arms and began to laugh.

Natalia, then Sarah, then John Rourke had showered. His body clean, his hair washed, Rourke sat back in one of the two identical sofas, across the table from Frau Mann and her husband. Wolfgang Mann sat, a towel across his neck, his bathrobe belted around him, hair wet from taking the last shower. Rourke wore clothes Frau Mann had provided for him—again the fit was perfect. A dark blue cotton-knit turtleneck shirt, dark blue beltless slacks and black fabric rubber-soled shoes. Beside him was a thin black waist-length jacket similar in design to the Members Only jackets which had been so much in fashion before The Night of The War.

"You look at ease, Herr Doctor."

Rourke smiled at the woman. "There is a saying—I suppose there is some equivalent in German—that looks are oft times deceiving." He studied her pretty face, as he had been for several minutes while she moved about the apartment paying attention to details that he had not followed. "On the other hand, you don't seem at ease at all." Across Rourke's shoulders was the harness of the double Alessi shoulder rig, the twin stainless Detonics .45s in place under each arm. He trusted the Manns by now—but had never considered himself foolish.

"You are right, Herr Doctor." She smiled. "This entire affair—it frightens me. While you were dressing and Wolf was showering—some distressing news came to me from another woman in the organization."

"What, my darling?" Mann asked her, taking the towel from about his neck, standing, rubbing at his wet hair in an attempt to dry it.

"Helene Sturm—she has been arrested."

"*Mein Gott*, but she—"

"Who is Helene Sturm?" Rourke interrupted.

Frau Mann ran her splayed hands along the tops of her thighs, stopping as her fingertips reached the hem of her dress. "She is—very important. Besides myself, she is the only one in The Complex who knows the overall plan."

"Aww, that's great," Rourke noted. "Drugs are available, I suppose—and other means?"

"She is pregnant with child. They would not force her to reveal—"

"Wolf," and Frau Mann stood, her arms going around his neck, then her forehead touching at his chin. "They

164

will use any means—regardless of the life she carries. Twins, perhaps. Perhaps you should break radio silence—and notify her husband in the field."

"He is a Nazi—I fear that he loves the party more than his wife." Mann almost whispered, kissing his wife's hair, then turning away from her and walking to the windows—the drapes had been drawn open partially while Rourke had showered. And through the windows which formed almost the entire wall, Rourke could watch The Complex.

It was a city, but built entirely inside a mountain. The engineering required to cut a shaft of such huge proportions into the earth, to blast so precisely as to hollow out much of the inside of the mountain without bringing it down—it was staggering to consider. But German engineering had always been among the best in the world. He estimated the height of some of the buildings to be in excess of twenty stories and the surface area covered perhaps three square miles, as best he could judge. "We have to get her out," Rourke remarked.

"Precisely so, Herr Doctor," Wolfgang Mann agreed, turning from the windows. "Precisely."

"Get who out?"

John Rourke turned to the voice. Sarah. He smiled. The last time he had seen her in nylons and high heels had been . . . he remembered. Their wedding anniversary, a few months before The Night of The War. She wore a gray dress now, the skirt straight and to just below the knee, the neckline high and collarless, the sleeves reaching to her wrists. A string of pearls hung from her neck and her hair was up, revealing pearl earrings. He stood. "You look beautiful."

She blushed.

She cleared her throat. She again asked, "Who do we have to get out?"

But before the question could be answered, Rourke

heard Natalia's voice. "She is beautiful, John."

He turned to look at Natalia. Almost predictably, she wore black, the dress almost identical in design to the one Sarah wore, but with a waist-length jacket. A single gold chain was at her neck—the gold earrings were her own, he recognized. Tiny—the pierced kind and when her hair would be swept back by the wind when they rode their bikes, or she would toss her head, he would see them. He saw them now, because like Sarah, her almost black hair was up.

"Your wife, Herr Doctor—and your friend as well—they are most beautiful. I was right," Frau Mann continued, Rourke not looking at her, "in assuming they would be able to pose as officers' wives or other women of the elite."

Rourke turned and looked at Frau Mann finally. But he said nothing.

"Who is it?" Natalia began, "that we must rescue?"

"Helene Sturm," Wolfgang Mann answered. "She is one of the leaders of the organization which opposes the leader. She alone besides ourselves of those inside The Complex knows the entire plan. And she is pregnant—"

"Her due date is very near," Frau Mann added.

John Rourke waited as Sarah and Natalia crossed the room, waited until they sat on the couch, then sat down, Sarah between Natalia and himself. "Do you know why, Frau Mann—why she was arrested?" John Rourke asked.

"And where she has been taken?" Natalia added.

Frau Mann wrung her hands, then sat, perched on the arm of the opposing couch, her husband sitting down beside her. "I fear that her son—her oldest son. She has three others. But I fear that her oldest son, Manfred—he is a member of the youth. I fear that he betrayed her. If that is so, then I fear she will be under interrogation even now. Not at the detention center. But she would be at the new government hall. It has recently been finished. On the surface."

"Confirm what you can—without arousing undue suspicion," Rourke told her. "Once we're certain where she is—then we go and get her. Deiter Bern will have to wait."

There was no choice. Even had she known nothing that could harm them, because of her condition there was no choice at all.

Chapter Twenty-eight

Annie Rourke had given up trying to undo the ropes about her wrists—they were synthetic, triple-stranded and so soft that she doubted that even had she been able to reach her hands with her teeth she could have tugged the knot free. And she could not reach her hands, because after she had been forced at gunpoint to the Soviet helicopter, Forrest Blackburn had—skillfully, she admitted to herself—crossed her jaw with his fist. Her jaw didn't even hurt now, but when she awakened, the Soviet helicopter had already been airborne. Her wrists were bound as they were in front of her and the safety harness had been put on her, in such a manner that it locked her arms to her sides and kept her shoulders in an upright position against the seat back.

"Soviet technology has come a long way," Blackburn remarked—she could hear him through the headset he had placed on her after she had regained consciousness.

"Paul will kill you for this," she told him simply, speaking into the teardrop shaped microphone in front of and slightly below her lips. "If Michael or my father doesn't get to you first."

"Yes, well—Annie? May I call you Annie? Well, your dear daddy is in Argentina. Your brother is flat on his back. And poor Mr. Rubenstein. If I didn't kill him when I knocked him out, I don't think he'll be in much shape to come after us either. Captain Dodd seems to have his hands full, doesn't he? And I doubt he'll send off valued personnel and equipment to rescue a troublesome girl and track down the last of the Soviet agents." And Blackburn laughed. "You know, I'll tell you something, Annie. Actually—you're better off. Stick with me and you'll live longer."

She knew her father'd be angry at her for saying it—not to mention her mother. "Fuck you."

"I'm glad you brought that up. I intend for you to do just that, Annie. I haven't had a—well, let's just say that I haven't for five centuries. It's ridiculous, isn't it? Five centuries—my goodness."

"I'm glad you didn't say 'My God,' " she hissed.

"You may prove too much like your father and mother. And if you do, I'll be very sorry for you, Annie."

"Where the hell are we going?" she began, trying to get him to another subject. "To Karamatsov?"

"No, no, the last man I want to see—just now, anyway." He cleared his throat.

She looked above her at the rotors, then below through the chin bubble. The ground was rockier than it should have been, and ahead through the windscreen she could see a blinking whiteness—they were heading north. "I thought Karamatsov was your boss," she pressed. Her wrists were hurting her and her fingers were falling asleep.

"He was. But I never did fully trust him, you know. Five centuries ago—that still amazes me," and she turned to watch him smiling as if to himself. He was doing something with the controls of the Soviet machine—she thought he might be preparing to land because through the chin bubble again she could see the ground coming up fast beneath them. "But five centuries ago," he continued, "when Vladmir Karamatsov first began getting suspicious that there was something like the Eden Project—well. When he asked me to get involved, I wanted some assurances. Future welfare, you might say. One of the things I got—but not from him because I don't know if he even knew about it—but I got the location of The Underground City."

"The what?" She cleared her throat. "Is this thing landing?"

"The Underground City—it was a project my employers had going for some time before what your family calls The Night of The War. Already self-sufficient—no longer an experiment. And, yes, we are landing. One of the things Karamatsov provided—and I spot checked that he hadn't lied—were personal supply caches for me. Aircraft fuel sealed in hermetic containers that were rot-proof. Individual weapons. And emergency food supplies. Surprisingly inexpensive. He had one hundred such little caches made for me throughout the continental United States since there would be no way to foretell where the Eden Project might land. Do you know how long it takes to memorize one hundred sets of compass coordinates?"

Annie felt herself starting to smile—but at least Blackburn seemed like a competent pilot. They were clearly about to touch down, and the ride was smooth as silk. She had never touched silk until Natalia had given her one of the teddies that she wore. Annie had not wanted to take it—yet wanted it very much. She wondered if she would ever get the chance to wear it.

She looked at Blackburn. He was laughing. "Now surely, Annie—you are thinking that with all that has happened, the magnetic coordinates will have changed. And you're right. But I took a reading off the Eden One's instruments and then wrote down the map coordinates from memory and worked a compass correction formula. We're right on the money."

The stolen—twice-stolen, Soviet helicopter touched down. She barely felt it. He began flipping switches and pressing buttons, shutting down the machine. "You see," he told her, not looking at her, "after I get the materials I need precisely located, I'll fly the machine closer if necessary and resupply. Then off we go to The Underground City where I will be a hero of surrealistic proportions. And should anybody follow us and by chance intercept us before we get there, well—" he turned to look at her, pulling his headset off, then reached across and pulled off hers. She screamed—he had caught some of her hair in it. He reached to her hair and began to undo it from the headset as he continued speaking. "Should we encounter difficulties, well, you're my hostage. If you're important enough to go after, you're important enough to be kept alive."

Her hair was free of the headset, and she shook her head to get her hair back from her face.

Forrest Blackburn climbed down from the machine, taking the key for the thing with him, then walked around the front of the aircraft, opening the side door beside her.

He drew another piece of rope from his pocket and reached down to her ankles. He began binding them tight together, then she could feel them being drawn back under the seat and being tied to one of the seat stanchions. "Where do you think I'm gonna go?" she asked him.

"Nowhere." He smiled affably.

He wore a large lined and hooded jacket that looked like it was military once. He reached to her shoulders and wrenched the shawl free of her arms and then twisted it into a rope. He drew her head forward and bound the shawl over her mouth between her teeth. She felt as if she would gag.

"Now—nice and safe, Annie." He smiled. "And just so you start thinking along the right lines," and he reached to her coat and unbuttoned it, pushing its skirts aside. Then he drew her skirt and her slip up, along her thighs. She started screaming—but only muted growls came out through the gag. He bunched her skirt and her slip up to her hips, the backs of her thighs suddenly cold against the

171

vinyl of the seat. He reached under her clothes and found her underpants, then pulled them down, along her thighs, over her knees.

Forrest Blackburn looked at her and laughed. "Get you cold enough—even you'll want a little warmth, Annie. Be back in a while." He slammed the door.

Nearly naked from the waist down, humiliated, frightened—she began to cry. But there was another word. She felt its meaning behind her tears. Defiance.

Chapter Twenty-nine

"Paul—answer me, damnit!"

"John?"

"No—Michael. What the hell happened?"

He watched as Paul Rubenstein opened his eyes. "Michael."

"They—they brought you in here unconscious. Something about Annie?"

Madison, her voice soft, low, began, "I told Michael he should not get out of bed."

"I'm all right," Michael snapped, leaning back on his perch at the edge of the cot where Paul Rubenstein lay. He had lain on his back since his surgery and working his stomach muscles pained him. His back ached as well from where his father had dug out some of the Soviet bullets.

Michael Rourke eased back further, standing then to rid himself of the pain, leaning against the center post of the tent, Madison beside him suddenly, her shawl falling from her shoulders as Michael looked at her. She reached to support him. "I'm all right, Madison," Michael Rourke almost whispered.

That his voice was like that of his father's was something he had been told before and that his own observation confirmed. But his father was not here—and his sister's fate perhaps rested on his and Paul's shoulders. And he looked at Madison—with Madison too.

Paul was sitting up, propped on his right elbow, his face very pale.

"What's, ah, what's going on, Paul," Michael began again. "Dr. Munchen brought you in—looked at me too. He looked at Madison—he told her he was good at looking in a woman's eyes and telling if she were pregnant."

Madison laughed. "No one can do such a thing—but I do, I do have life here," and she touched at her abdomen.

Paul shook his head. And then Paul sat up straight, his face showing pain. His right hand came from his hip pocket, a gleaming stainless steel derringer in it. "Munchen's a good guy—he knew I had this."

"What's goin' on, Paul? Where's Annie?"

"Munchen didn't tell you?"

"What—"

"Annie, ahh, Forrest Blackburn. He's the Russian agent. He kidnapped Annie—took a Soviet chopper and headed out. Ahh, Dodd—I think it was him. Said Blackburn couldn't get much more than a hundred miles or so—not enough fuel. But he, ahh, won't send anybody after her."

"We can go," Michael Rourke declared. "I can lie just as flat in the back of Dad's truck as I can here."

"And I can drive this truck," Madison volunteered.

Michael Rourke folded his arm about his woman's shoulders and drew her head against his chest. "You probably could."

Paul was sitting up fully now. "All right—this is what we do. I use this," and Paul Rubenstein gestured with the derringer, "and we get ourselves John's truck. I left that spare High Power I picked up—at The Place," and Paul smiled at Madison, then turned his face away. "Left that and some spare magazines and stuff in the truck. Just in case. We know where the strategic stores were located— Blackburn doesn't. We can catch him after that fuckin' machine of his runs outa gas."

174

"Madison'll stay—I can drive," Michael said grimly. He could barely stand.

"Well, I don't think so, Michael. And your dad wouldn't leave Madison alone here without someone to protect her—and he wouldn't take off all shot up with another guy in pretty much the same way and leave the only healthy person behind."

"Madison's pregnant, Paul."

"Good for her—if this were six months from now I'd agree with you. But it isn't—and I don't."

Michael exhaled a long sigh, finally easing down to his cot, Madison raising his legs, swinging his feet up onto the cot. Michael leaned back, straight, flat in his back, staring at the tent roof. "All right—you've got the experience, I haven't."

"Yeah, but you're a Rourke." Paul Rubenstein laughed, clutching at his abdomen.

Michael turned away again, looking upward. "What do we do?"

"All right," Paul began.

But Madison interrupted. It must be catching from Annie, Michael thought.

"I can take the derringer pistol—that is correct?"

"Yeah," Michael almost whispered. "But, no, you can't."

"Hear her out, huh?" Paul interjected.

Michael turned to look at her as she gathered up her shawl from the floor of the tent and cocooned it about her shoulders and upper body, then hugged her arms to her chest. She began to pace and he watched her—her long blond hair would swing to the left, her skirts to the right, and then vice-versa, as she walked. "I can take Annie's pistol and go to Father Rourke's truck. If it is unguarded, I will drive the truck here. If it is guarded, I will do something so it is not guarded any longer." Paul laughed. Madison stared at him a moment, then swept her hair back

175

from her face, continuing to talk. "I will return here and Paul and I can help you Michael—into the truck. We can then go to Captain Dodd and ask for the return of our guns. If he does not, well, then we shall steal them." And she nodded her head, as if deciding something, and then she smiled. "Is this good?"

Paul Rubenstein's face lit with a grin as Michael watched him. Paul laughed. "You know, Michael, your dad was right. We'll make a Rourke out of her yet." And Paul seemed to weigh the derringer in his hand. "All right, Madison—this is an American Derringer Corporation .45 ACP O/U derringer. John—Father Rourke, like you call him—he showed me once how these big-bore derringers work. The trick is to make sure the firing pins are set so the bottom barrel goes off first. That'll be your most accurate shot."

"Yes, Paul."

Chapter Thirty

John Rourke carried a briefcase—many men he had seen throughout The Complex carried similar briefcases. But John Rourke doubted that the contents were similar at all. In the briefcase was his Metalifed and Mag-Na-Ported six-inch Colt Python .357, and with it Safariland speed-loaders loaded with Federal 158-grain semi-jacketed soft points. With it as well were the twin stainless Detonics Scoremaster .45s he had liberated from The Place—there had been no way to return them, no one to return them to. Spare magazines for these as well as spare magazines for the twin stainless Detonics Combat Masters in the double Alessi shoulder rig under his waist-length jacket were in the briefcase as well.

The briefcase was heavy.

As he walked the narrow, spotless sidewalks, he could see ahead of him Frau Mann and Natalia and his wife, Sarah, the three women dressed to kill and out, it would have seemed, for nothing but a casual stroll. How Frau Mann was armed, he did not know. But Natalia's twin stainless L-Frame .357s were in the large leather-looking purse that hung so innocent-seeming from her left shoulder. The silenced PPK/S would be there as well. He knew where the Bali-Song was: under an improvised elastic garter inside her left thigh.

Sarah—the Trapper Scorpion she had adopted between

The Night of The War and the time he, John Rourke, had finally located his wife and two children. It was in her purse, and with it the battered, rust pitted 1911A1 she had carried since The Night of The War.

Rourke stopped at a shop window. He spoke German better than he read it, but the books in the shop window all seemed to have been written by the leader or written about the leader. Rourke saw his reflection smiling back at him from the glass—such books might soon become collector's items. And past his own reflection, curiously superimposed over a poster of the very Hitlerlike face of the leader, he could see the reflection of Wolfgang Mann, although he would not have recognized it had he not known. Mann wore a tight twenty-fifth century version of a business suit, the suit having seen vastly better days. A white wig and false mustache and a crushed cap, stooping shoulders and a cane accentuating the appearance of age. Mann's face would be the most recognizable and therefore had to be the one that was altered.

Rourke walked on, passing the bookstore—under Mann's arm had been a crumpled bundle. Inside the bundle was Mann's service pistol and a half dozen spare magazines. The cane was a sword, a relic preserved for five hundred years from his ancestor who had fought under Hitler against freedom, now to be used against Hitler's heir apparent in the cause of freedom if necessary.

There was, after all, a certain poetry to life, John Rourke mused.

He kept walking, watching ahead of him now—the three women further along because he had stopped for a moment at the bookstore window. Frau Mann, Natalia and Sarah were nearly to the exit of The Complex.

Sarah Rourke felt suddenly strange as she saw the reflection in the window of the dress shop. With Frau

Mann and Natalia, she had stopped to see the latest in Complex fashions. And somehow, seeing her own reflection in a shop window was somehow different than seeing herself in a mirror.

Subconsciously, after she had dressed in the clothes Frau Mann had provided for her, as she had watched herself in the mirror, it had all seemed unreal. An expensively made dress. Heels. Jewelry. Her hair up. Makeup—she had almost forgotten how it felt to wear lipstick. And now she wore eye shadow.

But suddenly seeing herself with two other women doing something that had once been so perfectly normal. It frightened her.

If her husband were successful here and the leader were deposed—would there be warfare here? Would these women—like Frau Mann and Helene Sturm whom they were on their way to rescue if possible—still have their shop windows to gaze in? Admiring what they did not have and perhaps more subtly admiring what they already possessed in themselves?

Her husband—she considered John Rourke. They had made love. He had ejaculated. She had felt it, sensed it—experienced it, and been happy for it. It crossed her mind. She should have been at her most fertile.

She wondered—not suddenly, but lingeringly and almost happily. What if even now she were pregnant by him?

Sarah Rourke licked her lips—tasting the lipstick, tasting something else she could not define.

Natalia, beside her, as exquisite a woman as Sarah had ever seen, began again to walk, and Sarah fell in between Natalia and Frau Mann. She thought of herself as a thorn between two roses. Frau Mann too was exquisite.

Natalia or Frau Mann—either of them could have been a model from the pages of *Vogue*. She tried to remember the last time she had seen a copy of *Vogue*. She remembered. It had been at the dentist's office when Annie had chipped a baby tooth.

If she were pregnant—they were approaching the entrance to The Complex and there were guards there—if it were a boy, all would be ideal for him. A Rourke, a natural leader like her husband and like her son. A man in a world where the manly virtues were what would make civilization take hold. But if it were a girl—then a woman, one of those who took civilization and made it stick after it had been planted. But it was not a world to be a woman in, Sarah reflected.

They were walking into the sunlight now, Frau Mann chatting idly in German with Natalia, Natalia responding. Sarah only nodded hopelessly and stupidly because she did not speak the language. What were they talking about? Nothing of consequence, because the German soldiers were too near. They would be talking about what was expected of them—hemlines and recipes and the sort of prattle that she, Sarah, had always detested.

But if she were pregnant—one of the guards saluted Frau Mann and Frau Mann stopped to talk with him. Sarah caught the introduction and smiled at the soldier. If she were pregnant, would it force John to give up all hope of Natalia? Did she, Sarah, really want that?

She had learned to live independent of him, to fend for herself. To be her own person and not live under the shadow of his greatness and his strength. She had found strength inside herself. And now was she perhaps forcing him through biological necessity to be with her?

What would he give up?

What would she give up?

Was it already given? But she loved him.

John Rourke stopped again, because the women had stopped, and he let Wolfgang Mann who was disguised as an old man pass him by.

180

He stared in a shop window. Cutlery. He saw no knife he would trade either his Gerber MkII or his Sting IA for. And he smiled. He had noticed, however subtly, that as Natalia and Sarah and Frau Mann had walked past the shop window, Natalia's head had turned almost imperceptibly. He saw no knife for which she would trade her Pacific Cutlery Bali-Song, despite its five centuries of use.

Natalia. Sarah.

He studied what was apparently the contemporary counterpart of the Victorinox Swiss Army Knives—a display of them, blades of all sizes, descriptions, functions.

Had he made Sarah pregnant? Why had he made love to her? Because he still loved her—of this he was resolutely certain. It had been all that had kept his sanity during those times between The Night of The War and when he had found her.

He wondered what she thought of him.

John Rourke had always felt discomfort in the objective realization that those about him saw him as tireless, possessing courage without measure. A hero. He saw it in Paul's face, in Michael's face, in Annie's. In Natalia's eyes.

He had never considered himself more than ordinary, and in some ways less. Ever since childhood he had retreated from humanity into reticence—it was interpreted as silent strength. His singularity of purpose was to avoid contemplating the alternative. That he planned ahead was his basic distrust in the efficacy of others. Confidence was a defense against the mass ineptitude of the world.

He valued Paul—courage, understanding, that rare love one man can show for another in friendship.

Natalia. His friend as well. But more—because she was a more sensuous lover than he, John Rourke, had ever imagined. But he had little more than touched her in all the time he had known her.

Sarah—he and his wife were unalike. But they loved. Had loved.

He found himself staring at a hunting knife with plastic handles—gone were stag or ivory.

John Rourke began to walk. He faulted himself. A fine and beautiful woman with strength and dignity and honor was his wife. And a woman of equal character was his mistress in his mind.

He had impregnated his wife.

His physician's mind considered the possibilities.

Decision would be lost in honor, because honor was something he had early learned, was all which elevated men among the beasts.

He kept walking. Sarah. Natalia. With Frau Mann, they had passed the guards at the open entrance to The Complex. He could see them.

Natalia Anastasia Tiemerovna stopped. She stared at the rising edifice of the government building which housed the headquarters for the youth. But she stared obliquely so her gaze would not attract attention. She felt her hands pressing down along her thighs, smoothing her dress against her undergarments, and these in turn against her flesh.

John. Sarah. They had been lovers again. She had told John she was happy for them. And she was. Lying was something she had abandoned long ago, and as one who had lived by deception, she could see truth.

John Rourke loved her. John Rourke loved his wife as well. John Rourke was and always had been bound by duty.

She, Natalia, would forever be John Rourke's bride, but only in her heart. Never in fact.

She looked at Sarah Rourke. The eyes. The hair. The figure. A beautiful woman, but not the sort of woman who considered herself beautiful.

Frau Mann whispered in English, "We should enter now—before we attract attention here."

"Your English is so very good." Natalia smiled at her.

"My husband—he taught it to me. It was his way of practicing when he trained for the officer corps. He was not my husband then. But he was my lover—always." Frau Mann smiled, almost seeming to blush, her pale cheeks reddening.

Natalia's eyes met Sarah's eyes. Sarah spoke. "Frau Mann is right—we should go inside."

"Yes," Natalia agreed.

And she began again to walk, her feet unused to heels after so long, but the discomfort somehow worth it as she saw herself approaching the government building, her reflection in the dark-tinted glass which composed almost the entire wall surface of the first or ground floor. Heels had always done something for her—accentuated her height.

Natalia knew she was beautiful. She had been told it often enough. She had used it often enough—her beauty.

She began to speak—to Sarah, her voice low so no one except perhaps Frau Mann would hear. And there was no way to avoid that because the words needed to be said lest one of them should die in the enterprise. "I am very happy for you and for John."

"Did John tell you?" Sarah asked, not smiling at all.

"He didn't have to tell me. I think—after we have finished here and we have stopped Vladmir, my husband. I think I shall go away."

"I don't want you to go away. That will solve nothing," Sarah whispered.

"There is nothing that can be solved, Sarah. You are his wife."

"He loves you as much as he loves me—maybe more. I don't know. Yes, he made love to me. But I know he'd like to make love to you."

"Thank you. He never has—I swear it," Natalia whispered, forcing a smile so that any casual observer would not become suspicious.

It was sultry, the temperature and the humidity. And Natalia was grateful the dress she wore was of a light fabric.

The sun shone brilliantly. The grass which flanked the walkway leading toward the main entrance of the new government building was bright green and as neat as a freshly vacuumed carpet.

"He's made love to you in your mind. You see, I know. Because when I first met him," Sarah whispered, "even though I didn't know him really—I made love to him in my mind. I know the look. And it's in your eyes too. He's very special."

"Yes," Natalia murmured. "He is your man."

"Is he?" Sarah asked, smiling, then quickening her pace. Natalia stopped for an instant, then she walked ahead, focusing her attention on the staccatto rhythm of her heels against the sidewalk.

Once they were inside the building, it would begin. It always did.

John Rourke started past the guards and stopped—they called to him, first one, then a second.

Rourke turned, drawing his briefcase closer toward his thigh with a downward pressure of his left arm.

In German, Rourke almost whispered, "Yes, there is something?"

"I have not seen your face before, sir."

Rourke made himself smile—his eyes were feeling the brightness of the sun beyond the entranceway, but he had elected not to use his glasses because he had seen no one with sunglasses in the entire Complex. "I've seen you, Corporal," Rourke answered. "You're on duty weekdays from eight until four. And I saw you once on Sunday. It is worthwhile to be observant, I suppose."

"Yes, sir. What is in your briefcase?"

John Rourke laughed. "Do you want to see boring things? I don't want to see them. Why don't you confiscate my briefcase and I can avoid all this paper work and blame you instead? Hmm?"

The soldier beside the corporal began to laugh.

The corporal shook his head, waving his hand toward the outside. "Go ahead, sir. I pity you the paper work."

Rourke smiled, "I pity you the standing," he answered sincerely, then turned on his heel and started ahead again.

The Sting IA Black Chrome A.G. Russell had sent him five centuries ago was up his right sleeve and a twist of his forearm would have sent the knife down into his palm.

It was the corporal's lucky day.

Rourke kept walking, the government building looming ahead of him now. It was imposing, if a bit overly utilitarian seeming.

He could just see, as he squinted against the light, Sarah, Natalia and Frau Mann entering the building.

Akiro Kurinami ran his hand nervously along the receiver of the M-16—Elaine Halverson watched him for an instant longer, then returned her gaze to the binoculars through which she had been observing The Complex. They had secreted themselves with the enlisted personnel from Wolfgang Mann's party along a ridge in high jungle overlooking the entrance to the Nazi stronghold below.

Without planning it, she began speaking, "Akiro—what are you thinking?"

"Ahh, what am I thinking? That this is a strange place for a Japanese naval aviator to be, in a jungle in Argentina, helping one faction of Germans fight against another."

It had been on her mind since the awakening—on many minds, she supposed. And it was like a time bomb, ticking. Soon, if the battling were over just to stay alive, then what had truly happened would sink in. It had already begun to with her. "I had a family. I mean, not a husband or children or anything. And they're all gone."

"A pretty woman such as you—" and she put down the binoculars—"should have been married, I think." Kurinami smiled as he said it.

"I'm not pretty—and anyway, nobody asked. Well," and she remembered something suddenly. "There was a boy once—but I was working for a Ph.D. and I didn't think it was all that urgent and, well, that—I thought there'd be plenty of time. I really did."

She studied his dark eyes. There was sadness in them.

"I had a wife. I had two children. I did not volunteer for the international corps of astronauts. I was requested by my government. It was thought that it would, ahh, bring honor to my country were I to pilot a manned craft that would someday touch the surface of another planet. Foolishly, I accepted the honor. Now—my uncle. He was in Hiroshima when the bomb fell there. Now . . ." And Kurinami fell silent.

"I didn't—"

"My wife—she was very beautiful. And she was very quiet. Very much what a Westerner such as yourself would consider a stereotypical Japanese woman. She was—I love her still. They, ahh, they were to come to America and join me. I had found a house—it was a little Japanese-looking and it had a garden. She—she would have liked it, I know. The children—they spoke English well, better than she. She would have learned though." He looked away.

"I know she would have," Elaine Halverson nodded. She tugged at her right ear lobe—Natalia had re-pierced her ears. "I, ahh, I envy you."

"That my family is lost to me?"

"That you had them," Elaine Halverson answered quietly. "The brash young man is just an act, isn't it? The reckless Japanese naval aviator."

186

"I—I suppose so, Elaine. But there is no reason to be cautious."

She could not understand why, but she reached out her right hand and touched at his left forearm. He did not draw his arm away. Instead, his right hand closed over hers.

John Rourke passed through the tinted glass of the doorway. A painting of the leader holding high the red, white and black banner of Nazism and rising, phoenixlike, from a sea of flames, dominated the far wall of the foyer. The ceiling was high, stylistic metal sculptures hung suspended at varying heights, the ceiling itself beneath which the sculptures were placed mirrored darkly.

Near the painting, but not so near as to clutter the heroic visage, was a high desk of the sort made to be stood behind because the considerable height would have totally obscured anyone sitting. Two uniformed men, seemingly weaponless (but Rourke knew better from experience and from the counsel of Wolfgang Mann) stood behind it. They were interviewing the tattered old man.

Rourke walked ahead, toward the guard desk, noting the door to the ladies' room opening.

Natalia stepped into the corridor first, then behind her Sarah—Sarah seemed to be searching for something in her shoulder bag. Natalia's right hand was concealed behind her right thigh. Frau Mann joined them, the three women commencing, it seemed, to chatter in hushed tones.

John Rourke smiled. He was near enough to the guard desk that he could make out the conversation between the disguised Wolfgang Mann and the two guards. "See Herr Goethler, supervisor of the youth. It is vital I speak with him."

"Sir, he does not see just anybody, Herr Goethler. You must move through proper channels and have an appointment. I shall be glad to give you his telephone number and you can perhaps call tomorrow."

"But I have walked all this way—from the far edge of the interior of The Complex. It is so important."

Natalia, in perfect German, her right arm sweeping up, the silenced stainless PPK/S American in her tiny right fist, said in perfect German, "You are being very rude to one so old."

The guard nearest her turned and Natalia shot him where the line at the height of the bridge of the nose would intersect the horizontal line of the eyebrows. He fell over dead as she lifted the pistol left, then fired twice more, once to the neck and a second time into the left eye of the second guard. Rourke was beside the guard desk as the second body fell, his sunglasses coming from inside his jacket, onto his face. His left hand released the briefcase and in one continuous motion swept out to the body of the guard, catching it at the scruff of the neck, holding it as Sarah and Frau Mann—Frau Mann seemed white as a ghost—caught the body from him and dragged it behind the desk.

Wolfgang Mann had the paper bundle open on the desk, drawing his Waltherlike service pistol from it, putting the spare magazines into his pockets, throwing the bundle—empty—down over the desk and behind it.

Sarah's right hand held the Trapper Scorpion .45. Natalia was changing magazines for the silenced PPK/S.

Rourke opened the briefcase, drawing from it his gunbelt with the Milt Sparks Six-Pack for the twin stainless Detonics Combat Masters, the full flap holster for the Python, the ammo dumps for it, the Gerber MkII. He secured the belt just below his waist, then took the musette bag from the case—it held his spare magazines for the stainless Scoremasters and his speedloaders for the Python. He slung it cross-body. Last from the case were the two Scoremasters—he stuffed these in appendix forward carries right and left in the front of his gunbelt.

Rourke looked to his wife—the second .45 was in her left fist. He looked to Natalia—she looked slightly ridiculous, the double Safariland full flap rig cinched at her waist. It didn't go with the dress, the jewelry and the high heels. Frau Mann held a military pistol in her right fist, identical to her husband's.

"Which way?" Rourke whispered getting the Sting IA from his sleeve, sheathing it inside the waistband of his trousers.

"Back along the corridor and then either the elevator or the stairwell to the second basement. It is where she would be held."

Rourke nodded only, breaking into a run. He glanced at the black-faced Rolex on his left fist. It would be more than an hour until the guard team at the front desk which Natalia had disposed of would be due for replacement. But anyone could come in at any time and discover their deaths.

He passed the elevator banks, then slowed. "Natalia—check there isn't an alarm. Hurry."

Natalia, running awkwardly in the heels and tight skirt, half skidded past him, dropping into a crouch before the door handle. Her fingers splayed out over it, touching at the handle, trying the knob slowly, gently. "I can't be sure—but I don't think so."

Rourke nodded. Natalia stepped back.

Rourke drew one of the Scoremasters from his belt, jacking back the slide, leaving the safety down.

He turned the knob. There was no sound, which of itself proved nothing. Silent alarms would be no stranger here.

Rourke stepped through the doorway, eyeing the frame first that there was no electronic eye.

He looked above him—a camera eye. It moved, following him.

"Kiss off secrecy," he snarled, stabbing the Scoremaster

toward the camera and pulling the trigger.

He averted his eyes as the camera shattered, lens material spraying downward.

The steps leading toward the basements—he ran toward them, glancing behind him once. Natalia and Sarah were through, Frau Mann, then Colonel Mann behind his wife.

The door slammed shut with a hollow, echoing sound.

And now, as Rourke took the steps downward two at a time, the Scoremaster's safety upped, he could hear the sounding of an alarm.

Chapter Thirty-one

Helene Sturm screamed.

"No one can hear you. These walls are soundproofed, Frau Sturm."

"I know nothing," she gasped, tugging at the straps which restrained her wrists and ankles, binding her to the cold stainless steel of the surgical table. The four walls, the ceiling and floor—all seemed made of the same substance. She could not see her feet for the swollen abdomen and the life inside it for which she feared. "If Manfred told you something it was some sort of lie, Herr Goethler—honestly, it was. I do nothing wrong."

The hand slapped downward and she tried to turn her face away, but when he struck her, her left cheek slammed hard against the table surface and she cried out, tears streaming along her cheeks, her vision blurring with them, the taste of salt against her lips. "Liar!"

"I am—"

The hand slapped at her again. And as she turned her face toward the doorway, praying, the door opened. She felt as though her heart skipped a beat.

But it was the face of the leader.

"I leave at once, Herr Goethler. My suspicions concerning a fifth column are confirmed. Armed men and women have invaded the structure. They will never get below the first basement. But I must leave. I have been watching the interrogation. It does not progress well."

"*Mein Fuehrer*—I am—"

"I can perhaps offer a suggestion," and she watched his dark eyes, his nostrils twitching above the comedy brush mustache. His hand reached out to her abdomen and he smiled as she felt the pressure there. "The child is kicking—but perhaps there are twins, hmm?"

Helene Sturm did not know what to answer, what to say that might not provoke him further.

She said nothing.

"There are several possibilities to get you to talk, *mein frau*. Several. Your three boys—they are in the next room, bound, ready for whatever we should choose. But if we were to take the youngest son—our loyal Manfred told us of your part in this conspiracy. What is the young one's name? Willy? But if we were to take Willy, perhaps you would only lie. No—I think there is a better way," and his hand flashed down from her abdomen to her thighs, and she felt it—she could not see—as he bunched up her skirt and reached.

Helene Sturm screamed, "What are you doing, *Mein Fuehrer*!"

"The unborn within her, Herr Goethler," his deep voice droned emotionlessly. "You shall have your surgeon prepare to probe the uterus." And then his face bent over hers, inches from hers and she could smell his breath—sour, somehow evil. "Perhaps, if there are twins, only one of them will be malformed by what is done here. It is your choice." And he smiled, his teeth yellow.

She closed her eyes—to make him gone.

One of the Scoremasters in each hand, John Rourke dodged past the corner and fired from eye level, emptying the twin adjustable sight full-sized Detonics pistols toward the SS security troops at the far end of the corridor beyond the stairwell.

"We must retreat," Wolfgang Mann shouted as Rourke tucked back, beside him. "Before they send troops down the stairwell and we are trapped."

"Yeah? And what about this Helene Sturm? If they are working on her they'll be working harder. No." Rourke had already replaced the magazines, dropping the empties into his musette bag.

The Python—he drew it as he resecured both .45s in his belt.

Natalia was on her knees by the corner of the doorframe, firing her L-Frames, wing-shooting.

She pulled back, automatic weapons fire hammering into the doorframe, chunks of plaster spraying around them, the black of Natalia's clothes splotched with chalky white.

Sarah reached to Frau Mann's hands, saying, "Give me that pistol of yours. It's selective fire, isn't it?"

Wolfgang Mann answered for her. "Yes—semi or three-shot burst. But the magazine is only eighteen rounds, Frau Rourke."

"How many spares you got?"

John Rourke felt himself smiling. "One or two of us stays here with her pistol set on burst, covering the others until they cross the opposite side of the corridor. They cover us with the second machine pistol."

"And I'm the one," Sarah said calmly. "I never did run worth a damn in heels and a tight skirt."

John Rourke looked at his wife. "Better way." More gunfire hammered into the doorframe. "OK," Rourke rasped. "Sarah and I stay here, Sarah with the space gun here. We cover the rest of you getting across, then Sarah and I go out together. Natalia covers us. Colonel—Wolf— you and your wife go on ahead. As soon as Sarah and I've crossed and linked up with Natalia, we'll be right behind you. Three-way fire and maneuver, sort of."

"It might work," Mann nodded, stripping away the pieces of his disguise, chunks of claylike substance shredding at his cheeks and the false gooseflesh of his neck. "The secrecy is lost, I think."

"Just hope that the way out of this place isn't lost." Rourke grinned.

Mann's wife was searching her purse, Natalia taking the double column magazines from it as Frau Mann found them—Rourke counted three. "That is all I have," Frau Mann barely whispered, her skin pale, her eyes seeming somehow sunken. Fear. Rourke knew the look.

"Good luck—to you both." Natalia smiled, handing the magazines to Sarah who proceeded to stuff them into the side seam pockets of her dress.

"It ruins the look of things." Sarah smiled.

"This is the position for burst control," Mann pointed out—it was a two-position safety, slide mounted.

"Right—put it here, all the way down into the lower notch."

"That is correct, Frau Rourke."

"Move it then—when Sarah says go," Rourke advised. The Python was in both fists, muzzle raised to snap it around the corner of the shot-up doorframe. Sarah held the Waltherlike German pistol, her right hand at the pistol grip, her left at the folded-down forward support—the gun on auto mode reminded Rourke of the Beretta 93R.

"Ready," Sarah hissed.

Natalia ran first, her high heeled shoes stuffed one into each side pocket of her dress, the L-Frames, one in each fist, spitting fire.

Rourke snapped the Python's muzzle down and out, double actioning toward what he had pegged as the greatest concentration of the SS security force, Sarah crouched beside him, the German machine pistol spitting three-round bursts, Mann was running now, pushing his frightened barefoot wife ahead of him, his pistol firing toward the SS position as well.

The Python empty, Rourke dropped it in the leather at his side and drew both Scoremasters from his belt, firing double taps with both pistols simultaneously as Sarah reloaded.

Two of the SS men—their uniforms charcoal-gray BDUs with lightning bolt collar tabs and swastika arm bands— dodged from cover, to get into better position to fire at Natalia as she dove behind cover on the opposite side halfway along the corridor. Rourke fired out both pistols, the bodies of the two assault-rifle-armed SS men almost dancing as they took the torso hits, then crumpled down-ward, their automatic weapons firing into the corridor ceiling, chunks of plaster and ceiling tiles spraying down like hailstones.

The Scoremasters were empty. Rourke rammed them into his belt, the slides still locked open, Sarah beside him again, the German machine pistol firing three-round blasts.

Two bursts cut into three of the SS security force, two of the men going down dead as they ran for cover, a third's left leg going out from under him as he sprawled forward.

The twin stainless Detonics Combat Masters were in Rourke's fists now, firing.

Natalia's revolvers—fresh loaded—tongues of flame licked from them at the midpoint of the corridor as more of the SS security force broke cover.

Sarah was ramming a fresh magazine into the German service pistol. "One more after this, John," she shouted over the roar of the gunfire.

The twin stainless Detonics .45s were empty in his hands.

Rourke dumped the magazines, pocketed the empties, ramming fresh spares up the magazine wells from the Milt Sparks Six Pack at his belt.

"Run for it—now—I'm with ya," and he shoved Sarah

forward into the corridor, his pistols blazing as he ran beside her, blocking her body with his as best he could.

He could hear the *phut-phut* sounds of Natalia's silenced Walther now, firing.

The sharp cracks of Wolfgang Mann's Walther P-38, in his left hand, the service pistol in his right hand.

The roar of assault rifle fire.

The three-round bursts at high cyclic rate of Sarah's borrowed machine pistol.

Screams, groans, curses—SS security personnel were going down.

Rourke shoved his wife ahead, the pistol in his right hand empty now, Natalia stepping from cover to draw fire toward her, the revolvers reloaded, at hip level, spitting death.

Rourke fired out the Detonics pistol in his left fist, one of the SS men hurtling himself toward him. Rourke backhanded the little stainless .45 across the man's face, teeth and blood spraying outward, the SS man's face seeming to compress as the body sagged downward.

Rourke threw himself forward, hitting the floor, skidding along on knees and elbows into cover, both pistols empty in his hands as he rolled onto his back, Natalia screaming, "John!"

He was up, to his feet, Sarah emptying the German machine pistol as the remaining SS security personnel—ten of them by rough count—closed.

The Bali-Song flashed into Natalia's right hand. A spray of blood appeared as an artery in the neck of the nearest SS security man ripped.

Rourke threw himself toward her, the big Gerber in his right fist now, hacking outward, an assault rifle's butt coming toward his head. The Gerber's blade bit first upward, thrusting into the crotch of the rifleman.

Rourke let go of the knife, snatching the assault rifle from the SS man as the body lurched backward, Rourke's right foot hammering up and out into the right arm to break the arm at the elbow and free the sling.

He swung the German assault rifle downward, no time to fire, the butt snapping forward and up in a long arc, the butt stroke contacting jawbone. Rourke drew the rifle back in a straight line, a vertical butt stroke to the face of another SS man.

Natalia's knife—Rourke caught a flash of gleaming steel in the ceiling fixture's light, then felt a spray of blood on the right side of his face as another of the SS men went down.

Rourke had the rifle on line now, his right first finger touching the trigger, the assault rifle burping a three-round burst, then another and another.

The German pistol in Sarah's hands—Rourke could hear it firing. She was blowing the third spare magazine—but there was no choice and some of the fallen SS security personnel wore side arms.

Rourke fired out the assault rifle.

Empty.

Three of the SS personnel were still standing, one of them firing as Sarah interposed herself between the SS man and John Rourke—the assault rifle spoke, and so did the machine pistol in her hands. Sarah's body slammed hard against him.

The SS man was down.

The sharp cracks of Mann's Walther P-38. A scream as Natalia's knife slashed flesh, Rourke catching his wife in his arms, sheltering her with his own body as Natalia's body seemed to leap over them, a flash of thigh, a blur in black—a shout of agony.

Rourke glanced toward her. She stood over one of the SS men, her knife imbedded in his chest, her left bare foot crushing his Adam's apple, the assault rifle still clutched in his twitching hands.

Rourke looked to his wife—blood.

Her left forearm. He pulled up her sleeve.

"I've never been—ooh, Jesus, he hurt me," she whispered.

"Flesh wound," Rourke whispered, feeling the arm for any broken bone, with his left hand reaching to the musette bag for a field dressing.

Natalia hissed, "I'll do it, John," dropping to her knees beside him.

"I'm fine. Hurts like the—but I'm OK." Sarah nodded, trying to get to her feet.

"Rest a moment," Natalia advised. "Let me get this dressing secure."

Rourke stood, Natalia attending his wife's arm, Frau Mann cradling Sarah's head in her lap. Mann was going over the bodies of the dead, scrounging weapons and magazines.

Rourke, ramming fresh magazines up the butts of his pistols, working the slides forward, almost whispered, "Clean wound—bullet just made a heavy crease."

Rourke took two steps forward, dropping to one knee, his left hand bracing against the body of one of the SS men, his right hand twisting free his Gerber.

He stood, then returned to his wife and Natalia, Natalia taking one of the aerosol sprays Doctor Munchen had sent with them. Munchen had explained it not only promoted significantly more rapid healing, but served as a disinfectant as well.

"Almost ready." Natalia smiled, looking up, her Bali-Song on the floor beside where she knelt, the Wee-Hawk pattern blade still glinting red with wet blood.

Rourke dropped to his knees beside Natalia, reaching out with his left hand, the right one still holding the knife. He touched his left hand to his wife's forehead. "You know, you've gotten pretty damned good in a fight."

"You're not bad yourself." Sarah smiled.

Rourke bent over his wife and kissed her lightly on the

lips. "You gonna be all right? We've gotta get moving—hmm?"

"Fine. It just took me by surprise."

"Bullets always do," Rourke whispered.

"I'll stay with her," Natalia whispered.

Rourke looked at Natalia—there were things he wanted to say to Natalia, to Sarah.

Mann's voice interrupted his thoughts. "I have five more of the machine pistols as you call them, two assault rifles for each of us, more additional magazines than we can carry."

"I can carry quite a lot." Rourke smiled, getting to his feet.

Rourke bent over one of the fallen SS men, wiping the blade of the Gerber clean of blood against the uniform front, then sheathing it. He took two of the assault rifles, checked their condition of readiness and slung them crossbody—he preferred his own weapons. He looked to his wife. Natalia was just finishing securing the dressing. "Sarah—you still handle one of these?"

Natalia drew back for a moment, Sarah flexing her left arm. "Yes, don't ask me to do it tomorrow though." And Natalia continued securing the dressing. Mann, murmuring something Rourke didn't catch, crouched beside Sarah and began dropping spare magazines for the German pistol into her purse.

Together, Rourke and Natalia helped Sarah to her feet.

Natalia picked up two of the assault rifles, checking their condition of readiness, then one of the German pistols. Holding the German pistol under her left arm, methodically, as they walked now down the corridor, Natalia began reloading her revolvers, reholstering them. It was only as he turned around that he noticed Natalia's dress—she had apparently used her knife and slit the skirt along the seam up to the waist for better freedom of movement, the slip slit as well.

Frau Mann clutched one of the machine pistols in both hands.

Her husband carried two of the assault rifles slung cross-body and a third in his hands.

Rourke edged past Wolfgang Mann, taking the lead now as they moved along the corridor. It would be a matter of moments until more of the SS personnel would begin flooding the corridor but at least, Rourke reflected, the five of them were better equipped now. Sarah—he could see the pain in her eyes, but she held the pistol ready as she walked, the purse sagging heavily at her left side, slung cross-body.

Rourke swung one of the assault rifles forward—from the plan of the first basement Wolf Mann had drawn for him before beginning the raid, the doorway ahead lead to the stairwell.

"I will go first. Perhaps if there are regular troops, I can reason with them."

"Yeah—maybe," Rourke agreed, but not feeling conviction for his words.

Rourke glanced behind them along the corridor—no one stirred. After turning the bend in the corridor it was no longer possible to see the dead they had left behind.

Rourke positioned himself beside the door, ready, Mann reaching out and turning the knob. The door swung inward—Rourke waited. Mann stepped through, his rifle, preceding him, the muzzle moving right and left, up and down, like a snake searching out prey.

"It is clear, my friends," Mann called. Frau Mann started after him, but Mann called, "Wait, *schatzie*— let the Herr Doctor follow me."

Rourke stepped through the doorway. It was a stairwell identical to the one leading from the first floor, but strange in that no stairs led upward. Mann was already moving downward, Rourke following after the German colonel slowly, peering down along the depth of the stairwell, waiting—there would be security personnel waiting, too, he reasoned.

Helene Sturm screamed. "No, I know nothing!"

Herr Goethler bent over her, large medical forceps of gleaming stainless steel in his hairy right hand. "I will do this myself, Frau Sturm—unless you tell me everything that I wish to know. We know that a fifth column exists. We have known this for sometime. And from our informant—"

"Manfred," she cried in anguish. Her own son.

"We know that Frau Mann, the wife of the *standartenfuehrer*, is somehow involved in the conspiracy as well. But I will make it easy on you—and your unborn children. Merely tell us that Frau Mann is involved in the conspiracy and you shall be unharmed, as will what you carry in your womb. We can obtain all the information beyond this when Frau Mann is interrogated. Now, admit to us that she is involved in this conspiracy. That her husband is the leader."

"No."

"Otherwise, Frau Sturm—" and Goethler brandished the forceps, and then she could no longer see them, feeling the cold of the steel against the lips of her vulva. She screamed. "I shall be forced to do something, *mein frau*, that we shall all regret."

"If—" she was breathing hard. She felt a contraction—her babies. "If—if—if my babies die—it's better—better than living in—in a society—where men like you—ahh!" First the contraction, and then the feel of the cold steel against flesh.

Chapter Thirty-two

John Rourke heard the sounds at the base of the stairwell. Three of the SS security men coming through the doorway there from the main corridor of the second basement. Rourke flipped the railing, crashing down into the center of the three men, his right hand snapping out, the middle knuckles impacting the man on his right at the base of the nose, breaking it, driving it upward and through the ethmoid bone and into the brain, the SS man dying on his feet as Rourke wheeled left. Rourke's right hand reached out, grabbing one of the SS men at the Adam's apple, Rourke's left elbow smashing back, bone contacting bone. As Rourke's right hand crushed the Adam's apple of the second man, Rourke's right knee smashed up, into the crotch, and on the downward motion, Rourke kicked back and up, a double kick into the crotch of the third man.

Rourke wheeled left 180 degrees, dragging the second man by the throat and hurtling his limpening body into the body of the third man.

As the third SS man fell, Rourke's left foot snapped out, the toe impacting just under the sternum, the third man's body snapping back, the head slapping hard against the concrete of the floor.

Natalia had vaulted the stairwell and was beside him now, the German machine pistol in her hands.

Rourke swung the assault rifle at his right side forward

on its sling, wrenching the partially open door past a dead man's errant left foot, then stepping slowly into the corridor.

No one. Rourke started ahead, Natalia moving on bare feet beside him, her stride as long as his now. Rourke glanced back once at Mann, Sarah and then Frau Mann. Sarah turned half around, covering the stairwell as they moved along the corridor, deeper into the bowels of the second basement.

"The interrogation room—it should be at the end of the corridor. There is a questioning room. Quite comfortable. And then a second room beyond it. It is supposedly an emergency medical facility," Wolfgang Mann murmured, Rourke not looking back at him. "But for some time there have been rumors of hideous experiments performed there by Herr Goethler and the youth."

Rourke licked his lips once—they were dry.

He drew his sunglasses from his face, putting them away, squinting for a moment against the artificial lighting.

"If they have Frau Sturm's children—they're likely in the outside room," Rourke hissed to Natalia.

"We can go in together. I will protect the boys."

"I'll take out any other guards not directly threatening them. And then we rush the second room—very fast."

"Agreed."

"Get Sarah to back us up—once we hit the second room, she keeps the boys safe if we find them.

"Right," and Rourke glanced toward Natalia as she sprinted back along the corridor. Her sheer stockinged legs seemed impossibly long—beautiful.

He turned his eyes toward the end of the corridor, quickening his pace now—because something inside him told him that he should.

John Rourke started to run. He smiled. Perhaps Annie's sometimes uncanny sixth sense was catching, perhaps The Sleep had something to do with it. He threw himself into the run, Natalia sprinting up along beside him now, the door closer, Rourke letting the second assault rifle forward now, almost to the door.

There was no time to worry if it were locked.

He fired both assault rifles simultaneously, the lock plate cutting out of the door, Rourke kicking it inward with his left foot, Natalia just after him as he looked right—three men and a tall, thin, effeminate looking boy smoking a cigarette. Rourke emptied both assault rifles into the three men. The boy dropped the cigarette onto his bare legs and screamed as he picked up one of the German machine pistols. Rourke drew the Python as he let both assault rifles fall empty to his sides, double actioning it once, then again as he side-stepped right. The boy's body crumpled and fell.

Gunfire behind him—the burping of a machine pistol, Rourke wheeling toward it, the Python tight at his right hip. Natalia's machine pistol was cutting down three men, Rourke double actioning the Python twice more to help put down the third.

Three little boys, looking less than two years apart in age, their bodies stripped of all clothing, then tied with what looked like wire, stickball gags in their mouths.

"Goddamned animals," Rourke rasped. To the door now leading to the interior room, Natalia beside him, the twin Metalife custom revolvers in her hands, in Rourke's hands the twin Scoremasters.

The door had a large knob. Rourke stuffed one of the pistols under his right armpit, cocked and locked, reaching the doorknob with his left hand.

He turned the stainless steel knob under his fingers, the feeling of the steel cold, like death.

The door was free—Rourke kicked it inward as he regrasped the second Scoremaster.

A woman, her clothes bunched up to her crotch, her abdomen huge seeming as she lay on a steel surgical table, her panties cut away, her stockings cut away, blood spraying from her crotch as she screamed, a man leaning over her with forceps, another dropping lit matches onto her face as she screamed, a boy—tall, effeminate-looking like the boy outside—one of the youth. The boy's hands were knotted in the woman's hair, twisting it, ripping out handfuls of it.

Natalia screamed, "Bastards!"

Rourke's Scoremaster fired into the body of the man with the forceps, the body already rocking as Natalia's machine pistol opened fire. Rourke shifted the muzzles—a shot from each pistol, blowing out the eyes of the man dropping the matches into Helene Sturm's face.

He shifted again—the boy screamed like the woman, picking up a surgical knife, hammering it downward toward Helen Sturm's throat. Rourke's pistols fired again, a double tap from each into the right forearm, nearly severing it, the knife clattering harmlessly to the blood-drenched table surface, the scream again issuing from the boy's lips. Natalia's machine pistol was emptying, the body pirouetting, stumbling, collapsing against the wall behind it, sagging downward, streaks of blood trailing over the dully gleaming stainless steel.

Helene Sturm screamed as she turned her burn-splotched face toward the blood-streaked wall. "Manfred!"

Chapter Thirty-three

Vladmir Karamatsov left his machine, feeling the warmth of the Argentina sun against his face. It was nearly sunset. His hat was in his hand and he thought better of what it should perhaps suggest to his officers and so he replaced it on his head, broadening his stride as he drew nearer to Krakovski and Antonovitch, the two majors striding toward him as well. They would intersect, he judged, at almost the exact center of the broad, grassy plane which was currently the helicopter landing field, the landing field for the jet fighter craft on the opposite side of a range of low, grassy hills to the west.

He stopped walking, so his field officers would have to approach him.

Krakovski and Antonovitch continued walking, stopping a few feet from him, simultaneously raising their right hands in salute.

Vladmir Karamatsov returned the salutes. "Gentlemen," he began, his voice upraised over the insect sound of the beating of the helicopter rotors. Over the keening of the wind the rotor blades only served to increase in force, the wind blowing hard from the north.

But the wind was warm on him still. "The potential for great victory lays before us. At dawn, our forces shall be properly assembled and we shall assault with full intensity this Nazi stronghold. Ground troops, helicopter gunships, jet fighter aircraft. I believe the Nazis coined the term—blitzkrieg. And this it shall be."

"All is in readiness, Comrade Colonel," Antonovitch began. "I have seen to it that surveillance data, photographs, revised maps—all are being properly disseminated to line commanders. Gunships are being programmed with the topographic features of the Nazi stronghold and its environs even as we speak, Comrade Colonel."

Krakovski spoke—Karamatsov disliked the younger of his two majors. "Comrade Colonel, the jet fighter craft under my command are refueling. Their weapons consoles are being programmed with Comrade Major Antonovitch's data even as we speak. My gunship crews are preparing their machines for battle. The ground forces are even now moving into their staging areas. All is in readiness but for your command."

Karamatsov studied the young major who wrote poetry. "Excellent—you have both performed admirably and it shall be reported so to the Central Committee. I have received word, by the way, that I have been promoted. Marshal."

"Congratulations, Comrade Marshal Karamatsov," Krakovski blurted out.

Antonovitch saluted, "Congratulations, Comrade Marshal."

Karamatsov allowed himself to smile. Antonovitch tentatively extended his right hand—Karamatsov took it. Krakovski did the same—Karamatsov clasped it with his left hand. Their hands still clasped, arms entwined over each other's, forming an irregular X-shape, he told his senior officers who themselves would now be in line for colonelcys, "Victory—over the entire earth shall be mine, mine." That, Karamatsov thought, or the alternative.

Akiro Kurinami and one of Mann's men, a Private Gessler, had moved back from the overlook of The Complex, taking the steep dusty trail that Mann had explained was carved from the jungle for just such a purpose—troop movement. Kurinami didn't envy a soldier moving upward along it with a full pack. He pushed his hair back from his eyes, shifting the M-16 to his left hand. Gessler spoke no English, and Kurinami spoke no German. He hadn't even entertained the thought of conversing in Japanese—for Gessler to have known it would have been as likely as Gessler knowing ancient Aramaic. They signalled intentions instead by hand and arm signals, and now Gessler did just that.

Kurinami stopped, edging back slightly.

He heard movement as well.

Kurinami shifted the M-16 to a hard assault position, his thumb finding the selector and moving it to full auto.

A uniformed man broke from the jungle cover where the road took a bend, Kurinami started to fire.

And then he breathed. The uniform—it was German. And the face, more importantly, was one he recognized. The officer under the command of Wolfgang Mann who had travelled with them.

The private, Gessler, came to attention and did a rifle salute.

The German officer, *Hauptsturmfuehrer Hartman*, returned Gessler's salute. And then in what Kurinami considered Hartman's all but perfect but somewhat strangely pronounced English, Hartman, saluting Kurinami politely, said, "Lieutenant Kurinami—all is in readiness."

Kurinami saluted and Hartman dropped his hand. "Captain—Elaine Halverson, myself and the remainder of Colonel Mann's force have been observing The Complex. There seemed to be considerable troop movement toward what we understand is the new government building. We detected what might have been gunfire. But there has been no signal from Colonel Mann."

"Then," Hartman began, drawing his gloves slowly from his hands, "I suggest that we continue with the *standartenfuehrer* and the Herr Doctor's plan as originally set forth." He slapped dust from his left thigh with the gloves. "I shall move my men into position—the bulk of my force is already moving up. We have, however, unfortunate news. Monitoring of radio signals from North America indicates that *Hauptsturmfuehrer* Sturm has acted independently of his orders and after suffering a significant defeat at the hands of the Russians upon returning and realizing that the *standartenfuehrer* was returned to Argentina, he attacked the *standartenfuehrer*'s remaining forces. The *hauptsturmfuehrer* then proceeded to attack the Eden Project site."

"Damn," Kurinami muttered.

"*Hauptsturmfuehrer* Helmut Sturm—he is a good officer. But, unfortunately, he is also a dedicated Nazi, among the most dedicated. But we idle here, I think, too long. Shall we?" Hartman raised his eyebrows, then smiled.

Kurinami shifted the selector of his assault rifle back to safety.

As he started back up along the road, walking at Hartman's left, he could not help but wonder how many of the Eden personnel were dead, had survived five hundred years of criogenic sleep to rebuild a world—but were senselessly slaughtered.

"Stupid," he sighed. The road was steep and long ahead and he was already tired.

Madison drew the shawl tighter about her shoulders, despite the coat beneath it. Cold—she thought it was not just the temperature, but fear. Concealed beneath her right palm was the small derringer pistol Paul had given her to use. A raw cold wind gusted along the plain now, the wind getting up under her skirt, billowing it, making her legs suddenly cold. She kept walking.

As she could see in better definition the two Eden Project personnel beside the camouflage-painted pick-up truck which belonged to Father Rourke, she forced her mind elsewhere. The baby—she was certain she carried life within her, life given her by Michael, life she would return to him. When he had been shot and she and the others had been taken off by the evil Russian man, she had craved death for herself and the baby. She had thought Michael was dead. And he had given more life to her than the life which would soon swell her abdomen.

Her left hand—the right held the derringer—felt at her body.

Madison raised her head, throwing her hair back into the wind, setting a smile on her face.

Michael and Paul had told her what to do, but she had her own ideas. She hoped they would work.

One of the white coveralled, green-coated Eden personnel—a man—turned from leaning against the truck and called to her, "What can we do for you, miss? This truck is off limits to your family."

"Ohh, please—I need something from inside the truck."

"What is it you need, miss? We'll get it for you," the guard insisted as she continued to approach. But she shortened her steps, to make them appear more hesitant, to make herself appear more fearful than she really was—which was a considerable amount.

"It's a very personal thing that I need. It's very small." She hadn't figured out what it was yet, but that wasn't important. Women, as she had quickly learned from the girl she considered like a sister, Annie Rourke, always had very personal things. And men were always eager to know about them.

"I'm sorry, miss, if you can't tell me, then you'll have to take it up with Captain Dodd, OK?"

Madison stopped six feet or so from him, smiling embarrassedly. "I, ahh, I really need it, ahh, can I tell just you—if I really have to. Can I whisper it to you, sir?"

She had learned also that men liked flattery.

The man she had spoken with looked at the second man, shrugged his shoulders, then nodded his head. "OK—what can I do for you, miss?"

She approached him, looking at the ground as though studying her boots. She stopped directly before him—he was very tall. "May I whisper it in your ear, please? I'm very, very—well, embarrassed."

"Fine," the man agreed and he bent slightly forward, Madison raising on her tiptoes, touching her left hand to his shoulder as she brought her lips close to his left ear—and she stabbed the ADC .45 derringer against his left cheekbone. "What the—"

"I will shoot you. It's already cocked. And the caliber is .45—drop your rifle and tell your friend that he should please do the same."

"Shit." She watched his eyes flicker—hers didn't. "Drop your gun, Harry."

She heard his hit the ground, saw the second man—Harry—do the same.

She had one of the duplicate sets of keys Father Rourke had wisely had prepared for his fine truck. She would tell them to lie down on the ground, then she would take their rifles and then she would drive the truck away. Paul would have his second High Power pistol, Michael would have an assault rifle. She would have one too. And then they would, the three of them, get the other weapons and the things they needed and go after her friend, Annie.

211

But Madison was always raised to be a polite girl and not to be rude. So, as she held the derringer just below the man's left eye, she smiled and said, "Thank you both so very much." Neither said, "You're welcome" or anything even remotely like that.

She was cold—and she felt horribly embarrassed, sitting there trussed into the seat of the Russian helicopter, unable to move, unable to pull her clothes into position. She had no idea how long Forrest Blackburn had been gone—but she found herself wishing for his return. She was powerless to free herself—and if he were not to return, she would die here, strapped into this seat with her clothes up to her crotch and her panties pulled down. She would simply die of starvation or exposure—or perhaps the new world held other terrors she couldn't imagine. For him to violate her, he would have to free her—at least she assumed that he would.

And then she would have a chance. Maybe.

She kept repeating to herself that even though soon her last name would be Rubenstein, inside she would always be a Rourke. And a Rourke never gave up. She squinted her eyes shut—if she could concentrate on something besides fear and the cold, she would be all right, she knew.

She pictured Paul's face. It was a good face. She realized she was smiling. Someday the thinning hair would probably be gone and there would only be a fringe of hair and she could kid him about being bald and rub the top of his head and tell him she was shining it for him.

She wondered how it would be to make love.

Paul—he had told her one night, when he had spoken to her and there had been no light at all by which to see his face, that he had never.

She wanted—she wanted to give herself to him, not after

someone had taken her.

Annie Rourke opened her eyes suddenly—she had seen Forrest Blackburn in her mind and now he stood beside the bubble, opening the passenger side door. "Miss me, Annie?"

"Go to hell," she snapped as he undid the gag.

"No, I found my supplies. We'll fly there now. Should take us about two minutes or so. Then we load up." He rested his right hand on her naked right thigh and she tried to recoil from him but couldn't. "And then we're off to old mother Russia. And by the time we get there, Annie—well. You'd better decide. Either you warm up to me or you're dead—and I'll make sure it's very unpleasantly dead."

She wanted to tell him—go ahead, kill me now. She didn't. She said nothing. She had something else inside her that was a part of being a Rourke—patience. She focused her attention on Natalia. Natalia would know what to do. Annie had learned that her mind, in ways she had always heard were impossible, could see—see what could not be seen. She remembered the dream of Michael in danger. And he had been.

Annie Rourke closed her eyes—she tried to see Natalia. Natalia would know. And after a while, she felt the pressure of Blackburn's hand gone from her thigh and heard the whirring of the rotor blades. In her mind, she thought she saw Natalia, wearing a once-pretty black dress. But there was white powder on the dress and the dress was somehow torn from the hem to the waist. Natalia—Annie focused her mind on one thought. Natalia . . .

Natalia Anastasia Tiemerovna, regretting for the moment her abilities, walked ahead of the seven others. Frau Sturm carried one of the healthy if somewhat small twin

213

girls, Hugo the other one. Sarah Rourke towed along the other two Sturm children, Bertol and Willy—her wounded arm in a makeshift sling. John Rourke and Wolfgang Mann carried the stretcher—it was plastic and inflatable, making a transparent air mattress with an integral pillow which was supported by lightweight stretcher rods made of some type of high tensile-strength aluminum she guessed. On the stretcher was Helene Sturm. She had delivered two babies.

And Natalia, because of her abilities, had let the other two women carry babies or shepherd the children while she carried a gun.

Barefoot still, she moved along the tunnel, her stride no longer impeded by the dress she wore—the skirt, slit with her knife from hem to waist to give freedom of movement during the fight with the guards in the first basement, was stained with plaster dust now.

In her hands she held one of the German assault pistols—it was a decent weapon, but the magazine capacity was too small for selective fire, she thought, even with the enforced three-shot burst control.

And she had never liked weapons with built-in burst control. Somehow the feel wasn't right.

And she knew a great deal about the feel of weapons, moreso than the feel of babies. She looked back once—the infants, wrapped in towels taken from the torture chamber where Helene Sturm had delivered them, were so tiny and fragile.

Natalia had watched as John Rourke had brought the babies from Helene Sturm's body, watched the pain in Helene Sturm's eyes, and the joy there too.

She envied other women—their fragility and their strength. She kept walking.

Over her head, pipes ran, the pipes steaming, the air around her cold as she walked ahead. "Up ahead, there,

214

Fraulein Major—take the turn to the right," Wolfgang Mann called from behind her.

By the dim light of the bare, bulblike fixtures overhead interlaced between the pipes, Natalia began following the tunnel where it forked to the right.

Troops had been coming as Wolfgang Mann—Natalia had carried the stretcher with John Rourke until they had entered the tunnel—had led them to the far end of the second basement. A panel of concrete blocks moved on weights when Mann had inserted a bayonet into one of the seams between the blocks. And they had passed through into the tunnel. Then with John Rourke helping, the stretcher set down, Frau Mann and Hugo holding the twin girls, Mann had pushed the panel of blocks back into position. She had lent her own strength to it as well.

Mann had explained, smiling in the light of the hand torches which were necessary in that portion of the tunnel because there was no overhead light, that all construction was supervised by the army engineers and he had been able to have the secret passageway built into the foundation.

They had climbed for some time—the younger boys tiring, their capture and subsequent rescue taking its toll— the tunnel rising sharply. There had been another panel of concrete blocks that had to be moved aside and they had entered the service tunnel where water, electrical power and communications lines were run. Closing the panel as they had the first one, they had moved ahead, Mann warning that troops could have anticipated them and be waiting along the tunnel.

Barefoot except for the stockings which were little better than shredded now, she was grateful that animal life—at least here—was gone. Because the tunnel would otherwise have been infested with rats. Dark beyond the dull glow of the lights spaced every fifty yards or so, damp, warm enough.

She kept walking, and the tunnel bend stopped at another block wall.

"This is the last of the panels," Wolfgang Mann called from behind her.

She could hear John telling Frau Sturm in what sounded to her to be perfect German to rest easily, that all would be well. She heard the click of John Rourke's boots as he approached. Mann was beside him. In Mann's hand was the bayonet that had been secured to his left shin with strips of elastic. He operated one of the hand torches, scanning along the seams between the blocks. "Ahh— here," he murmured, as if speaking to himself, inserting the tip of the bayonet—it was similar to those used with the M-16, she noted mechanically—and prying. The concrete blocks began to move, as though somehow an irregularly shaped section were being cut from a chessboard.

Natalia threw her weight to it, as did John Rourke, and the panel moved move rapidly.

"Let's go," John Rourke whispered, running back toward Frau Sturm and the stretcher. Mann ran behind him, Natalia stepping through the opening in the wall surface— a cave, at the end or mouth perhaps a hundred yards distant, gray light. She moved the muzzle of the machine pistol left and right against the darkness. There was no movement.

"Come ahead," she whispered into the opening behind her.

John, carrying the base of the stretcher, Frau Sturm— Rourke had given her a B-Complex shot and a mild sedative as a relaxant—and then Wolfgang Mann, his handsome face in sharp contrast to the stained and ill-fitting old man's clothes he wore.

The stretcher was set down again as Frau Mann and Hugo passed through carrying the mercifully silent newborns. Then Sarah with Willy and Bertol. Then with John

Rourke and Wolfgang Mann, Natalia worked her weight against the panel of blocks, pushing it back into place.

For some reason, she began thinking of Annie.

What a wonderful young woman Annie had become.

They began moving through the cave, Natalia again taking the point. Mann called out, "Just outside, we travel up a path and then into the trees. There is a cave concealed there where there is safety."

Natalia nodded only, her eyes adjusting to the gray light—it must be sunset, she thought absently.

Annie.

For some reason, Natalia thought back to her youth. She had been on her first assignment with Vladmir, in Latin America. They had been working through Communist sympathizers who were heavily involved in the cocaine trade. She had asked Vladmir about the morality of this— serving the people of the world by dealing with such men. He had shrugged it off as necessity. But she had made a mistake—and she had fallen into the hands of the cocaine dealers and one of them had made no secret of his intention of raping her. Then he would kill her and explain that her body had been discovered, that she had been murdered by the secret police of the established government.

Natalia remembered the feel of his breath on her face. He had told her that if she were good to him, he would see to it that she died well. If not—if she resisted—she would die very hard.

She had done the only thing logic and training had dictated. She had made him feel good, aroused him and just prior to penetration, she had murdered him with his own knife. Then, her clothes torn from her body, nearly naked, she had taken up his assault rifle and fought it out with his three henchmen, killing them all and escaping in a stolen truck.

For the life of her now, Natalia Anastasia Tiemerovna could not imagine why, after so many years, she had thought of this while walking through a cave.

And for some reason again, she thought of Annie.

She could hear John Rourke, his voice little over a whisper, "After we reach this other cave, then Wolf, Natalia—the three of us—we'll go to to free Deiter Bern. It's now or never."

There was wisdom in his words. The Nazis would never expect them to attack so soon after the raid on the new government building.

But her thoughts—they drifted again to Annie Rourke and, suddenly, Natalia was unreasonably cold.

Chapter Thirty-four

The detention area was one side of a gothic-looking structure of twin towers located at the exact center of The Complex, the first official building erected there five centuries ago.

John Rourke sat, reloading the magazines for his pistols, at the mouth of the cave hidden at the fringe of the jungle, Wolfgang Mann sitting opposite him. Both men had changed to SS dark gray BDUs Mann had ordered brought there to the cave along with other supplies. Rourke was convinced of one thing—Mann was terribly thorough. While Natalia changed at the rear portion of the cave, after reminding the boys to keep their voices down, lest they be heard, Rourke and Mann discussed their predicament. Mann sketched out once again the structure of the detention area, with a stick in the dirt between their feet.

"So the only entrance to the building is through the courtyard at the center, one gate at the front and one gate at the back."

"That is correct, Herr Doctor. And entering from the front as we must because the rear gates are not used, it is then somehow necessary to enter the building at the left side of the courtyard. When you first view the twin towers, do not be mistaken by their antique appearance. The exteriors are quite medieval, but the interiors are thoroughly modern. The walls on both the outside and the interior are cylindrical. In the tower at the very top is the detention area for political prisoners such as Deiter Bern. He is the only one there now unless new arrests have been made since I departed with the expeditionary force. It is fourteen floors above the level of the ground. But I like your idea for escaping once Deiter Bern is freed."

"It's the only way." Rourke nodded. "This vehicle— freshly stolen?"

"Yes, it will not be recognized as stolen from the internal security forces."

"But the guards will recognize your face, know that Natalia and I aren't in the SS."

"By then the gate will be opened." Mann smiled. "And we have weapons. Remember, Herr Doctor, it is not important that I survive. What is important is that you reach the fourteenth level of the tower and free Dieter Bern, you and Major Tiemerovna, and then get him from the tower to the communications center which is across the street. On the ground floor, there are guards. There is the high staircase which leads to the upper level. There, the communications facility is actually located—television and radio. The engineering controls are there as well. Major Tiemerovna, you are certain, can operate these controls if necessary?"

"She's very good at electronics. Don't worry. It's getting there that's hard, and fast enough that they don't cut the power on us. Where should the leader be?"

"After one has entered the courtyard, the building on the right is his headquarters. It is also where he lives. It is very secure, the twin towers."

Rourke started to speak—but he turned, Natalia approaching. Her hair was caught up under the peaked BDU cap, her uniform identical to theirs except that it buttoned to the left, as women's clothing normally did. At her waist was a holstered German machine pistol. Slung from her right shoulder, the uniform purse—he knew why it appeared so heavy.

John Rourke stood. "Ready?"

"Yes." And Natalia laughed.

The vehicle was electrically powered, little larger than the golf carts of five centuries earlier and Wolfgang Mann was at the wheel, Rourke sitting beside him, Natalia in the seat behind, the warmth of the air in the open top vehicle a good sensation.

The vehicle slowed, The Complex main entrance guard quadrupled since Rourke had passed it on the way to the new government building to free Helene Sturm.

Two guards approached the vehicle on Wolfgang Mann's side. Rourke's hands were between his legs—he sat on one of the twin Detonics .45s and his hands were within inches of it.

The closer of the two guards, his voice loud, filled with authority, proclaimed, "Papers!"

Wolfgang Mann handed over a folded set of documents, and as the man who had spoken a second earlier took them, Rourke could hear the man's hushed whisper, "All is in readiness, Herr *Standartenfuehrer*—the signal has been received."

"Very good, Hartman," Mann whispered.

And then the voice of the guard was raised once again. "These papers are in order—allow this vehicle to pass," and the papers were returned. Mann eased the controls and the electric vehicle glided ahead.

Mann, not turning his head, said over the wind around them, "We are fortunate my men were able to insert themselves as planned. Hartman—he is my most trusted captain—he transferred to my unit from SS security two years ago. When I gave the radio signal for the attack to begin, he carried out the first phase personally as instructed. We are fortunate he was successful in taking over the guard barracks located by the main entrance. Otherwise . . ." Mann let it hang.

John Rourke moved the little Detonics from beneath him. A fine gun to shoot but uncomfortable to sit on. He didn't like being dependent on good fortune—because it had never been anything on which to depend . . .

Mann's troops had not moved beyond taking the main entrance. It was the plan that they hold the front entrance under the guise of the SS security team and go no further lest word reach the leader and Deiter Bern's immediate execution be ordered.

It was a good plan as plans went for insanely dangerous activities, Rourke mused as again the vehicle slowed. Once again, the Detonics mini gun was beneath his rear end. He glanced down between his feet. The gray canvaslike bag contained his musette bag, the second Detonics Combat Master, the two Scoremasters, the Python, the Gerber (the A.G. Russell Sting IA Black Chrome was beneath his uniform) and, more important than the weapons, his medical gear. Clamps for the artery. The scalpel for the incision. The small forceps for removal of the capsule which contained the electrode and the explosive charge which would release the curarelike synthetic into Bern's bloodstream.

And he knew the contents of Natalia's bag—her revolvers, spare magazines for the machine pistol, and more important than her weapons, the lock pick set which she would use to remove the shackle from Bern's neck after the operation was completed.

On the seat between Rourke and Wolfgang Mann was another gray canvaslike bag identical to Rourke's, and Rourke knew the contents there as well, like the medical equipment and the uniforms, brought to the cave by military personnel loyal to Wolfgang Mann. The special gear needed to cross the booby-trapped room, special gear

222

Rourke had requested of Mann after agreeing to go with him to Argentina and attempt the rescue of Deiter Bern.

The vehicle stopped, the gates to the twin towers and the courtyard closed. They should not have been. "We have trouble," Mann murmured.

It was a trouble Rourke was well familiar with.

"We cannot crash through the gates with such a vehicle. And I will be recognized as soon as the guards approach."

"Follow my lead," John Rourke almost whispered.

His hands moved closer to his crotch, so he could reach for the small Detonics pistol he sat on. He cleared his throat three times in rapid succession. It was a signal to Natalia.

She cleared her throat twice in response.

The guards approached.

The nearest of the guards—a lieutenant in the SS—started to speak. And then his jaw dropped. He started to run. John Rourke stood to his full height in the vehicle, firing the little Detonics .45 across the windshield top and into the face of the SS lieutenant. He kept firing, a single shot for each of the men in the guard detachment, Natalia's machine pistol opening up from behind him, cutting down more of the SS security personnel, three-round bursts, a burst per man.

Rourke jumped to the ground from the front seat, shouting to Wolfgang Mann as Rourke jammed the little Detonics into his beltline and grabbed up his case, shouldering it. "Better be right that fence isn't electrified!"

Rourke started to run, the distance to the gates some ten yards still, the German machine pistol in the holster at his belt coming into his hands, no time to fold down the forward support. As both fists tightened on the pistol grip, Rourke stabbed the pistol toward the nearest of the enemy and fired, a three-round burst nearly severing the man's head from the neck. The SS man fell back.

Rourke was at the gates, turning, more guards streaming

from the guard station just outside the gates. Natalia had mentioned it to him earlier—in passing—that she didn't like burst control. Neither did John Rourke as he fired the machine pistol, wasting three rounds on one man when a four-round burst would have taken out two. He fired a third burst, conscious that only three more bursts remained.

Natalia was running now, firing her pistol, Mann beside her, one of the machine pistols in his hands as well.

Rourke stabbed the weapon into the holster at his hip, took three steps back from the ornamental wrought iron gates and ran, jumping, grasping for the pointed spikes at the top of the fence.

Both gloved fists closed over them. Rourke's right leg found a purchase, his right foot bracing between two of the verticals as he pulled himself up, then rolled over, dropping to the flagstones on the far side in a crouch, his legs taking the spring, the machine pistol back in his hands.

Guards from the entrance to the tower on the left—their destination.

Rourke fired the machine pistol, cutting down one, then another, then a third guard—the pistol was empty now.

Rourke buttoned out the magazine and rammed a fresh one up the well, working the slide release, the slide trailing forward as Rourke touched the trigger—the pistol would not fire until in battery. Another burst—another guard dead.

Natalia was coming over the fence, jumping like a cat to the ground beside him, the machine pistol firing in her hands while she was in midair.

She rolled across her back, coming to her knees, firing again.

Mann—was clambering over the fence—his right sleeve was stuck. "Go," he shouted.

Rourke rasped, "Bullshit," firing out the remaining bursts in his machine pistol toward the onslaught of guards.

Natalia was running for the entrance to the left tower, a machine pistol in each hand—she wasn't strong enough to fire them accurately that way, Rourke realized. She was spraying both weapons toward the oncoming guards.

Rourke reloaded.

Mann jumped, clear of the fence, hitting the flagstone hard, Rourke glancing back to him once. But Mann was already up, running, limping badly on his left foot. "Broken or sprained, I think!"

"Wonderful—*wunderbar!*" Rourke shouted, running too now, turning, backing around, firing the machine pistol behind them toward the gates as guards from the outside frantically worked to open them, Mann limping past him.

Rourke emptied the weapon, downing six more men.

He turned and ran—gunfire hammered into the flagstones beneath his feet, impacting the exterior walls of the tower.

He threw himself through the doorway, Natalia in a crouch there, one of the machine pistols on the floor beside her, the second firing toward the guards at the far end of the cylindrical first floor.

Rourke picked up her weapon, reloaded it with one of his magazines, then reloaded his own.

Mann began firing. Rourke opened fire, Natalia's machine pistol empty—throwing it down, she picked up the second machine pistol.

Rourke rammed a fresh magazine up the butt of his weapon, charging forward, Natalia running beside him, Mann limping after them as Rourke glanced back.

Three guards remained blocking the elevator banks—three guards went down.

At the elevator banks, they stopped. "Gonna have to be," Rourke proclaimed, glancing toward Mann's injured foot.

"Agreed!" Natalia pushed the call button and the eleva-

225

tor door to their left opened, Rourke reloading as Mann limped past. Natalia snapped, "Cover you."

Rourke dodged inside, his left hand working the buckle to loosen the uniform gunbelt and let it drop to the elevator floor, his right hand, still holding the machine pistol, punching the floor button. As the doors slapped shut, Natalia slipped through between them, the elevator beginning to rise.

"If they should cut the power, Herr Doctor . . ."

."If they cut the power, Dieter Bern's dead anyway."

The bag on the floor beside him, Rourke crouched, drawing out his gunbelt with the Python and the magazine holder. He slung the belt around his waist. Then the double rig for the twin stainless Detonics pistols.

Already reloading the fired-out Detonics Combat Master, Rourke eyed the floor counter above the doors.

He glanced to Natalia—she was buckling on her own guns. As she finished, she ripped the peaked BDU cap from her head, her almost black hair cascading to her shoulders.

Rourke threw off his own hat. He smiled. It somehow wouldn't have the same effect to someone watching.

Mann was on his right knee, reloading the machine pistol. "Ready!"

Rourke nodded, licking his lips.

The elevator stopped—the doors opened. Rourke had one of the Scoremasters in each hand as he stepped through—two uniformed guards at the far end of the corridor. Rourke did a double tap with each pistol, at hip level, both guards going down, one man's machine pistol discharging into the ceiling, chunks of accoustical tile littering downward.

Rourke ran forward, shouting to Natalia, "Fix the elevators!"

"Of course!" The sound of rapid bursts of machine pistol fire. "They are fixed!"

A doorway at the far end of the corridor—Rourke ran for it. No one visible—a switch on the wall beside it.

Rourke twisted half right, his left foot snapping up and out, a double *tae kwon do* kick and the glass panel over the switch smashing, then the button depressing. The door glided open.

Mann's information was good so far, Rourke reflected.

He ran through the open doorway—at the far end of the well-lit room was a cot, and a very frail-seeming form was on the cot, a chain leading from a collar around the figure's neck to the wall. It was Deiter Bern and two feet in front of where Rourke stood were the first of the photoelectric eyes that would release the synthetic curare-tipped spikes.

"To further diminish any chance of Deiter Bern being freed, the entrance to and from the section in which he is confined—the only means in or out, and my best commandoes have confirmed this—constantly broadcasts an identical electronic impulse. Should the current at the doorway be disrupted, an effect occurs similar to that of the claymore-type mines used prior to the warfare between the Superpowers. Thousands of tiny needles the size of slivers which have been positioned at strategic locations throughout the walls and ceiling and floor of the room are released, traveling at such high velocity and of such infinitesimal size that they will penetrate up to a six millimeter thickness of armor plate."

Wolfgang Mann's words when he and Rourke had first spoken that night at the outskirts of the camp—for some reason Rourke remembered them, he felt, almost verbatim.

But John Rourke had planned ahead.

Photoelectric eyes were visible framing the room, on both walls and on the ceiling and on the floor, forming what he realized and had realized from the start was an impenetrable spider web of light.

But John Rourke had planned ahead.

"Natalia—let's get at it."

She nodded.

Wolfgang Mann lay prone by the entry door, four machine pistols beside him, one in his hands. He looked up. "Be careful—both of you."

"Do you want something for your foot? A pain killer—there's not time to do much else," Rourke asked him.

"Pain will sharpen my senses, Herr Doctor. I will take nothing which would dull them now."

John Rourke only nodded.

The figure chained to the wall, lying prostrate on the couch, began to stir—Rourke looked back to Wolf Mann. "Does Deiter Bern know you?"

"Yes, he was my professor many years ago."

"Call to him. Tell him to lie still—that help is coming," and Rourke turned on his heel and walked past Mann and from the room into the corridor. Mentally, he was calculating how long it would take impassioned fully equipped storm troopers to race up fourteen flights of stairs with some infuriated Nazi officer shouting at them.

He shrugged it off—time had always been the critical factor at any event.

He started to jog toward the cylindrically shaped outside wall at his right. Natalia was already there, setting charges of the German equivalent of plastique. "I think it is ready. Mann explained the chemical composition of their explosives—they are roughly sixty percent more potent than what I am used to with American C-4. We should take cover," she said, turning, running as she strung out wire behind her. Rourke joined her, running toward the main corridor, rounding the corner there, taking cover alongside the useless elevator banks.

She touched two exposed wires together, Rourke folding her into his arms as the explosion rocked the floor beneath his feet.

He looked around the corner from the elevator banks—a cloud of smoke and dust, and there were acrid fumes on the air.

He ran toward the source of the explosion, Natalia's boot heels clicking on the hard floor surface beside him.

A hole—approximately five by five—had been blown in the wall.

Rourke peered out. Below him troops were forming—but no marksman would hit a moving target fourteen floors straight up.

He took Natalia's bag from her, securing it cross-body with his musette bag, opposite the heavier bag which contained his medical equipment and more spare ammo.

Natalia had Mann's bag, open, uncoiling rope from it and setting the rope beside it.

She extracted what looked like a large CO2 pistol, a three-bladed spearlike object protruding from the muzzle.

Natalia pushed past him, leaning out the hole in the wall. Gunfire cracked uselessly from below.

Natalia looked upward. She raised the pistol with the peculiar projectile toward the parapets which crowned the tower, some twenty feet above them.

"*Merde.*" He grinned.

"Hmm." She smiled, settling the pistol in both hands. She fired.

The spearlike projectile shot upwards, the rope secured midway along the shaft uncoiling from the light grasp in Rourke's hands. Rourke tugged at the rope then, the rope going taut—the rappelling hook had taken hold along the parapets. He hoped.

Natalia took the rope from his hands, Rourke helping her up into the sill of the five-by-five hole made by the explosion. Mann's bag—was slung again from her side, a length of rope knotted about her waist. Rourke still held the other rope.

"Be careful."

She looked at him and laughed, then kissed him hard on the mouth, swinging out on the rope now, her legs extending, her feet impacting the stone wall of the medievallike structure, pushing her off again. She swung out into air space, then toward the wall again, her feet wide apart, the rope secured around her waist in a hitch.

Natalia's gloved hand reached to Mann's bag. Rourke looked beneath her—some sort of heavy equipment was being brought in below.

He looked back along the corridor toward the main corridor—no movement there.

Rourke turned his attention back to Natalia—she was edging over slightly, a surveyor's transit, only smaller. She began securing an amorphous mound of plastique against the wall. Mann had shown her photographs of which building to site on to be certain of the spot where to place the charge.

She was connecting the wires now.

"Ready," Natalia shouted.

Rourke tugged at the rope, drawing Natalia back along the wall surface, Natalia using her feet to rappel along it, near to the hole in the wall now. Rourke reached for her. His hands closed around her waist and he pulled her inside.

From her belt, she unhitched the wire connections.

"Stand back," she whispered, touching the wires together. The building seemed to tremble, the floor beneath Rourke's feet shaking.

Rourke peered through the opening again—a hole, almost five feet in diameter, in the exterior wall—he hoped blown all the way through.

Below them, fourteen stories down, men were scattering, bricks and debris raining down still.

Rourke felt a smile cross his lips.

Gunfire from the main corridor. It would be Mann, repelling SS security forces.

"Ready?"

He looked at Natalia. "Yeah, ready."

Natalia with Rourke's help climbed back into the opening, Rourke climbing up behind her. Her arms folded around his neck, her face inches from his. He kissed her, then closed his gloved hands along the rope and launched himself outward, Natalia's legs tucked up, his feet taking the impacts of both their body weights against the wall, then pushing out again. Again, their bodies crashed back toward the wall surface, Rourke's feet taking the impact, his knees flexing with it. Three feet from the hole leading into Deiter Bern's cell.

Rourke could see the cot through the hole.

His arms ached with the combined weight of Natalia's body and his own. He edged along the wall surface, looking down once. Whatever the piece of heavy equipment was, it seemed in position.

The hole—he was nearly to it. Another foot.

He could barely straddle it, one foot at each edge. Natalia—she edged her feet out, slipping down, through the hole. He could feel as she drew in the slack from the rope.

Rourke swung his feet outward, then through the hole, bracing with his left hand, edging off the base of the hole in the wall, then dropping down to the floor.

Sixteen feet from Deiter Bern's bed, debris less than a foot from the bed. It had been a gamble with Bern's life— but so far they had won, he reflected. Good luck always worried him.

Rourke ran toward Bern's bed, setting down his medical and spare ammo bag, opening it as Natalia bent beside Bern on the opposite side of the cot. She touched gingerly at the shackle ring around Bern's neck. "I've never seen a lock quite like this. I don't know, John."

"Just be ready," Rourke hissed, handing her the surgical gloves. Natalia held them as he inserted his already powdered hands inside them. The clamp for the artery—if he left it clamped too long, death. He was gambling that he could work without it.

The carotid was located approximately one and one-half inches below the surface of the skin. Unconsciousness would result if the artery were blocked for five seconds. Death would result in twelve.

Natalia scrubbed over the incision mark with antiseptic, Rourke drawing the pre-sterilized scalpel from the sheath which Natalia held for him. "If I ask for that clamp, be real quick."

Bern asked in German, "How are . . ." Rourke merely nodded, Natalia administering the injection which would render the old man unconscious.

He looked at her eyes—their blueness—love, assurance. Even if Sarah were pregnant, he still couldn't abandon Natalia, because she had surrendered the rest of her life to be with him. And he loved her in a way he had never loved, never could.

He touched the scalpel to the skin, beginning the incision over the exact spot of the scar. "Sponge," he hissed, reaching to Natalia's outstretched hand, drawing the sponge from the sterile packing—blood. He threw down the sponge. He thought he could see the device—set beside the artery in a cyst cut in the flesh. Its mere presence—he shuddered thinking. There was no way to tell if dislodging it would cause it to explode—and cause Bern's death and the loss of Rourke's fingers.

He folded back the skin flap, using the tiny forceps. It was like removing a bullet, and no more complicated than that. Unless . . .

He closed the forceps over the capsule—slowly now, he started to extract it. The forceps caught against the steel collar circumscribing Bern's neck. "Damn," Rourke snarled.

"Here, I'll tug up on it. It's—it's coming," Natalia

whispered.

Rourke twisted, Bern's body lurching once—it was not a proper anesthetic, but had it been there would have been no time to revive him. Rourke tugged—the forceps came, and with them, the pellet.

Rourke rose from his knees, running toward the hole in the wall, flinging the pellet and the forceps out through it.

He recrossed the room, gunfire again from the doorway beyond the invisible web of photoelectric eyes. Mann was returning gunfire. A stray shot could trigger the photoelectric eyes.

Rourke dropped to his knees beside Deiter Bern, Natalia already offering a sponge, Rourke filling it with blood, throwing it down to the floor beside him. He folded back the skin flap, looking to Natalia again. He took the surgical stapler from her, stapling the wound closed—no time for stitches. He drew his hands back, Natalia spraying the wound with the antiseptic/healing agent Munchen had given them. The instruments were Munchen's as well.

Rourke threw down the stapler; Natalia began to bandage the incision. Rourke tore the surgical gloves from his hands, casting them down.

"Here—let me finish," Rourke told her, completing the dressing. He glanced at Natalia's hands—the left held a probe, the right a pick as she attacked the lock on the collar around Bern's neck. To have severed the chain by some other means and interrupted the electrical current could have triggered the claymore-type devices secreted in the walls and ceiling, Mann had told them—and Rourke had no idea of the range or direction.

"This isn't a normal lock, John. I don't think—"

"You've got to," Rourke told her quietly.

She looked up at him. "Yes, I do, don't I?" She exhaled loudly, peering again at the lock, working the probe. "Wait—wait a minute. Maybe—yes."

Gunfire again. Mann shouted, "Herr Doctor, I can't

hold them much longer. Hurry!"

Rourke didn't answer, securing the dressing in place with tape.

Natalia was twisting the pick. "This could take hours, but—I don't think—I don't think that it will." She withdrew the pick and twisted the probe once, the lock popping open. "Five points," she said, smiling, "for the KGB's Chicago espionage school, hmm?"

Rourke leaned across Bern's unconscious body and touched her face with his hands. "I love you very much. Remember that always. I don't know what's gonna happen, but remember that—now help me with him." Natalia put away her picks as Rourke pried the collar open and slowly removed it from Bern's neck, lest some booby trap were present even Wolfgang Mann hadn't known of.

None was.

Natalia threw down Mann's bag, Rourke reaching into it for the web harness, slipping it onto his shoulders, Natalia straightening the straps. It gave him a feeling of *déjà vu*— the rescue of Paul from the burning helicopter. How many days ago?

The harness strapped across his chest, he eased the frail-seeming old man from the cot, propping him up, Natalia taking his weight then as Rourke stooped. Rourke hauled Bern up, onto his back, Natalia buckling the straps as Rourke settled into the added weight.

"Hurry," she hissed, running toward the opening in the wall, Mann's bag slung again at her side.

She was already clambering through the opening, the rope in her hands—and she swung away.

Heavy caliber fire from the ground below—Rourke looked down to the crew-served weapon. Some sort of recoilless rifle, Rourke realized. "Natalia!"

But she was already climbing along the wall, upward, the weapon discharging again, a chunk of the wall surface blowing away under the impact, mere feet from her body.

Rourke tucked back, Bern's weight heavy on his back.

He peered through the opening again. Natalia was nearly to the parapets, the recoilless rifle discharging again, another chunk blowing out of the wall.

Natalia—he looked up—was gone, but the rope snaked down. Rourke reached for it, the crack and whine of the recoilless rifle from below. Rourke drew back, a chunk of wall two feet to the right from the hole blowing away. The rope snapped back, Rourke reaching for it and catching it. He locked it into the rings at the front of the harness, then climbed through the hole, ducking lest he injure the unconscious man on his back.

He tugged at the rope, feeling it draw upward as he swung out, his hand gripping it through his synthetic BDU leather gloves. The winch from the bag Mann had carried and Natalia had taken from him. He could hear it cranking upward, then the crack and whine of the recoilless rifle again. Chunks of brick and mortar were pelting him as he shielded his eyes, but faced the explosion to protect Deiter Bern with his body.

The winch—his body wrenched with it—but he was nearly to the parapets, Natalia's arms reaching down to him, his hands taking hers. She threw her weight back and he half fell over the parapets, to his knees.

"Are you all right?"

"Think so," Rourke breathed, Natalia already freeing Bern of the harness. "You stay," Rourke told her, shrugging out of the harness as he stood, Bern safe for the moment unless the accurate range of the recoilless rifle could make it this high. They were on the roof of the tower, one of the highest points in The Complex, the parapets protecting them from view. He began feeding the winch rope down through his belt.

Rourke ran to them now again, taking the single rappelling rope, knotting his hands into it, then vaulting over, rappelling downward, toward the opening into Bern's ceil, kicking away. slamming back, then kicking away again, feeding out the rope, the gloves starting to fray with it. Leather was better than any synthetic for gloves, he thought absently.

He was down, to the level of Bern's cell, and he swung out now, along the wall laterally, for the first opening Natalia had cut, the second rope attached through his belt still. The recoilless rifle fired again.

But he was nearly to the first opening. He pushed away again, swinging toward it, his right foot near the opening—he walked it off, dropping through, hooking one hand into the rope which had taken him down, one of the Scoremasters in his right fist, the thumb safety wiping down as he fired into the SS security force barricading Mann into the cell from which he could not escape. One security man down, then another and another, Rourke tucking back along the wall as gunfire hammered toward him. The first rope was drawn in after him and he released it now, ramming a fresh magazine up the butt of the Scoremaster, plaster flying around him. A fresh-loaded pistol in his right fist, a nearly loaded one in his left, Rourke stepped forward, firing, cutting down more of the SS security personnel. "Wolf!" Rourke shouted. "Run for it!"

The Scoremasters empty, Rourke stuffed them into his waistband, and as each hand became free, drew one of the twin Detonics Combat Masters, firing into the knot of security men. Mann was coming now, running along the corridor, dragging his left leg, firing the machine pistol behind him. Rourke reached to the floor, grabbing a handful of empty shell casings from his .45s.

Mann passed him, half diving for the rope at the opening. "Use the double rope for the winch," Rourke shouted as Mann disappeared through the opening. Rourke fired out his pistols, men going down, reaching for the single rope, grasping it, hurtling himself through the opening, the recoilless rifle firing again, chunks of the wall surface powdering under the impact.

Mann was swinging free, the rope going taut—the winch was working.

Rourke rappelled along the surface of the wall, laterally, reaching the second wall opening. Mann was nearly to the parapets above now, the double rope trailing behind him.

Rourke took the handful of brass from his BDU trouser pocket, hurtling it through the opening into Bern's former cell, the cartridge casings flying toward the invisible lattice web that would trigger the poisoned wire fragments—he heard explosions, screams of SS security personnel too close to the door opening.

The double rope snaked downward, Rourke catching hold of it, his arms nearly wrenched from his sockets as the rope was winched upward. Gunfire beneath him—Rourke glanced back and down. One of the SS security men was firing his machine pistol through the first opening.

Rourke held to the rope with his left fist, drawing the Python with his right hand, double actioning it downward, two slugs into the face of the SS man, the body tumbling through the opening and downward fourteen floors.

Rourke reached the parapets, hurtling himself over, rolling to the momentary safety of the rooftops.

"John?"

Rourke looked at Natalia and smiled. "So far so good, huh?"

Rourke began feeding fresh magazines into the .45s. The Scoremasters were freshly loaded now. Then the Combat Masters. He dumped the cartridges from the Python, using a speedloader to replenish the cylinder, casting aside empty brass, pocketing the four still-loaded ones.

"Now what?" Natalia asked.

But Mann was already answering the question, a pocket transmitter in his hands, in German almost shouting over the roar of the recoilless rifle, "This is the Wolf—attack. Attack! Send in the Condor! Attack!"

There was an opening on the roof from below. Rourke knew what to expect, catching Bern—the old man was beginning to stir—up into his arms, running with him toward the far edge beside the parapets, air conditioning units built into the roofline, a small shed as well. He secreted Bern beside the best cover he could find.

Natalia was helping Wolfgang Mann, whose left foot was dragging badly now.

Rourke settled the Python in both fists, waiting for the inevitable.

"We are ready, Herr Lieutenant!"

Kurinami nodded, settling back, giving the webbing harness of the seat a good luck tug. Elaine Halverson was shouting something to him from beyond the perimeter of the mini-copter's rotor blades. It sounded like, "Be careful!".

He had every intention of that.

He spoke into the headset's teardrop microphone. "Colonel Mann—the Condor is flying!" He pulled on the throttle and the rotor speed increased, the mini-helicopter airborne suddenly, skimming over the grassy plain where Mann's troops had stayed—and they were already moving ahead, Kurinami flying low over them, toward the main entrance of The Complex. It would be the most intricate flying of his life. He had studied the plans for The Complex on the flight down from Argentina, memorized the height of every building—and the width of the opening.

He was nearing The Complex entrance now, fighting on the ground below him, men dressed in the steel-gray BDUs of SS security but with white arm bands, fighting hand to hand with men dressed identically except for swastika arm bands.

Groundfire was being aimed toward him, the wind lashing at his face now, tearing at his skin. If he slowed, he'd have a better chance of threading the needle and getting through The Complex doors. But if he slowed, the ground-fire would have a better chance of getting to him.

He heard a ricochet against the framework for the fabric body of the fuselage—his decision was made. Kurinami throttled out all the way, threading the needle. He breathed, judging he'd missed the wall surface with his rotor blades on the portside by less than a foot.

Ahead—the twin towers, what looked like a recoilless rifle firing up toward the one on his left, fighting visible on the rooftop.

The Python fired out, Rourke hammered it down across the skull of one of the SS men. Natalia's knife flashed open, a scream as steel contacted flesh. Wolfgang Mann fired a machine pistol.

Rourke found the butts of the Scoremasters, the Python fallen from his grasp—he fired both pistols simultaneously point-blank into two SS security personnel.

Natalia sprang past him, rolling, catching up an assault rifle, her right hand hurtling the Bali-Song—it buried up to the hilt in the chest of an SS man coming up onto the roof.

Natalia, to her knees now, firing, the assault rifle spitting death from her hands. The Scoremasters in Rourke's hands were empty now and he smashed one of the pistols into the forehead of an SS man charging for Natalia's back.

He stabbed both pistols into his belt, drawing the twin Combat Masters, firing simultaneously with both hands. Bodies fell.

Natalia was to the roof hatch, firing an assault rifle from each hand down the ladder leading from the fourteenth floor below them.

Rourke looked skyward—the mini-helicopter. Kurinami.

Rourke ran toward Natalia, snatching up one of the German assault rifles, firing down the ladderwell at the SS personnel, Natalia firing beside him.

He heard an explosion from the courtyard below. Gunfire—automatic weapons.

Beneath them, SS men were fleeing now—downward.

Rourke stepped back, kicking closed the roof hatch. He threw the empty assault rifle to the roof surface.

He walked backwards away from the hatch, Natalia wrenching her Bali-Song from the chest of a dead man, wiping the blade clean against the man's fatigue blouse, then flicking it closed.

She began speedloading her revolvers.

Fresh magazines for the .45s—two guns loaded, then all four.

He picked up his Python from the roof surface. It seemed unscathed. He speedloaded it, dumping the emptied Safariland unit into his musette bag.

Kurinami—the mini-chopper dubbed Condor was coming, hovering now.

Rourke ran across the roof, Natalia guarding the hatchway, a captured assault rifle in each hand.

He dropped to his knees beside Deiter Bern. He had given Bern a B-Complex shot, then a mild stimulant, guessing at the overall state of the man's health. Too strong a stimulant could have caused death. Bern was stirring now, talking as though half asleep, Mann cradling the old man's head in his arms, speaking soothingly to him in German. "We've gotta get him airborne," Rourke cautioned.

Rourke looked overhead—the Condor was settling.

In the jump seat behind Kurinami, Rourke finished tightening the restraint harness, the semiconscious Deiter Bern talking incoherently. Rourke rolled back the eyelids—

the eyes were nearly closed. He tapped Kurinami on the shoulder. The Japanese turned his head, nodding as Rourke jumped back, falling into a crouch. The machine started airborne—Natalia was still near the hatchway, Mann lying on the roof beside where she stood, a machine pistol in each hand, Natalia with an assault rifle in each hand.

Natalia smiled.

Rourke reached up, the helicopter hovering, his hands closing over the skid as the helicopter lurched fully upward, his arms feeling momentarily as if they would be wrenched from their sockets. Suddenly nothing was below him except the street, more than fourteen stories below, the wind of the slipstream tearing at his face, his hair, the collar tabs of the BDU blouse lacerating his cheeks and his neck.

The communications building loomed ahead, the Condor beginning to drop, downward, downward—Rourke jumped clear, landing on the flat tarmac of the roof, rolling, coming to his knees, then to his feet, a Scoremaster in each hand as he ran to get clear of the landing helicopter.

The chopper was down.

Rourke looked away for a moment, toward the street six stories below him—fighting—but civilians were joining now, joining to fight beside the uniformed men with the white arm bands who fought for democracy.

Rourke ran back along the roof, toward the landed helicopter. Kurinami was already free of the pilot's seat, unbuckling Deiter Bern. "Starting to regain consciousness, John!"

"I hope he does in time to at least talk," Rourke shouted back.

The wiry Japanese naval lieutenant caught the frail Deiter Bern up into his arms. "I'm ready," Kurinami shouted.

Rourke only nodded, running now toward the roof egress, the artificial lighting of the dome of The Complex several hundred feet above him casting eerie shadows on the rooftop, giving his stainless steel .45s a dull, coppery glow.

He reached the doorway—a double *tae kwan doe* kick with his left foot at the glass of the doorway, the glass shattering. Rourke reached through, hammering down the panic bar and wrenching the door open outward.

The communications center.

Chapter Thirty-five

Paul Rubenstein had taken what he considered the direct approach—with the Browning High Power Madison had found for him in the truck, he had approached Dodd just as word of Madison's stealing the truck had reached the Eden Project commander. He had put the muzzle of the High Power to Dodd's head. After that, it had merely been a matter of keeping it there while Dodd had ordered the truck loaded with provisions from John Rourke's second pick-up truck, the gear in the tents they had used and, most important, the weapons.

The cammie-painted pick-up truck was less than eight feet from him now, Michael already aboard in the back of the truck, Madison with the truck started. It was simply a matter of walking eight feet with the gun to Dodd's head.

Paul Rubenstein started to walk—and Christoper Dodd's right hand slapped toward the pistol. Paul turned, recovering his balance, but started to fall, the sickening feeling in his stomach that suddenly all was lost.

But as he fell, he heard a clear, German-accented voice.

"You will not move, Captain Dodd—or you will be shot."

Munchen.

"Doctor Munchen, stay outa this," Dodd snapped. "We need these people's vehicle, their weapons. We may need them if your German friends attack again."

Paul Rubenstein turned his eyes away, a dust devil rising as Doctor Munchen fired a three-round burst from his machine pistol. "The next time, Captain Dodd, you will be dead. As ranking officer here, I represent the interests of my commander. And hopefully also, the interests of reason. No helicopter can be spared to aid them—this is a military necessity. But it is a moral necessity that they be allowed to try—to rescue Annie Rourke. Help Herr Rubenstein to his feet, Captain—and do nothing which will provoke your death."

Dodd's eyes flickered in the lamplight from the nearest tent pole—and then Dodd, very slowly, began to move. He reached down, stopping, Paul Rubenstein holding the High Power in his right hand, his left arm going over Dodd's shoulders.

To his feet. With Dodd half supporting him, Paul moved toward the truck, reaching it then, shaking his left arm loose of Dodd, Madison reaching down to him. Paul clambored aboard.

As he settled behind the wheel, he told Madison, "Keep your rifle on Dodd—he moves, kill the son of a bitch."

"Yes, Paul." She nodded, thrusting the muzzle of the M-16 through the open passenger-side window.

Paul Rubenstein released the brake, putting the Ford into gear. He shouted past Madison and through her open window. "Doctor Munchen. God bless all of you—I hope you find what you want."

Doctor Munchen pulled himself to attention, then curtly bowed his head, nodding. "And to you, Herr Rubenstein—this God, may He bless you as well in your endeavors. I am sorry that no more can be done to help."

"I know that." Paul nodded, then cut the wheel hard left as he eased clutch pressure, turning out of the lamplight and toward the night. Annie . . .

Annie Rourke had made her decision. She watched now as Forrest Blackburn loaded supplies aboard the helicopter. When he made his move, she would make it seem as though she realized there was no choice but to surrender to his desires. She would not make it obvious. Tears—they would help.

And he would undo the straps which bound her. She would hesitate, then pretend that she would accept him.

From the gear he had found cached, she had noted several objects of interest. Two M-16s. A full flap military holster of some fabric material, inside the holster a pistol. She had watched him as he had checked it, cleaned it of the cosmolenelike substance that had protected it. It was something she recognized from her father's arms locker—a Beretta 92SB-F, the military 9mm adopted just before The Night of The War. But the object of greatest interest lay in the sheath on the opposite side of the belt—a bayonet for an M-16.

A knife. She could kill with that as he folded his arms about her, as he touched her.

Natalia.

It was what Natalia would have done—had done?

Chapter Thirty-six

Rourke kicked through the glass door at the base of the steps, an alarm sounding now, high pitched, agonizing to the ears, his left hand wrenching down the panic bar. He threw open the door, passing through first. Gunfire hammered toward him and he drew back, shards of glass left in the doorway shattering now under the impact of assault rifle bullets. Rourke snapped both Scoremasters through the open doorway, firing in tandem, emptying both pistols as he dodged to the side of the corridor opposite the doorway. Two of the SS security personnel were down.

Past them, around the bend in the corridor and then down a single flight of open stairs—the second floor was the communications center.

But to get past them. Kurinami—Rourke could see the Japanese in the doorway, having rested his burden of Deiter Bern.

One of the German machine pistols was in Kurinami's hand. "What do we do?"

Rourke reloaded the Scoremasters, nodding toward the end of the hallway.

Kurinami smiled. "I was afraid you would say that. "Let's go," and Kurinami charged forward, Rourke beside him, the .45s spitting, the German machine pistol firing bursts, a cry issuing from Kurinami's throat. *"Banzai!"*

Security men going down, gunfire hammering into the

corridor walls, Rourke feeling something tugging at his left rib cage, firing out both Scoremasters. He stabbed the empty pistols into his belt, drawing the twin Combat Masters, firing as they closed with the remaining SS.

Kurinami's right hand flashed outward, then his left, a bayonet in each—Rourke had seen them on the man's belt earlier. The knives arced outward, downward, right to left, screams from the SS security personnel.

Rourke's little .45s empty, Rourke stabbed them into his hip pockets, grasping the butt of the Gerber MkII, hacking with the spear point blade into flesh.

One of the SS men raised his assault rifle, a fresh magazine slapping home. Rourke's right arm punched outward, like a rapier thrust, the knife biting into the SS man's throat, pinning the man to the wall.

Rourke drew the Python—the SS security team was no longer a threat.

"I'll guard here—get Bern."

"You are wounded, John!"

Rourke touched at his rib cage. "Very perceptive of you—go on," and Rourke snatched up one of the assault rifles, starting to hunt for spare magazines. He found four fully loaded, ramming one up the empty magazine well of the rifle, working the action.

He started forward, breaking into a run along the corridor, halting by the edge of the bend, pulling back.

The assault rifle slung at his side, Rourke reloaded his pistols. He glanced behind him. Kurinami, an assault rifle suspended below his right arm, carried Deiter Bern in his arms.

Kurinami was beside him then. Rourke started around the bend of the corridor. But Kurinami hissed, "Hey—about shouting, '*banzai*' back there, you know?"

Rourke looked at the young lieutenant. "What about it?"

"Well, I always wanted to try it."

Rourke nodded. "Kinda like somebody born in Texas shouting, 'Remember the Alamo,' huh? Don't sweat it— come on, stay behind me," and Rourke took the bend in the corridor, tucking back as gunfire hammered into the wall near his head.

"What do we do now?"

Rourke was just about to tell the Japanese, "I don't know," when the volume of gunfire dramatically increased, but somehow sounded wrong.

Rourke peered past the corner. "Hartman—all right!" And Rourke broke into a run, shouting to Kurinami, "Come on—hurry!"

Captain Hartman and his team of counterfeit SS personnel. At least a dozen of Hartman's men were locked in combat with the genuine SS security team, and they were closing, the real SS falling back. Rourke opened fire, into the backs of the SS, some of them turning toward him now to return fire, Hartman's men closing at hand-to-hand range, machine pistols discharging at close range, the smell of burning flesh on the air, mixed with the acrid smell of the chemical propellent from the German weapons.

As Rourke narrowed the gap, emptied his Scoremasters, Hartman's men beat down the last of the SS, Hartman firing two bursts from his machine pistol into the commander of the SS unit.

Hartman stepped over the body as Rourke slowed, stopped.

Hartman rendered a military rather than Nazi salute. "Herr Doctor, the way is clear to the nerve center of the communications area. The leader and a dozen SS hold it as the leader utilizes the television system and the radio system to appeal for support. We must go at once."

And Hartman turned to his men, pointing to one, then another. "You. You—relieve the Japanese officer of his burden, quickly."

Hartman turned again toward John Rourke, bowing

slightly, his heels clicking together. "Herr Doctor, if you would accompany me?"

"What about Natalia?" Rourke began, walking beside Hartman, stepping over the bodies of the dead SS. "And your *standartenfuehrer*."

"I think perhaps he should be called colonel, now, hmm, Herr Doctor? Both the colonel and the Major Tiemerovna are well—they wait with the rest of my unit by the broadcast area for us to join them. You are wounded?"

"Creased my rib cage—I'll be stiff as hell tomorrow," Rourke began, starting to take the steps downward two at a time, "but I'm fine now. Anybody's got a field dressing and some tape I wouldn't mind it."

Hartman nodded, then in German, "You there—attend the Herr Doctor's wound—quickly!"

Rourke stopped beside the railing, looking down toward the position below. Natalia waved up toward him, and then so did Wolfgang Mann—he was at the head of his troops, his men barricaded on both sides of the walls which funneled toward the broadcast studios. At least two dozen personnel were with him, more joining him from Hartman's unit. Rourke had the BDU blouse opened, pulling back the left side, holding the shoulder rig back, gingerly touching at the wound. It was shallow, but bleeding heavily. He shrugged, closing his eyes against the sudden cold of the antiseptic/healing agent the trooper sprayed against the wound. He let the man position the field dressing, then held his breath as the tape was applied to secure it. He looked at the German soldier. "Thank you for your care," Rourke told the man in German.

The soldier snapped to attention and nodded. "Herr Doctor!"

Rourke started again down the stairwell, surveying the position below. There were enough personnel for a frontal assault. But it would take a heavy toll. Before he reached the base of the stairwell, Mann was to his feet, shouting to his men as he limped ahead "Follow me!" Hartman's force was moving, Mann and Hartman at the forefront, a machine pistol in each of their hands. Glass shattered in the front of the broadcast studio, the leader's voice—it could be no other—audible now.

The voice—fear edged—called for defeat of the fifth column, adherence to the strict principles of Nazism which had brought them so far, for the people to rise up in his defense.

Rourke took the stairs downward, Natalia meeting him at the base of the stairs, one of her revolvers in her left hand. Rourke leaned against her, one of the Scoremasters in his right fist. They walked ahead, in the wake of Mann—helped by two of his troops—Hartman and the anti-Nazi force.

Gunfire. Screams. As Rourke and Natalia passed through the shot-out entryway, he heard a new voice. "This is Colonel Wolfgang Mann. The leader is dead. I bring to you a man we all trust—Herr Professor Deiter Bern."

The voice matched the body—frail, old sounding, but though the words of Deiter Bern were older, their strength—democracy, freedom, equality, tolerance—was not diminished.

Rourke sat in the leatherette swivel chair, his feet propped on one of the communications consoles, a cup of coffee beside him. Deiter Bern's words were long since concluded. And so, except for a few pockets of SS resistance at the far end of The Complex, was the fighting. Wolfgang Mann had refused medical care, attempting instead to contact the remainder of his forces in North America. A voice crackled over the speaker. Rourke sat more erect.

"This is *Hauptsturmfurhrer* Helmut Manfred Sturm. I announce this to you, *Standartenfuehrer* Mann, and to all other traitors. The remainder of my force, what is left after combatting heavy Russian forces, shall embark this hour in a final attack against the Eden Project base. We know their strength and they cannot resist our attack. Then, Herr *Standartenfuehrer*, my men and I shall return to The Complex and fight you and all other traitors to fully restore our rightful system of Nazism."

John Rourke was sitting beside Wolfgang Mann. There was pain in Mann's eyes, but not from injury. "Helene Sturm's husband—*mein Gott*."

John Rourke took the microphone into his hands, Natalia beside him. "Captain, this is John Rourke. You don't know me. But I know your wife. I'm a doctor—I delivered twin daughters to your wife, Helene. Both your wife and your daughters nearly died at the hands of the SS under the personal direction of your leader who is now dead, after your son Manfred betrayed your wife to the leader of the youth. When Colonel Mann, others and myself rescued your wife, your oldest son was assisting in your wife's torture and your infant daughters were about to be mutilated before they could be born. Your three remaining sons were already prepared for torture. But they, like your wife and twin daughters, are safe now. Your son Manfred—he had to be killed to prevent him stabbing your wife in the throat with a surgical instrument. Rourke over."

There was silence from the speaker, only the crackle of static—then panicked shouts that were unintelligible, and the roar of a single gunshot.

Rourke handed the microphone to Wolfgang Mann. John Rourke said nothing.

He started walking away from the communications console, picking his way over the shards of glass, the unmoved dead SS personnel. Natalia walked beside him. His left hand held her right hand—tight.

In the foyer beyond the communications studio was a small white column, rising perhaps four feet, and atop the column—identical except for materials to one he had seen earlier outside The Complex—was a bust of Adolf Hitler.

John Rourke still held Natalia's hand, but with his right hand he drew the Python. The hydrostatic shock characteristics of the .357 Magnun over the .45 ACP made it the logical choice. His voice a whisper as he raised the Python to eye level, he told Natalia Tiemerovna, "I don't think anyone will want to worship him anymore." And John Rourke pulled the trigger, and the face of Hitler shattered into dust.

THE SURVIVALIST 10: THE AWAKENING

JERRY AHERN

Checking the Geiger counter, John Rourke, CIA-trained weapons and survival expert, edged out into the thin, cold air. Squinting, in spite of his dark-lensed glasses, against the sudden sunlight, he crouched, action-ready, hands poised to reach for the twin, shoulder-holstered, Detonics ·45s.

Nothing.

He could feel the comforting hardness of the black, chromed hunting knife against his left hip bone.

Still nothing. No sign of life.

Slowly, slowly, he relaxed. Behind him in the living quarters of the lair, the children slept. Before him was an empty world.

The other survivors he discovered later. Survivors who had become animals. Who ate human flesh and killed with a pitiless lust for death.

THE SURVIVALIST 13: PURSUIT

JERRY AHERN

John Rourke, CIA-trained weapons and survival expert, looked down at the man's body, half-buried in the snow. Multiple stab wounds in the back — most likely caused by the bayonet of an M-16 assault rifle. Lying nearby: a Beretta 92SB-F 9mm Parabellum. In the abandoned tent: a couple of M-16s and a scattering of survival gear. In the background, black and threatening against the white Arctic emptiness: the Russian-built helicopter.

Rourke had found everything he was looking for — except for the most vital item of all. Annie, his daughter, kidnapped by the man who lay dead at his feet. Annie who had vanished into the wilderness.

THE 'SURVIVALIST' SERIES
BY JERRY AHERN

All these books are available at your local bookshop or newsagent, or can be ordered direct from the publisher. Just tick the titles you want and fill in the form below.

Prices and availability subject to change without notice.

Hodder and Stoughton Paperbacks, P.O. Box 11, Falmouth, Cornwall.

Please send cheque or postal order, and allow the following for postage and packing:

U.K. – 55p for one book, plus 22p for the second book, and 14p for each additional book ordered to a £1.75 maximum.

OTHER OVERSEAS CUSTOMERS – £1.00 for the first book, plus 25p per copy for each additional book.

Name...

Address..

....